# A Long Way from You

Dear Mr. and Mrs. Folboff,

# A Long Way from You

GWENDOLYN HEASLEY

Happy reading!

Gwendolyn Heasley

HARPER TEEN

An Imprint of HarperCollinsPublishers

HarperTeen is an imprint of HarperCollins Publishers.

A Long Way from You
Copyright © 2012 by Gwendolyn Heasley
All rights reserved. Printed in the United States of America. No part of this book
may be used or reproduced in any manner whatsoever without written permission
except in the case of brief quotations embodied in critical articles and reviews. For
information address HarperCollins Children's Books, a division of HarperCollins
Publishers, 10 East 53rd Street, New York, NY 10022.
www.epicreads.com

Library of Congress Cataloging-in-Publication Data
Heasley, Gwendolyn.
A long way from you / Gwendolyn Heasley. — 1st ed.
p. cm.
Sequel to: Where I belong.
Summary: Seventeen-year-old Kitsy Kidd learns that there is a lot more to making
original art—and relationships—than she thought when she leaves Texas behind for
a prestigious summer art program in New York City.
ISBN 978-0-06-197885-2
[1. Interpersonal relations—Fiction. 2. Artists—Fiction. 3. Self-Actualization
(Psychology)—Fiction. 4. Moving, Household—Fiction. 5. New York (N.Y.)—
Fiction.] I. Title.
PZ7.H3467Lon 2012                                                    2011044630
[Fic]—dc23                                                                CIP
                                                                            AC

Typography by Alison Klapthor
12 13 14 15 16 CG/RRDH 10 9 8 7 6 5 4 3 2 1
❖
First Edition

To Sarah Dotts Barley, my editor.
Kitsy and I wanted you to have this dedication
as a small thanks for working so hard
(and brilliantly) on our story.

# Prologue

I remember where I was when I learned about Santa Claus: in my parents' closet.

I remember where I was when I learned about sex: the Broken Spoke Elementary School playground.

I remember where I was when I learned that my dad had left: in the backseat of our maroon Buick.

But most vividly of all, I remember where I was when I decided that I wanted to live in New York City.

It was the first Christmas without my dad. Kiki, my three-year-old brother, and I had gathered around the TV to watch the updated version of *Miracle on 34th Street*.

When the camera pans around to New York City at Christmastime, with all of its festive lights and cheer, Kiki, in his Grinch pajamas, turned to me and said in a serious voice, "That place is so beautiful it must be make-believe."

"No, it's real," I said. "It's a place for dreams. One day, I'll figure out how we can move there and our wishes will come true."

"Really?" Kiki asked. His eyes were as big as ornaments.

"If miracles happen anywhere, it's there," I whispered.

# Chapter 1

## I'm a Waitress, Too

"FLIGHT FIVE-OH-FIVE TO NEW YORK CITY, LaGuardia Airport, is now boarding business class and Advantage Executive Platinum cardholders. All other ticketed passengers please remain seated until your zone numbers are called," blares over the loudspeaker.

I look down at my ticket. It doesn't say Advantage Executive Platinum anywhere, but it does say "Business." What kind of Business (with a capital B) does American Airlines think I, Kitsy Kidd, have? I'm only seventeen. Hopefully, this isn't the mistake-that-ruins-my-trip. I've known about my summer in New York City for two months now, and I keep waiting for someone to say there's been a mix-up and that this is too good to be true.

I've been sitting at gate 9 in the same uncomfortable

plastic seat for over an hour. I wanted to buy a trashy magazine, get a strawberry milkshake at Burger King, and most importantly, go to the bathroom, but I was too afraid that I'd miss my flight.

"Kitsy, pay attention at the airport and don't go wandering around," Amber, aka my mother, instructed. "They ain't going to hold back three thousand pounds of steel just because you aren't on it." In a rare bout of parenting, Amber offered me a lot of advice before I left, but not much of it seems to be true. "Dress up, Kitsy," she had said. "You are supposed to wear your best clothes to fly." I wanted to argue with Amber that even celebrities fly in sweats according to *Us Weekly*, but I just let her go on. It's easier that way. So here I am wearing my Easter outfit in July, surrounded by people traveling across the country dressed like they're shopping at Walmart.

With all the emotion of a robot, the airline employee begins taking and scanning the Business tickets from a line of men dressed in two-piece suits. Maybe there *was* some merit in Amber's advice about dressing up. People in the Spoke only wear suits if they are going to a funeral. Just follow them. Just do exactly what they do. It's like a cheerleading routine. Synchronize yourself to everyone else. I just wish there was a beat. I hand my ticket to the airline lady; she scans it and passes it back.

"Thanks, Ms. Kidd," she says without a smile. "Have a nice flight."

Ms. Kidd? That's *Amber*, not me. I give her a big grin, which seems to startle her, and I go down the hallway. At the end of it, to get onto the plane, I'm forced to step over a big gap. Hands, my boyfriend, forgot to mention this. I asked him to tell me everything he knows about aviation because, after all, he's flown six times! I can't believe he left out this part, which seems crucial, not to mention life-threatening. Yet I shouldn't be surprised: You can only be tackled so many times before you have some residual effects. As the quarterback of our football team, Hands has spent the majority of his life in a heap of turf and defensive linemen.

A flight attendant looks at my ticket, smiles, points, and says "Four C." That's when I realize: Business class is first class! Unlike buses, where the back is cool and coveted, the front of airplanes is distinctly superior. I know this from the movies. The seats are bigger, not to mention leather, the people richer, and the bathroom closer. There's even a curtain divider. I can't believe that *I'm* flying first class like a movie star. I sit down in 4C next to the only other woman. She's dressed in all black, including a silk eye mask, and appears to be either unconscious or sleeping.

The flight attendant swoops over to me and asks, "Would you like a drink?"

"Yes, ma'am. I'd love a Coke please," I say.

"Oh, honey, today we only have Pepsi products. Is that all right?" she asks, and then proceeds to pour me a

Pepsi and set it down without waiting for my answer. In my whole life, I have *never* drunk a non-Coke product. Everyone I know calls all carbonated beverages "Coke": It's a Texan thing. My friend Corrinne tells me that in New York a carbonated drink is a "soda," which does not sound refreshing or delicious the way "Coke" does.

I sip my Pepsi, which tastes acidic compared with Coke's carbonation perfection. Hands told me that there would be a demonstration about safety procedures, so I decide that I don't need to memorize the safety card just yet. Instead, I text him.

> On the plane, I made it. Thanks again for the ride. Call you in New York, New York. XXX.

He responds right away.

> I told you it'd be easy. Call when you land, and don't forget about the Spoke or me. OOO.

Before long, the flight attendants give a performance on how to properly fasten a seat belt. The scary thing is no one even looks up from their cocktails or BlackBerrys even when the pilot instructs us (for the second time) to turn off all electronic devices. I'm pretty sure that I'll be the only one on this flight prepared if there's an emergency. Life with Amber is always an emergency situation, so I reckon that I'm doubly prepared.

I listen as the flight attendant explains how in an emergency to put on our own oxygen masks before assisting others. I think she's made a mistake because I've never lived in a world where we worry about ourselves first, then about others. Maybe that place is New York. And maybe that's what this trip is about for me. Some people say that New Yorkers are heartless. I don't think that's true at all; just like it was with my friend Corrinne Corcoran, it might take a while to locate their hearts under their chic designer clothes. I'm the opposite: I pin my heart on the outside.

When the plane takes off, I hold my breath.

"Good-bye, Old," I whisper. "Hello, New . . ." I pause. ". . . York." I giggle at my own lame joke.

Real flying feels a lot like flying in your dreams. My body seems light and disconnected, but it also feels like I could crash to the ground in an instant like the sensation you get when you wake from a dream with a jolt.

Since Corrinne's parents are paying for my flights and my summer art classes *and* letting me stay with them in their apartment, I want to do well and prove to them that I can make art with more than just Wet n' Wild makeup. So I pull out my sketchbook and a charcoal pencil and start drawing my favorite painting, Vincent van Gogh's *The Starry Night*. I have an old, semi-torn poster of it hanging above my bed. It's the only piece of art displayed in my entire house, and I know nearly every inch of it by memory. I focus carefully on my sketch because I shouldn't waste time watching movies or eating airline food that Hands told me tastes like rubber anyway. (Although my menu, with an option of steak or salmon and some dessert called tiramisu, doesn't sound like rubber at all. It sounds exotic and fancy, two adjectives that I am not very well acquainted with.)

The man across the aisle from me orders a Jameson and ginger. Good thing Amber isn't here: Amber plus free drinks would be a dangerous combination. This reminds me that I need to text my eight-year-old brother, Kiki, when I land. I want to make sure that he's doing okay since I left and that he remembers to start his assigned summer reading, four books from the Boxcar Children series.

"What would you like for dinner?" the flight attendant asks, bringing me back from thinking about the Spoke. I politely request the salmon. Eventually, I'll need to sleep. After all, this flight is billed as a red-eye. But my mind's racing. Four weeks in New York City taking art classes at Parsons with other students who are hopefully as passionate about art as I am. Four weeks away from Texas heat, housework, and Amber . . . but also Hands, Kiki, and free ice cream from Sonic. The longest I have ever been away from home was three days camping with my fifth-grade class. Somehow, I think this trip will be a little different.

When Hands dropped me off at the airport, he told me, "I hope you like it there, Kitsy, but not too much. We're Americans by birth—"

I finished for him: "And Texans by the grace of God."

That also happens to be the slogan of the bumper sticker on Hands's truck, Yellow Submarine. (Corrinne also mentioned that no one names their cars in New York and that most people don't even own cars. That's *almost* as weird as the calling-Coke-soda thing.)

I didn't say what I *really* thought, though: If God graced Broken Spoke, it must've been long before I was born. Unemployment, unforgiving fundamentalists, and struggling farms don't look like grace to me. . . . Of course, I know that's wrong to think. The Spoke's just going through a rough patch. And we did win the state football tournament last fall, the answer to fifty-two years of unanswered prayers to win another title. I even got to be on TV with the Mockingbirdettes, my cheerleading team, *and* I was interviewed since I'm team captain. I need to work on being more grateful in my thoughts and not just my words.

Reminder to Kitsy: You can't be all pep and go, *school spirit, rah-rah,* with your pom-poms and everyone else, and then be all Debbie Downer in your own head.

I start to sketch the middle-aged woman sitting next to me. With one hand, I cover my paper just in case she wakes up and thinks that I'm a stalker or something. People ridin' high and walkin' in the tall cotton with clothes and looks like hers probably need to worry about things like that.

When my salmon arrives on a tray with a fancy doily, I'm glad that I watch a lot of Food Network on TV so I know that salmon is supposed to be this pink color. Food like this exotic fish isn't on my grocery list, which I compile only after figuring out what's on sale that week.

The man across from me slurs to the flight attendant that he wants another drink. When she comes by again with my dessert, which looks like a dirty sponge with whipped cream on top, I smile at her. I know all about annoying customers from my job.

"I'm a waitress, too," I say and smile. "It's harder than people think, right?"

The flight attendant flares her nostrils (not a pretty view) and asks, "Do you want another *Pepsi*?" Something about the way she pronounces *Pepsi* makes me know that I overstepped some airplane etiquette.

"Sorry. I'm not exactly a waitress. I'm a carhop. I roller-skate. Actually, I Rollerblade. I never could get a hold on roller skates. Kept tripping over the toe stop. Have you been to a Sonic Drive-In? That's where I work."

The flight attendant, whose name tag reads MEREDITH, walks away without a word. I wanted to tell her that I like

8

her name and her perfume. That's what I do when I'm nervous: talk and compliment. In the Spoke, that routine helps make up for people's preconceived ideas about me.

Just then, the lady by the window pulls up her eye mask and smiles a fourteen-tooth grin, one like Julia Roberts's. That kind of smile is extremely rare. I only have an eight-tooth smile, and it's crooked because I never got braces. "Straight teeth don't make a difference," Amber said. "Look where my perfect teeth got me. Nowhere." Amber isn't exactly a fountain of optimism.

"So, I imagine you're *coming* from Texas and *going* to New York," she says.

"My accent gave me away?"

"Yes . . . ," the lady says very slowly. "Your accent. Let me tell you something. Don't worry about the stewardess. Stewardesses come in two types. The type that wanted to be models and settled for this, which makes them bitter"—she gulps a clear drink and continues—"and then the husky type who never thought they'd become stewardesses because of the weight limits. After they eliminated the weigh-ins, that type got the chance to see that being a stewardess isn't actually glamorous—not to mention, the aisles are narrow. That type is sour, too. Of course, there are exceptions."

I nod slowly and scan for Meredith. I don't want her to overhear this and get the pilot to reroute us back to Texas.

I also want to tell the Lady in Black that although this is my first flight, I'm pretty sure they are called flight attendants, not stewardesses. This is 2012, after all.

"Meredith's probably real sweet," I say. "I just got too personal. My mother says I've never met a stranger. She thinks I get nosy quickly and talk too much, which might be especially true when I'm nervous. Am I talking too much? I'm sorry if I am."

"Who's Meredith? And why is a pretty thing like you nervous? We're landing in the city created for Bright Young Things like you."

"Meredith is our flight attendant," I answer. "And I'm nervous because I've never flown before. Actually, I'm nervous *slash* totally thrilled."

Right there and then, I want to launch into what Corrinne calls a *Kitsy Monologue*. I want to tell this woman, a complete stranger, how I'm leaving Broken Spoke for the first time and attending Parsons for a four-week art program for promising young art students. That's exactly how the acceptance email put it: "promising young art students."

I want to tell her about Corrinne, a native Manhattan girl, who had to move to Broken Spoke and how it changed my life more than hers. She moved in with her grandparents because her dad lost his big Wall Street job. (Her mother's originally from the Spoke although you'd never guess it looking at her.) Corrinne stayed in the Spoke for six months until her dad got another job and could move the family back to New York. And I want this lady to know how the Corcorans were so grateful for my friendship with Corrinne—who was initially not too happy to be living in the Spoke—that they bought me a ticket, my first plane ticket, to New York, so I could attend art school.

Up until now, my only formal art education has been taking one class a year at my high school. It's taught by Madame Williams. She's very supportive but has no art background. She only started teaching art three years ago when the school slashed the French program. I want to explain to this lady how this opportunity is the most amazing thing that's ever happened to me, and how I'm certain that there's going to be a jolt and I'll wake up because it just must be a dream.

I also want to tell her about Kiki and Amber. In Broken Spoke, everyone thinks they know my story, and here is someone who doesn't know it. I want to narrate it for the first time and go further than the obvious parts like the fact that my dad left and that Amber drinks and smokes too much.

This woman's eyes grew Super Sonic Cheeseburger-size when I told her that this was my first flight. Does she not understand the cost of a plane ticket when you make $5.50 an hour at Sonic? Actually, *I* don't even know the cost of the ticket, especially one like this. I told the Corcorans that I'd keep track of how much I'm costing them and pay them back just as soon as I can, but they wouldn't hear of it. Mrs. Corcoran said, "After the recession, we figured out what's worth spending money on. And you, Kitsy, are a solid investment." When she said that, I held the phone away from my ear and tried not to cry. No one, not even Hands, has ever said anything like that about me.

"And all that stuff I said about the stewardesses, I only know that because I was one—a stewardess—back when there was still a bit of glamour left at forty thousand feet," the woman tells me with a laugh, and puts her hand on my mine. "You're going to have a fabulous time in New York."

"What do you do now?" I ask. I wonder if she got discovered, became a model, and is now an ambassador for a third-world nation like Angelina Jolie.

"I got saved," she says and waves her left hand, which is weighed down by a ring with a sapphire center stone sandwiched by two gumball-size diamonds. It's even bigger than Mrs. Corcoran's, which was the biggest one I'd ever seen until now. "I got married, honey."

Considering my own parents' situation, I've never thought about being married and getting saved in the same breath.

"What a *beautiful* ring." Talk and compliment. And then repeat.

"Thanks, darling. Are you meeting your man in New York? Will you be wined and dined?"

I don't bother to tell this woman that the only wining and dining I've done is "borrowed" Arbor Mist with some BBQ, and that I'm only seventeen.

"No, ma'am. I'm taking a course at Parsons. It's an art school," I say proudly.

The closest I've ever been to Parsons before this is watching Tim Gunn on *Project Runway* tell contestants to "make it work." I can't believe that I'm actually going to school there. *Fierce.*

"Oh, good for you," the woman says. "You have to have a career these days. Thanks to my generation." She rolls her eyes as if she's *not* thankful for the feminists' efforts for equal rights.

Art as a *career*? Maybe in New York with all of its galleries and museums, but it's so not possible in Broken Spoke. It could happen only if Madame Williams would finally retire and I became the art teacher. I try to make eye contact with Meredith, the flight attendant, so I can apologize with my eyes for the whole I'm-a-waitress-too comment, but she's flirting with the Jameson-and-ginger man in 4A.

The woman beside me pulls her eye mask back down, rests her head against the window, and snuggles up with her black cashmere blanket. "Get some rest," she mutters.

"You'll need it. You know, New York is the city that never sleeps."

I think about pulling out my sketchbook again, watching a bad movie, or asking for another Pepsi. But then . . . I'm not thinking at all.

I wake up sleeping upright, which is a first for me. The only person I know who sometimes sleeps sitting up is Amber, and I think that's called passing out.

There's a fabulous bacon smell wafting throughout the cabin. The aroma reminds me of weekends at Corrinne's grandparents' and brunches at Hands's, which always beat Cheerios at my place. My watch says it's only four a.m. Central Time, but I sit up with a hunger. The Lady in (All) Black next to me is reapplying her makeup, using a monogrammed gold compact. Definitely nothing you can buy at our local Piggly Wiggly. But I've learned that drugstore makeup is just as good if you know what you're doing.

The lady looks at me directly for the first time, then pulls open the window shade. Light floods our seats.

"Darling," she says, "switch seats with me. We're going to fly over Manhattan at sunrise. This is something that you *must* see. I'm still awestruck by its beauty even after living here for twenty-five years."

After some awkward maneuvering, I have my nose

pressed up against the window of my new seat. Its imprint leaves a mark that I try to rub away. Right now, the view is houses and more houses but Monopoly-size ones.

But then I see water, and I spy it: a tiny green statue.

The lady nudges me and says, "*Give me your tired, your poor, / Your huddled masses yearning to breathe free, / The wretched refuse of your teeming shore. / Send these, the homeless, tempest-tossed to me. / I lift my lamp beside the golden door!*"

"The inscription on the Statue of Liberty," I say. "I read about it at the library when I tried to learn everything I could about Manhattan."

"Somehow, I think you'll still end up surprised," she says. "I'm going to give you an aerial tour of the island of Manhattan. It's going to be quick because the island is only—"

"Thirteen miles long." I'm beginning to like this lady even if she's a bit un-PC.

"The green patch—that's Central Park. There's the Empire, the Chrysler," she says, pointing to different skyscrapers. "Oh, that's the Brooklyn Bridge," she adds, nodding toward a stunning suspension bridge. "Make sure no one sells that to you."

I laugh, but I'm not worrying about anyone trying to scam me. I've been waiting for this chance my whole life. I only wish the plane would slow down because I somehow feel that this experience is already going by too fast.

"Don't worry, honey," she says. "It's better from the ground. By the way, I'm Mary Carter Hubbard. It's very nice to meet you."

I'm happy when Mrs. Hubbard extends her right hand for me to shake. I was worried that her ring would cut my hand.

"I'm Kitsy. Kitsy Kidd. Thank you for the window seat and for the tour." Quickly I look away from the window and gobble up the muffin and bacon that have appeared in front of me. It's free, after all.

"Good God. I wish I still had your metabolism." Mrs. Hubbard sips her water daintily as if she's worried that even water could make her fat.

The pilot makes a few announcements—and then we start to descend.

Hands was right: The landing part feels like driving on a dirt road in an old, rickety truck. Real flying was just as much fun as it was in my dreams. I hope the real New York is as good as the one in my dreams, too.

When we get off the plane, Mrs. Hubbard stops me. "I'm originally from Charleston, South Carolina," she confides softly, as if it were a secret. "But New York belongs to *all* of us." She gives me a small hug, then walks a few steps before she turns around. "Kitsy, make sure you remember this."

"Remember what?" I ask.

"Youth. Savor it."

I smile and wave good-bye. I don't tell her that I haven't felt young in a long time.

I text Kiki, Hands, Amber, and Corrinne that I made it to New York. I'm a bit nervous to navigate the taxi thing, but Corrinne said even people who don't speak English can do it. "Kitsy, you'll figure it out, even speaking Texan. If you need help, just try to be careful of the *y'all*s and other Texan-speak, especially all those phrases that no one outside of Broken Spoke understands."

I begin following the baggage claim signs with the pictures of suitcases on them.

As I ride down the escalator, I see a mob of people beyond security. It's only six a.m.! Most of the crowd is wearing black suits and holding signs. Then I see a giant poster board with a picture of an apple that says KITSY KIDD, TAKE A BITE OUT OF THE BIG APPLE. Then Corrinne, dressed in white linen pants and a black tank top, steps out from behind it.

Because I can't help it, I find myself running down the escalator, pushing people out of the way (gently, of course), and grabbing Corrinne in a lasso-tight hug. I figure New York is used to a little aggression anyway. Even though I've read that nothing shocks a true New Yorker, people are staring and covering their ears because of our squeals.

*"Kitsy Kidd!"* Corrinne exclaims. "Surprise! We're going to be your taxi. You're the only person who I'd wake up this early for. I hope you slept on the plane—we don't have much time."

I light up, glad that Corrinne is here and I don't have to deal with New York by myself quite yet.

Unfortunately for me, Corrinne is going to be a counselor at a sleepaway horse camp in Virginia this summer and leaves in two days. She's like a total cowgirl but a preppy one. Corrinne's going to be in New York with me for only a few days: first this weekend and then my last three days in the city. I'm pretty much on my own other than that. Freaky, but exciting, since I'm in the greatest city in the world, and I only have to worry about looking out for myself.

"What's your bag look like?" Corrinne asks. "Tell Ivan." Corrinne points beside her to a tall man dressed in a black suit and wearing a cap.

"I'll go with him," I say quickly. I borrowed a suitcase from Corrinne's grandparents. You don't exactly need luggage unless you have somewhere to travel. And before this, I've never had the opportunity to go anywhere outside of Texas.

"All right," Corrinne says. "I'm totally back onto coffee. Don't tell my grandma. You know how she feels about caffeine being the gateway drug. What do you want from

Starbucks?" Corrinne points to a green awning with a line that's already ten people deep.

"Um, coffee," I answer, shrugging.

"Oh, Kitsy. I forgot that the Spoke's like the last place on earth untouched by Starbucks. They should make it like a national preserve. *The last frontier, completely unscathed by Frappuccinos!*" she broadcasts as if she were an announcer for a travel channel, and dashes off to Starbucks.

I follow Ivan to the spinning baggage thing. Unlike most of the other bags, which are black wheelies, Corrinne's grandparents' faded floral one is easy to spot.

We find Corrinne balancing her welcome sign and two large green-and-white cups. Immediately, I wish we had asked Ivan if he wanted anything. I'm in New York only two minutes, and I'm already forgetting my manners. While waiting for my bag, I learned that Ivan's from Bulgaria, where his wife and two kids still live, and he used to be a pharmacist. I guess it's true when Amber says that I've never met a stranger.

She hands me a massive green-and-white cup. "I got you a venti skinny mocha latte with three Splendas. Memorize that. You need a signature drink. Everyone has one," she says with Corrinne authority.

I take the cup from her and slowly sip. It pretty much tastes like a burnt chocolate bar. I don't say this, of course. Starbucks, like most bad things, probably just takes a few times to get hooked. Amber says she hated her first cig-arette; she started at twenty-one, right after I was born. "Got lonely in the house with just you," she told me once. It's now seventeen years later and she smokes two packs a day. Hopefully, I don't get addicted to Starbucks. I defi-nitely can't afford to be buying fancy, semi-gross coffee every day.

We follow Ivan to the car. The July air is cool. It feels like the Spoke does in April. I look at the clouds and think it might even rain. Back home, it's so dry that the bark is bribing the dogs. We could use a little of this New York weather.

Corrinne squeezes my hand and says, "It's going to be *fabulous*. You know that's East Coast for cool, right?"

We hop into the back of a black sedan with leather seats. Ivan navigates his way through the mass of taxis, buses, and pedestrians, and then we're Manhattan-bound. Once I spot the city in the distance, I realize that my life is finally moving at sixty miles per hour in the right direction.

How fabulous.

# Chapter 2

## Ladies Who Lunch

AS WE CROSS THE QUEENSBORO BRIDGE, Corrinne launches into a spiel of what she calls EMK: Essential Manhattan Knowledge.

"Bridges and tunnels," Corrinne explains. "That's what you call people who visit Manhattan from off-island. And it's *not* meant as a compliment."

"Corrinne, since I'm not from Manhattan, am I a bridge or a tunnel?" I ask.

Ivan and Corrinne both shriek with laughter.

Corrinne pulls on her seat belt to loosen it. "I'm like having a heart attack, Kitsy. Ivan, do you know CPR? Tell me this town car has a defibrillator!"

Corrinne stops cackling to explain: "Bridges and tunnels refer to people from Jersey and the boroughs. You, coming from Texas, are a *tourist*."

Corrinne pronounces *tourist* as if it weren't a good thing, but I've waited a long time to be exactly that—*a tourist in New York*. And in my wildest fantasies, I didn't think I'd get to be a tourist *and* an art student.

As Corrinne goes on and on, I wish she'd be a tad quieter so I can try to absorb these images to sketch them later. I'd try to draw now, but unfortunately I've learned from school bus trips that sketching while in motion makes me totally carsick.

Corrinne has now launched into a spiel about Williamsburg and how the whole Williamsburg-equals-the-new-cool thing is only true if you're a celebrity and are hiding out from the paparazzi. Otherwise, it's still un-cool . . . unless you really like poetry or music that's supposedly hip just because no one's ever heard of it. "It's a weird place," she says and exhales. "Stick to Manhattan, Kitsy. Everything you need is in Manhattan."

*Everything you need is in Manhattan* echoes in my head. That has always been my hope, and now I have the chance to see if it's true.

After about thirty minutes, which I mostly spend with my head hanging halfway out the window like a dog, Corrinne squeezes my hand. "We're, like, *walking-distance close*," she announces and points down the street. "That's how you measure distance in New York, *walking-distance*

22

*close* versus *taxi-* or *subway-distance far*. Good thing we're almost there because I'm out of coffee. I'm totally up to three doses a day. Still can't believe that Grandma Houston didn't let me drink coffee in Texas. Truthfully, it's shocking I functioned there at all without it. I've heard about celebrities who've had to go to rehab just to wean themselves off it. It can be pretty dangerous just to quit cold turkey like that."

I shake my head at Corrinne. I'm pretty sure no one has ever died coming off caffeine, although I'm already anticipating New York withdrawal when I return to the Spoke.

After Ivan executes an illegal U-turn, we pull up to a beautiful glass building with a gated courtyard. I know from my research that the West Village used to be the home of struggling artists and that now lots of famous and successful artists live here. I already feel inspired to be in the same space as some of my heroes.

"Morton Square," Corrinne says, pointing at the building. "Remember that if you get lost. It's one of the only modern buildings in the West Village, so people will know what you're talking about."

A doorman wearing a crisp green suit opens the gate and welcomes us in. In Texas, men open our doors all the time, but the uniform reminds me that here they're paid to do it. I feel culture-shock tingles in my neck.

"Rudy!" Corrinne exclaims to the doorman, who is basketball-player tall. "This is Kitsy, my friend from Texas. Treat her like she's me . . . but you're lucky because she is not as much trouble."

"You're one-of-a-kind, Corrinne," Rudy says and carries my bag to the front door.

Corrinne takes the bag from Rudy. "I've got it from here. Hot, sculpted arms are the new thing." She flexes her arms like a weightlifter.

Rudy shakes his head and pushes open the door to the building.

"Nice to meet you, Kitsy. I'll be seeing you around."

I like the sound of that.

The inside of the building looks like a hotel. Scratch that, I've only stayed at two hotels, and they were technically motels since the rooms' doors were on the outside of the building: This place looks like a hotel from a movie or a dream. There's a mahogany front desk staffed by *three* people. Overflowing flowers in *Shrek*-size vases sit on the entry tables, and giant canvases hang on the wall. I fight the urge to walk up to the large modern paintings and get lost in them for the morning.

After I realize that I haven't said anything since getting out of the car, I look at Corrinne and say, "Pretty," which sounds lame the second it lands in the air. *Pretty* is a dirt road at sunset. This is sexy, sleek, not-of-my-galaxy—anything but *pretty*. Maybe there's a word in

New York-speak that could adequately describe it, but I haven't learned it—yet.

I follow Corrinne to the elevator.

"The city must've got your tongue," Corrinne says. "Or alternately, it's jet lag. Don't worry. You know I like talking, too, but I'm excited to hear a Kitsy Monologue. And get the newest gossip on Bubby. First, we've got to do the meet and greet with the parents. I can't believe you've never met my dad!"

Bubby was Corrinne's Broken Spoke love interest. He's the star running back, a newspaper reporter, *and* the son of her mother's high school boyfriend, Dusty. It was like a total romantic comedy; all it needed was a song-and-dance number.

"I know Bubby misses you almost as much as I do . . . although he'd never admit to it because you ripped his heart out when you broke up with him three seconds after you rolled up to your fancy boarding school. Hands is worried that all of Bubby's obsessing over you is going to hurt his football game."

Corrinne turns and smiles as if that were good news. "I'm glad I had such an impact," she says. "It's nice that I can affect people."

"Hands isn't feeling so Team Corrinne," I tease. "He wants another state ring, so maybe send Bubby a text saying hi once in a while."

"I'd do that for Broken Spoke," Corrinne says seriously.

Unlike Corrinne, who switches boys with the seasons, I've been with Hands for five years and one month, ever since our very first school dance at the end of sixth grade. Of course, we had known each other forever before that. That's the Broken Spoke way. When we danced to our first slow song, his palms were all sweaty, but I didn't mind because he said I was the nicest and cutest girl there. He's still the only boy I've slow danced with, and he doesn't even get sweaty while dancing anymore. I can't imagine life without Hands. This will be the longest I've ever been away from him.

The elevator door opening snaps me out of my thoughts. We step in and Corrinne pushes 5.

"Before Texas, we owned the penthouse," Corrinne says. "When we moved back, we rented this place on five. It's called getting recessionated. I'm just happy to live in the same building." She adds, whispering, "Some people had to move to the *suburbs*. That's nearly as bad as moving to Texas." She gives me a gentle nudge.

"Just joking," she says, and puts on her I-can-say-any-thing-and-you'll-still-love-me smile.

"We aren't all lucky enough to be born in the core of the Big Apple," I gently remind her, and hope that she hasn't reverted to Corrinne version 1.0, pre-Texas snob.

The elevator doors open and Corrinne ushers me into 5D.

Standing in the doorway is Mrs. J. J. Corcoran, better known in Broken Spoke as Jenny Jo Houston, the Spoker who went to Manhattan to model, married a rich New Yorker, and never came back.

"Kitsy!" Mrs. Corcoran says in a voice that still holds the last threads of a Texan drawl. "Don't you look gorgeous. Corrinne usually wears sweats when she flies."

I look at Mrs. Corcoran. Back in Broken Spoke, she did the jeans-and-cowboy-boot thing. At eight a.m., she's wearing kitten heels, a black skirt, a white blouse, and white pearls. I'm guessing Mrs. Corcoran doesn't wear her bedazzled rodeo top in New York.

Mrs. Corcoran ushers us through the door. Mr. Corcoran, gray in a Clooney-handsome way and dressed in a suit, stands in the kitchen and drinks a cup of coffee.

"Kitsy," Mr. Corcoran says and shakes my hand. "Nice to meet you. Happy to have you here this summer. It would be lonely with both kids at camp. I still can't believe Tripp suckered us into skateboarding camp in California. I'm pretty sure there aren't any colleges looking for skateboarders to fill their athletic rosters. Wish he would do crew like his old man, but alas."

"Dad, calm down, he's prepubescent," Corrinne says. "Besides, I'm glad he's slowing down on the chess hobby. That was even hurting *my* PR."

Tripp is Corrinne's thirteen-year-old little brother,

although sometimes I doubt that they are blood relatives since "he's all sugar, and she's all spice" as my nanny always said before she died. *Nanny* in Broken Spoke is another name for *grandma*, and not a paid, usually foreign, substitute mother, as Corrinne explained to me it is in New York.

"Unfortunately, my husband has to go to work even though it's Saturday," Mrs. Corcoran says. "But his business is picking up, which is a good thing."

Corrinne pulls me away from her parents.

"Mom," she whines, "I'm giving Kitsy a tour. We're on a tight timetable."

"Heavens," Mrs. Corcoran says and steps out of the way. "Let Kitsy rest, Corrinne. She's here for art school, not to be a guest on *The Corrinne Corcoran Show*."

As Corrinne and Mrs. Corcoran bicker, I'm hypnotized by the apartment's views of the river. I walk straight up to a row of windows.

"Ohmigosh," I say. "There's a cruise ship, *The Princess*. Just like the one on the commercials with the cheesy music. I've always wanted to take a cruise. Oh, look at the people running and biking on that path. And over that way, there's a park just for dogs!"

Every way I look, there's something else to take in.

Mrs. Corcoran walks up next to me and puts her arm around my waist. "That's what I missed the most in Texas:

the river. Wait until you see tugboats, Kitsy. They come in all different colors, red, blue, yellow. The river is captivating. I don't know how I grew up without having water nearby."

I'm sure after living this fancy life, Mrs. Corcoran probably wonders how she grew up in Broken Spoke at all. To be fair, in the Spoke, there's one pond, which people do swim in despite the rumors of the swimming nutria aka water rats. Northern Texas is not known for its waters, and southern Texas, by the Gulf, is like a different state since it's at least eight hours away by car.

Corrinne grabs my shoulder. "Remember, absolutely no swimming in the Hudson River unless you're looking to catch a disease or find a dead body."

I roll my eyes at Corrinne.

"*Tick tock*. Time for me to be the tour guide on, as my mother puts it, *The Corrinne Corcoran Show*. . . . I'm not going to lie. I like the way that sounds. Catchy!" She throws open her arms and continues, "This is our apartment. It's very modern and minimalist. We have a great room, which is a combination of a living and dining room, and our kitchen is what you call a galley kitchen. Now on to my fortress," she says and whisks me through the hallway.

"My room!" Corrinne opens the door. Her room is about the size of my entire house, which is really just a trailer with a foundation dug underneath it.

"Corrinne, I thought New York apartments were small," I say softly.

"New construction," Corrinne explains and opens a closet door. "Thank *God* for new construction. Some of my friends live in old prewar places that don't even have walk-ins. I mean Holy Holly Golightly, even my dorm room at boarding school has a walk-in."

I ignore Corrinne's walk-in comment because her closet blinds me. Dozens of dry-cleaning bags hang in a row and all the clothes are organized by color.

"Corrinne?" I ask. "When did you get all these clothes?"

Corrinne looks a bit embarrassed and shuts the door.

"Oh, it was all in storage when I was in Texas," she says and claps her hands together. "Time's up. Get dressed. We have reservations soon. And '*mi ropa es su ropa.*'"

I raise my eyebrows and try to translate.

"I'm totally forgetting my Spanish since I'm back in Latin class. I think I said my clothes are your clothes. Anyway, you get yourself dolled up."

I follow Corrinne's commands and set my cell phone on Corrinne's dresser. "I'll call nights and weekends," I promised Hands, Amber, and Kiki. "It'll be cheaper." I didn't add that it would be easier, too.

We're standing outside Morton Square when Corrinne says, "You know that saying about taking off one accessory

30

before you leave? That's not true in New York. You put another on." I'm in a white button-down dress, to which Corrinne has added her own rope belt and warfare-type sandals.

I've never heard that expression, but I nod.

"Guess where we're going?" Corrinne asks excitedly.

I hold my breath and pray that it's not shopping. I need to save my money, not blow it on the first day. I imagine shopping in New York with Corrinne qualifies as an Olympic sport, one that I am definitely not trained or sponsored for.

Before I can even try to guess, Corrinne answers: "MoMA! I love you enough to go to a *museum*." She pronounces *museum* in the tone most would refer to a Porta-Potty, but I ignore her pitch as I feel my cheeks get red with excitement. While I knew this would be the summer that I'd finally go to MoMA and see the works from my very worn used book *MoMA Highlights: 325 Works from the Museum of Modern Art* in real life, I didn't think it would happen today. I also never dreamed that it'd be Corrinne who would take me.

This is *so* going to be the best summer of my life.

"I knew that'd get a big smile. I bet you wish you had your pom-poms. You could give me a cheer. M! O! M! A! Rah, rah!" Corrinne sings and shakes an invisible pom-pom. "We'll walk down to Houston to get a cab. Too hot for the subway," she says. "And Kitsy, remember, it's pronounced *Hows*-ton, not *Houston* like the city. I don't want you to end up back in Texas."

I don't tell Corrinne that I actually *did* pack my pom-poms, but I only brought them because they remind me of the Mockingbirdettes and the best parts of home. Right now, I don't need any props to help me channel excitement because I'm headed to the Super Bowl of art museums: MoMA. Touchdown!

Corrinne hands a twenty-dollar bill to the cab driver. I try to pay but she pushes my hand away.

"I know what minimum wage in the Spoke is," she mumbles, referring to her job as a stable hand in Texas.

MoMA is a large glass building; I immediately recognize it from my book. The street's already bustling with both car and pedestrian traffic. I'm amazed that people can walk right by this place. How can they keep moving on, knowing that the great works of Pablo Picasso, Henri Matisse, and Frida Kahlo are housed inside? If I lived here, I'd have to stop in every time I passed by. Then I remember that, as of today, I do live here! I'm definitely still waiting for the jolt.

Corrinne grabs my arm and pulls me in through the doors. She holds out her iPhone. "Kitsy, I'm sorry, but I have to do this." She sets her iPhone timer for two hours. "We have lunch at the museum restaurant at one. And I know you won't agree, or at least not until you try it, but ninety percent of the point of going to this museum is eating at the restaurant. If I don't give a time limit, you'll still be in here when I get back from camp."

She's probably right. This place is sure to be my cloud nine on earth. Corrinne always says her fantasy mental happy place is in Nantucket wearing a Hervé Léger bandage dress while hanging out with her horse, Sweetbread, but I never could figure out where mine would be. But now I know: MoMA on West 53rd Street is my mental happy place. I'll pretend to visit here long after I'm back in the Spoke.

"First," Corrinne says, getting down to business, "we buy tickets, then we go to the museum shop where I'll explain the rest of the details. I already have this all planned out, *not* that you're surprised by that." Planning, plotting, and scheming are three of Corrinne's favorite activities.

At the ticket counter, Corrinne buys us two student tickets. They're *fourteen dollars* apiece, so I promise myself to soak in as much as I can since I can't afford to come back often. Corrinne walks me into the gift shop and straight over to the postcard rack, which she spins like a contestant on *Wheel of Fortune*.

"Pick four," Corrinne commands as she stops the rack's spin. "Four that you must see now, and we'll visit those and only those. You'll have time for the rest with the artsy friends you'll meet at school. I'm sure you guys will come here and be *artsy* together. Artsy, artsy, artsy," Corrinne sings. Corrinne's interests are fashion, horses, and boys.

"Okay," I say, laughing, "I'll play, but I have a book on MoMA, so I know already which ones to pick. Plus, I want to see the ones that aren't in my book and the ones that are here on loan from other museums."

Gently, Corrinne places her hand over my mouth.

"There it is," she says. "A Kitsy Monologue. *Tick, tock.*" She releases my mouth and wipes her hand on my dress. Ew!

Focusing, I scan for my four favorite works. Corrinne takes the cards from me and moves to the checkout line to buy them.

"Souvenirs," she explains. "Don't forget that a good tourist always buys them. It's a vital part of our city's economy. We need to get you an I ❤ NEW YORK shirt. Not that I'll let you wear it in public, but your brother will want one."

Corrinne's right; Kiki would want one. For a second, I wish he were here, too. But it's one thing to take care of him in Broken Spoke, and it'd be a whole other thing to do it in New York City. I definitely would need to invest in a kid-leash.

"Let's get a map," Corrinne says. "I could do Bendel's with a blindfold on, but here I need some directions."

I don't ask what Bendel's is. Knowing Corrinne, I'm sure it's a fancy store. I also don't tell Corrinne that I've done the MoMA online tour about ten times, *and* I follow the museum on Twitter. I know that there are six floors, that *The Starry Night* is on the fifth floor, that photography's on three, and the big installations are on two and five. I let her continue on her choose-your-own-museum-adventure because it's fun, and it's kind of her to do.

Corrinne looks down at the first postcard, *Gold Marilyn Monroe* by Andy Warhol. She smiles. "I would've, like, totally wanted to be an artist's muse if I lived in the sixties," Corrinne says and locates the work on her map. She pauses. "Too bad that Rider ended up being a loser. I could've been his music muse. I still can't believe that he's living in New York for the summer. *At least* he's in Brooklyn. I wouldn't want to run into him. Promise me you won't call him, Kitsy? I can't believe that he's playing with an actual *New York* band."

"Sure," I answer, "I'm not here to hang out with people from home anyway—and definitely not the ones who were mean to you! I want to meet *new* people."

Corrinne keeps talking, but I'm not really

listening—because I see it. Against a gold backdrop, much bigger than I thought it'd be, is Andy Warhol's portrait of Marilyn Monroe. It's as if she's fading away into the gold.

"Corrinne," I say. "It's her. Do you know what Warhol said about her? 'I see Marilyn as just another person.' Isn't that beautiful?"

"It might be beautiful, but it is a total, mammoth lie," Corrinne says. "No man, even if he was gay, saw Marilyn as *just another woman*." She sticks out her chest and asks, "What size boobs do you think Marilyn had?"

Looking away from Corrinne, who has cupped her chest with her hands, I get close enough to touch it. "That's the thing. He didn't use a photograph of her body, just a headshot."

Corrinne's not listening; she's already locating the next stop on the map. I give Marilyn one last look and chase after my friend.

Next up is *Map* by Jasper Johns. *Map*, which is painted with only primary colors, looks more colorful than a rainbow. I never knew that in person you have to stand three feet back in order to take it all in. It's *that* big.

I study *Map* and count in my head: I'm, at the very least, seven states away from Texas. I look around and see the other museumgoers, some in chic clothes, some speaking foreign languages, some with sketch pads. Wait, only seven states away? It feels farther.

"*Next*," Corrinne says in a bored voice. "I don't get

this modern art thing, Kitsy. The piece of art next to Marilyn was a giant fan. How's *that* art? Couldn't you just say everything is art? Is Facebook art?"

I mull it over. "I think you could argue that Facebook is art, and that we're all creating multimedia self-portraits of ourselves."

Corrinne exhales and hands me the stack of postcards and the map. "I never realized what a nerd you were. Those pom-poms and cheerleading outfits were awesome disguises. Very Double-O-Seven of you. Maybe you should be the next Bond Girl. How about you do the rest on your own? I know that you'll enjoy it more. I'm going back to the gift shop to practice my passions: browsing and charging. Meet me at the restaurant on the first floor at one o'clock *sharp* for our reservation," she says with a big grin.

I let Corrinne go because it makes sense. She likes to move quickly, use her iPhone, and talk loudly. Although this is my first real museum visit, I know that's not proper etiquette. *Dear Abby*, who I read in the *Spoke Star*, would have a field day with Corrinne.

Next up is Georgia O'Keeffe's *Abstraction Blue*, a watercolor of blues and purples. I'm glad that Corrinne's not here because I wouldn't want her to ask me to explain it. I've looked at it a thousand times in my MoMA book, but I don't know what it is or what it means. When I found out that I was coming to New York, I Googled *O'Keeffe* because Madame Williams told me she once lived in

Texas. I found out that she taught in a public school in Amarillo, which really isn't any bigger or better than the Spoke. Later, Georgia O'Keeffe was discovered in New York. I'd like to be discovered here. Or at least be recognized. I look at my watch: *Tick, tock*, got to keep moving.

I've saved *The Starry Night* for last. Approaching the gallery, I can already tell which painting it is because there's a large crowd gathered around it as if it were a celebrity and the crowd the paparazzi. Now isn't the time to be meek, I tell myself as I maneuver around the flock and edge myself into a corner spot with a perfect view. I go into a daze staring at and absorbing the palette of blue, green, and yellow swirls that make up the painting of a village at night. Even after memorizing every detail from the reproduction above my bed, the real thing still seems completely different.

Next to me, I notice a young guy with a faint five o'clock shadow wearing a fitted blue flannel. Objectively, he's totally hot, so Corrinne's going to be mad she missed spotting him, even if he's wearing a flannel in July. I turn away and try to figure out Van Gogh's techniques. Dissecting and replicating is how I've taught myself to do art, so it's always what I focus on.

"You look stunned . . . like you've seen a ghost," I overhear someone male say. I turn and realize the hot guy in the blue flannel shirt is staring directly at me.

38

I smile happily. There are friendly New Yorkers despite everyone's warnings.

"It's just pretty cool to see the real thing after looking at so many reproductions of it. None of them did it justice, not even close. *The Starry Night* has a fourth dimension or a sixth sense or something. There's definitely something magical going on."

"I agree," he says with a smile. "I've been coming here since I was a kid, and it still blows me away."

Wow, I think, a cute guy who's a regular at MoMA. He'd totally be my fantasy if I didn't already have Hands and I wasn't from Texas.

I wave my index finger. "Did you know that Van Gogh sold only one painting in his life?" I ask.

The guy shakes his head. "No, but I did know that Van Gogh became famous *only* after he died. I guess it took everyone a while to appreciate his unique style. I read that he painted *The Starry Night* at an insane asylum."

Even though I knew all that, I smile and nod, attempting to continue my one and only discuss-art-at-an-art-museum convo with *anyone*, not to mention a cute guy. As I'm about to introduce myself, I look at my watch and realize that I'm now five minutes late to lunch with Corrinne, which is going to cause her to flip out.

"Nice talking to you!" I blurt out. I give *The Starry Night* and Art Boy one last look and dash away. I think I hear him say something after me, but I'm probably just imagining it since I do kind of want to skip lunch and instead talk with this guy who gets it all afternoon.

I fly down the stairs toward the restaurant. The cafeteria I spotted on the second floor would have been perfect, but Corrinne told me earlier that she made reservations at this place—The Modern—weeks ago. She said that most of the people who eat there don't even *visit* the museum. That's hard for me to believe, but I know not everyone loves art like me. Hands would definitely choose to go to the NFL Hall of Fame in Dayton, Ohio, way before he'd elect to visit Manhattan.

When I arrive at The Modern, the first thing I see is a beautiful crystal bar with black leather stools. I feel immediately underdressed. Corrinne's shoes start to feel like I'm wearing actual artillery, not gladiator sandals, and I'm worried that I'll trip. Corrinne waves at me from a round table with crisp, white linens. This is undoubtedly the nicest place I've ever been to.

I'm about to become a lady who lunches.

"You have a museum glow to you. It looks strangely similar to a post-make-out, rosy face," Corrinne says as a waitress pulls out my chair. I try not to stiffen, but I have never had a woman pull out my chair. Thanking her, I sit down with the grace of a bull in a china shop.

"Oh, Corrinne! It was wonderful. How can I ever

thank you or your family? You don't—you don't know how much this means to me," I finally say breathlessly.

"Kitsy," Corrinne says, "stop that. You're the one that taught me to be hospitable. Remember when you bought me that Sonic Blast when I hurt my arm? Remember when you took me bargain shopping? God, you made a heaven out of hell." Corrinne quickly corrects herself. "Not that the Spoke is hell—or well—not exactly."

I laugh even though Corrinne's comment hurts. "Compared to this," I say and look around, "the Spoke is looking pretty dark, like Dante's *Inferno* dark."

"Please don't reference schoolbooks outside of school," Corrinne says matter-of-factly. "It's summer; I need some distance from learning."

"You missed *a cute boy*," I tease.

"In this museum?" Corrinne asks, giving me bug eyes. "You might be seeing things, Kitsy. And on the slim odds it's true, I have a feeling he'd be more *your* type. I'm not so into the museum-faring kind."

Corrinne's right. She's definitely into a variety of guys, but probably not any that frequent MoMA.

Pushing the image of the Art Boy out of my head, I tell Corrinne, "I only have one type: Hands."

Corrinne gives me a mysterious eyebrow raise and says strangely, "You mean you've only *tried* one type."

Since I know Corrinne and I have different views

about relationships, I don't respond, and look down at the large, leather menu.

"Speaking of heaven, the food here is otherworldly. We'll do the three-course prix fixe. When we lunch, we lunch," Corrinne says.

Corrinne and I play the parts of ladies who lunch over a meal of mozzarella and mint salad, Berkshire pork chop, and a jelly thing called panna cotta. When the bill comes, I realize that it costs as much as I earn in my weekly paycheck, and I work the maximum hours. But Corrinne charges it on her AmEx without a second thought.

"It's almost time to spa. We have a party to grace." When Corrinne stands up, she grabs a small paper bag with black handles from under the table. "I bought myself a necklace at the store, and you get a discount if you become a member of the museum. So I purchased a membership and put it in your name because I have had my fill of museums for a while. Maybe, like, forever."

Corrinne hands me a card with my name on it and a pamphlet about the perks of membership—like the fact that you can visit for free whenever you want.

I get all choked up. "Thank you, Corrinne," I say and hold the card out in front of my face. "I've never been a member of anything but the Mockingbirdettes."

I am *so* taking to New York.

# Chapter 3

## Kitsy, Phone Home

CORRINNE AND I ARE HEADING back downtown in a taxi when she asks the driver to stop at Spa Belles on Christopher Street.

"We're getting our nails done," she announces as we step into the salon, complete with at least ten nail stations and an entire room for pedicures in the back.

"I'll just watch," I say, eyeing the price board. "Or we could go to your apartment and I could do our nails for free. I just bought Canary Yellow polish, which magazines say is the hot color of the summer."

"No," Corrinne says. "Sometimes, Kitsy, you need to let other people do stuff for you. I'm going to do this for you. Well, actually, Joy will do it, but you know what I mean."

As Joy gives me a shoulder massage at the end, I think

how I could totally get used to this. Corrinne is right. It *is* a nice feeling to have someone do something for me. One thing I will never adjust to, though, are these prices: Thirty-eight dollars plus tip for a spa manicure! Do these ladies have a PhD in nail art or something?

All of a sudden, I'm no longer relaxing but thinking about tips and my last day at Sonic.

*Looking out of Sonic's front windows, I sigh when I recognize the red Mustang that's pulled into spot eighteen. Everyone in Broken Spoke knows that car. Peggy Brooks has paraded it around town 24/7 ever since her daddy brought it back from Dallas.*

*Because Ruth Ann broke her ankle and Kerry is on maternity leave, I'm the only carhop. I have no option other than to wait on Peggy even though she rallied to replace me as Mockingbirdette captain on account of my "reputation." The only thing is that it's Peggy, not me, who has a reputation; she was just trying to use my family's situation to her advantage. It didn't work, but it still burns, especially since I'm forced to act all peppy and zesty around her at cheer events.*

*I count down, three, two, one. Then, as if on cue, I hear through my earpiece:*

*"Hello. Hello. Is this thing on?" Peggy yells. Through the window, I see her sticking her whole head out of her car to talk to the intercom, which is totally unnecessary.*

"Yes, it's on," I say politely. "Welcome to Sonic. Would you like to try one of our four new all-beef hot dogs?"

I always follow the script because our manager, Rob, gets mad if we don't, and I can't risk losing my job.

"Kitsy, is that you?" Peggy cackles. "I didn't think you still worked here."

What I want to say is "where else can a high schooler get a job in Broken Spoke?" Truth is, I'm lucky to have this one. I'm the youngest person who works here, and every day people come in asking for job applications.

"Hi, Peggy. Yes, it's me. I hope you're enjoying your summer. What can I get for you?" I say with as much energy as possible.

"Does the low-cal diet limeade have calories?" Peggy asks. I watch her stare at the giant, electronic menu.

"It has twenty calories," I answer. I want to say if it has no calories, it would be called calorie-free, not low-cal.

"Twenty?" Peggy repeats, horrified.

"Twenty for the thirty-two-ounce drink," I clarify.

"Okay, fine, I'll have a medium one. And I'll have a double cheeseburger. That's for Taylor," she says proudly. "I could never eat the food here."

Taylor is a player on Hands's football team. Peggy's been chasing him for years. Everyone says he just likes her car. I try not to gossip, but I secretly agree.

"That's funny because I love the food here. It's Sonic

good!" I exclaim. That's our company motto.

Maybe if Peggy spent less time joyriding and more time walking, she wouldn't be so worried about eating a cheeseburger here and there. Truth is, Sonic is delicious and cheap, especially with my employee discount. I think the whole reason I'm Kiki's hero is that I usually bring him home a Sonic shake. Unlike Peggy, he thinks it's awesome that I work at Sonic.

"That'll be four dollars and eighty cents," I say, ringing it up. "I'll skate over real soon. Is the order to go?"

"Yes and hurry," Peggy demands. "Taylor doesn't like it when his food is cold."

I think Peggy ought to tell Taylor to get his own food then.

After grabbing a burger from the heat lamp and filling a cup with limeade, I Rollerblade out the door. Usually, I don't do any tricks, but I decide to skate backward to her car. I want to remind her that it's not just my sunny disposition that earned my team captain spot, it was also my athletic abilities. Next year, I'm definitely auditioning for Sonic's So You Think You Can Skate competition.

Peggy rolls down her window barely enough for me to fit the bag and drink through. Maybe she's worried about catching my reputation.

Handing me a five-dollar bill, she says with a smile: "Keep the change."

Doing the math quickly, I realize that she's given me a 4 percent tip.

All of a sudden, I find myself saying, "No thanks," and

handing her two dimes back. *"I'd prefer you to keep your tip, just like I kept my captain title."*

*She shakes her head, throwing the change in her cup holder.*

*"My momma and I are praying for you and your family,"* *she calls out as she puts her car in reverse.*

*Tell your momma to save her prayers for you, I think.*

*But I say, "Tell her thank you. I'll need them when I'm spending the rest of the summer in Manhattan. I hope you have a great time in the Spoke."*

*Peggy screeches on the brakes and her mouth drops open. Now it's me who's smiling. She might care about being queen bee in high school, but I don't. What I'm concerned with is pursuing my passion and seeing the world outside this town.*

"Kitsy Kidd, Kitsy Kidd," Corrinne is saying again and again. "Kitsy, are you okay?"

I come to and smile at Corrinne.

"You were so zoned out," she says. "You must've fallen asleep after Joy finished the massage."

"I'm fine," I say, standing up from the chair and looking out of Spa Belles's window to New York's streets.

You've made it to NYC, Kitsy, so why can't you leave the Spoke and girls like Peggy Brooks behind?

When we get back to Corrinne's apartment, Mrs. Corcoran is there. She's dressed in a different black skirt (this time pleated), white top, and strand of pearls (this time black).

"Remember to call your mother. She'll worry," Mrs. Corcoran says before slipping out the door to a party. "All of us moms worry."

I don't correct her.

I follow Corrinne into her room and I grab my phone off the nightstand where I left it. Eight new text messages. Three missed calls.

Hands: Call me. I'll pay the phone bill if you go over minutes.

Amber: Glad u made it. Which one is the fuse for the bathroom? Text me back soon.

Kiki: Hiiiii. Have you seen King Kong yet? Call me.

Hands: Call me.

Amber: Did you take my black heels? I hope not. . . .

Kiki: Made popcorn like u showed me. Hot here.

Amber: Call your brother. He's asking for you.

Hands: That's it. I'm calling the NYPD blue. Caallllll me.

I sit on the floor of Corrinne's bathroom so I can call Kiki back. He is my most important baggage. He answers on the first ring.

"Did you see him yet? Did he destroy the city? Are you okay?" Kiki asks me breathlessly.

"Kiki, calm down. Don't you remember that King

48

Kong was just misunderstood? He didn't mean to hurt all those people," I explain. The last thing I want when I'm in New York is for Kiki to have nightmares about a hairy beast gobbling me up. I already feel guilty enough about leaving him at home.

"Oh no," Kiki exclaims. "I hope you didn't fall in love with King Kong like that lady in the movie. Hands would be so mad. What about the Marshmallow Man from *Ghostbusters*? You see him? He'd be impossible to miss. . . . Does he smell sweet?"

Kiki has an incredible imagination both because of and in spite of growing up in the middle of nowhere.

"I'm pretty sure the Ghostbusters took out all the ghosts back in the 1980s, but I'll keep my eye out for anything suspicious," I answer seriously.

I'll have to remember to take some photos of *Ghostbusters* landmarks for Kiki.

Amber forgets to pay a lot of bills but never forgets the cable. She's a serious fan of the Home Shopping Network, which she watches from late night to early morning. Having cable is a good thing since Kiki's already an amateur film buff and studies *TV Guide* like it's the multiplication table. Classics are his favorites. I think I know why Kiki's so into movies—because Amber once said that our dad loved film and TV and wanted to be in show business.

I don't remember that about our dad, but I'd never tell Kiki that. He thinks that it's their thing. He hopes one day that our dad will show back up, he'll impress him with his movie savvy, and the last six years will be forgotten. I know that's ridiculous, but Kiki's only nine years old. All third graders believe in ridiculous things.

"Don't watch too much TV, Kiki," I counsel. "Remember that Corrinne's grandparents said that you're welcome there anytime. Did Mom go out today?"

"Kits," Kiki whines, "it's too hot for anything but TV. No, I don't think Mom went anywhere. Why?"

"Oh, nothing," I say and breathe deeply. "You'd love it here, Kiki. We'll visit Manhattan together someday. Today, I got to see the real *Starry Night*, the painting on the poster above my bed, and I was so close I could almost touch the painted stars." I already want to ditch Corrinne's party and try out my new membership to MoMA. I wonder how late the museum stays open.

"Wow," Kiki exclaims. "Mom says I can sleep in your bed tonight, and I'm going to stare at your poster all night. It'll be like we're looking at the same stars."

Tearing up, I squeak, "I'm always thinking about you here." My guilt that I didn't call earlier overwhelms me.

"What are you having for supper?" I ask as I wipe a single tear away.

"Stouffer's lasagna," Kiki answers. I can hear Amber

saying something in the background.

"Okay, Kiki," I sigh. "Make sure you eat some veggies as well. You want to be tall and strong, right?"

"Okay, Kits," Kiki says. "I love you. And remember: *Who you gonna call?*"

"Ghostbusters," I answer, blinking a few times. I suddenly remember that I saw *Ghostbusters* on TV with my dad right before he left. The movie gave me nightmares, and he stayed up all night trying to convince me it was actually a comedy. "A green gooey sidekick named Slimer? Kits, c'mon, how's that scary? A marshmallow man? How's that scary? One day, I'll take you to New York and you'll see it's not scary."

I found out a few weeks after we saw that movie that real life is what is actually scary.

"I miss you," I say, and hope my voice doesn't crack. "Put Mom on."

I hear some scuffling in the background, and Amber picks up the phone.

"Kits, any celebrity spottings? And did you take my black heels?" Amber rants.

"I'm not here to see celebrities," I say and then lower my octave level, so Corrinne can't hear. "The black heels are under your bed. And where are you going in black heels anyway? Remember, the bathroom fuse is the top left. And don't blow-dry your hair in the bathroom. Do it in my room."

"Okay, Kitsy. What am I going to do without you?" Her voice trembles a bit, and I realize she's really nervous about being on her own.

So I keep my mouth shut and don't let any of my ten thousand worries escape. Just last month, I spent the money I was saving for a watercolor set to pay our overdue electric bill. It would've been hard to paint in the dark anyway.

"Y'all will have a great summer, Amber," I say cheerfully. "Do something fun with Kiki. You know that Rob will give you free Sonic food. Take Kiki over there sometime. And make sure you actually go you-know-where."

With my foot, I push Corrinne's bathroom door all the way shut. You-know-where is the unemployment office, and Corrinne especially doesn't need to hear this part. Of course, I know Sonic isn't any better for Kiki than frozen lasagna, but at least he'll get out of the house. And Rob, my manager, would never make Amber pay. He knows from my willingness to take over anyone's shift without a second thought that money's pretty tight in our family.

"I'll go tomorrow," Amber promises quickly. "And that rumor about the factory is starting up again. Not that someone with my qualifications should have to work on the assembly line, but maybe there will be some management positions available."

The speculation about the farm equipment factory reopening goes around every year. I stopped believing in it around the same time as I stopped believing in Santa Claus. Amber went to college for two years, so she thinks she's too good for most jobs because of her *qualifications.* I even tried to get her to work at Sonic with me, and she said, "Kits, I don't think you understand. I don't work because there aren't jobs in the Spoke for my degree. If your father hadn't forced me to stay here, I'd be a successful career woman by now. I'd probably even have my own business."

Sometimes what I hear is *if I didn't have to be with you and Kiki, I'd be happy and successful.* Sometimes it sounds like she's blaming not just my dad but Kiki and me, too.

"A job is a job," I say, which is always my answer. This time I add, "I feel bad I can't work while I'm in New York."

"You deserve a break," Amber says with a sigh, and I hear her rustling around. "I have to go. Lasagna is in the oven."

"Amber," I coax, "remember, easy on the wine."
*Click.*

It's not that I worry about Amber driving drunk or running off to a bar and leaving Kiki home alone. She has never done any of those things. The problem with Amber and her Arbor Mist habit is that she just checks out mentally. When she's drinking, she's always around but never *actually* there. Truthfully, I feel relieved not to be at home supervising, but that makes me feel guilty, too. I wish just once I could be happy in a normal, teenage way without having a conscience about it. I remind myself that's one of my goals while I'm here in New York.

I hear Corrinne's voice through the door. "Wardrobe time!"

"Okay," I call back to her. "I've just got to dial Hands real quick."

Hands also picks up on the first ring. "Hey, doll," he says, "I got worried. Don't tell me New York City doesn't have cell phone reception."

"Sorry," I apologize, and I mean it. Hands is always there for me. "I went to MoMA, the museum I have the book on. The place is amazing, Hands, better than I ever imagined."

"That's great, Kitsy," Hands says, pausing. "I do want you to have a vacation . . . just not one from me, too."

Breathing in deeply, I remind myself that Hands isn't trying to be a nag and that I should've called when I landed, but I was too caught up in the excitement. Just because I wanted to get away from the Spoke and work on my art doesn't mean I want to get away from Hands. At his house, I can forget for a few minutes all the stuff going on back at home. Hands is always pushing me to ask for help and telling me to remind Amber who the mother is. The only thing is, it's nothing that Hands can completely understand—because *he's* an only child of two with-it parents, whereas I'm the part-time mom, part-time teen to one single mom and one little brother.

"Promise me you'll check in on Kiki," I urge.

"Kit-Kat," Hands says, "I already promised twice that I would. I'll go by tomorrow after practice. . . ."

I hear Corrinne rummaging through her closet and I feel like I should get off the phone and hang out with her. But I hear a strain in Hands's voice, something off in his tone.

"Something wrong, Hands?" I ask.

"No," he says and pauses. "It's just you didn't call and I was worried about you getting to Corrinne's okay. Plus, when Bubby and me were tossing around the football, he mentioned that there's a transfer from Bulston . . . and I know this kid, Kits. He plays quarterback, too. I think I'll definitely have competition for my spot this fall."

"Oh, Hands," I say, and take a breath.

Football is not only Hands's thing. Football is all of Broken Spoke's thing: It's also our *only* thing.

"I'm sure you're better than him. Y'all won state, don't you forget that. No one is going to take that or your position away. You got all summer to work out. It'll be okay," I say, trying to sound confident. I notice it's a little hard to be a cheerleader with major pep-and-go on a long-distance call.

"I gotta go," I say. "Corrinne has big plans for us, and I can't be late."

"What kind of plans?" Hands asks.

I pause. "We're going out for supper," I lie. Corrinne

told me over our manis (Corrinne's word, not mine) that it was a huge party, and that there might be college kids and live entertainment. It will not be a supper at all, and if it were, they'd call it dinner. "No one uses the word *supper* here," Corrinne said. "*Trust* me."

"Okay, I'll let you go then. O O O," Hands says, and he almost sounds like himself again. "Call me later. I know it's only been a day, but it's weird not doing stuff together. Bubby even asked me what it's like to have *Hitsy* separated for a month. Get it, *Hitsy*? But really, Kitsy, I do feel I'm missing part of me without you here."

"That's sweet, Hands. X X X," I say softly and hang up. I put my cell phone down on the bathroom counter.

I don't feel like I'm missing part of me in New York. Instead I feel like I'm finding new parts of me here.

I breathe in and look in the mirror. My blond curls look a little frizzed out, and the bags underneath my eyes aren't doing anything good for my normally bright blue eyes. I feel tired, as if I'd space-traveled from one world to another rather than flew across country, but I do what I always do when I have to cheer tired: I smile bigger and add more concealer.

"Corrinne Corcoran!" I chirp as I open the door. "How about the best night of our lives?" And part of me thinks it could actually happen, since anything can happen in New York.

Corrinne's face breaks out into a giant smile. "Thank God, I thought you got homesick. You freaked me out until I remembered that you're good person, and you were acting like one by calling home."

And as soon as she finishes her sentence, she swings open her closet door.

"Pick out whatever you want!" Corrinne says. With all the incredible clothes she owns, Corrinne could open a boutique right out of her closet. Luckily, I get to go shopping there for free.

I find myself wishing my real life was always as easy as it is at this moment.

# Chapter 4

## When I Was Seventeen, I Went to a Party at The Pierre Hotel

DRESSED IN CORRINNE'S WHITE SLIP dress and black tights and wearing a feathered hair extension, I know I don't look like myself, and I definitely don't feel like myself. And I'm pretty sure that's a good thing.

We step out into the cool of a summer night. I can see people strolling, biking, and jogging down the Hudson River Park. Summer in Texas basically means avoiding the outdoors and opening car doors with pot holders so you don't get scalded. We have heat advisories and you can be arrested for jogging because it's dangerously hot. If I were wearing tights in Texas right now, they'd melt permanently onto my legs. I think I could get used to the New York version of summer.

"Are we going to take that underground train thing?" I ask Corrinne.

Corrinne stops strutting up the block in her three-inch wedges and bends over at the waist. I wonder if something is wrong until I hear her high-pitched laughter.

"It's called the subway. Oh Holy Holly Golightly, I don't know if I can leave you in New York alone," she cackles.

Blushing, I fib easily, saying, "I knew that. I was just practicing the part of a naïve country girl. How'd I do?"

"Aced it," Corrinne says, throwing her hand in the air. A yellow cab comes barreling toward us.

"Here's the thing about the subway, Kits. It's fine for getting from place to place, but it's no good for making an arrival. Think about celebrities and how sexy they look getting out of cars."

"Corrinne, you can usually see those celebrities' privates, which isn't sexy. And they ride in limos, anyway," I argue.

"Kitsy," Corrinne says as she climbs into the cab, "we can't be going places in limos. We were just in a recession. It would be insensitive. East Sixty-First Street and Fifth, please. The Pierre Hotel."

I slide into the cab next to Corrinne and buckle my seat belt, even though Corrinne tells me nobody wears seat belts in cabs. "It's a cab, Kitsy, not a pickup truck." I'm not sure I follow her logic, and there's no way that I'm letting anything, especially a taxi collision, mess up my summer and my chance at becoming a real artist.

The cab zooms off into traffic. I stay quiet in fear of saying something else stupid and watch the city out my window. Bike messengers wearing twenty-pound chain locks around their waists weave through traffic. Several almost collide with our cab, and each time I white-knuckle grab the door handle. Corrinne keeps on calmly typing on her iPhone.

Once I can relax, I stare out the window at all the places I want to visit. There's an entire restaurant devoted to dumplings and a store that sells only jeans! I'm also shocked by all the different types of people I see. There are little kids by themselves on scooters zooming around. *Adults* on skateboards. I could paint the rainbow with the many different-colored Ray-Ban sunglasses I spot. I see a couple, the woman in an evening gown and the man in a tux, walking casually down the street as if they got that dressed up all the time. Every single person I notice seems interesting enough that I want the cab to stop, so I can ask them: "Who are you? How did you get to live here? Why not me?"

We approach a green forest, which I immediately recognize as Central Park.

"Ohmigosh," I squeal. "It's the park. It's from *Sex and the City* when Carrie and Big fall in the water, not to mention it's in every movie about New York. It's so beautiful. I read all about this statue called *Angel of the Waters* above a fountain in the park. A sculptor named Emma Stebbins created it in the late 1800s! I must see it."

Corrinne looks up from her iPhone, which she had been obsessively typing on throughout the entire ride, not even noticing the incredible city outside.

"There's my Kitsy," she says. "I was beginning to worry that the city turned you into a mute. And who's Emma Stebbins? Hopefully, your art friends understand you, since I've no idea what you are saying."

That reminds me of Art Boy from MoMA. I hope that was just the first of a whole summer of conversations about art.

We pull up in front of The Pierre, a white hotel with arched windows and two beautiful awnings. Men dressed in green suits with top hats guard the hotel as if it were a palace and they its protectors. As Corrinne hands a wad of cash to the taxi driver, a doorman swings open my door and grabs my hand to help me out. I'm having a total princess moment.

"Does your friend live in a hotel like Eloise?" Corrinne and I, teetering on her highest heels, enter the lobby.

"No," Corrinne answers. "Vladlena's just renting a suite for her birthday. It's totally winning. No one has to use a fake ID, and we can still party in style without getting caught by someone's parents. Besides, Eloise lived at the Plaza."

I don't ask about how Vladlena, a high school exchange

student from Russia at Corrinne's boarding school, can afford to host a birthday party like this. I think that this must, like most things here, fall under the category of T.N.O.M.W.: Things Not of My World.

In the white-and-gold-marble-adorned lobby, complete with shiny black-and-white-checked floors, people whisk in and out accompanied by bellmen carrying their luxury logo-stamped luggage. One lady, with hair as red as a barn, makes a silk T-shirt and leggings look as beautiful as a ball gown. She could wear a potato sack and get away with it.

"Is there a model convention going on?" I ask Corrinne in a hushed voice.

"Get used to it, Kitsy," Corrinne says. "It's the way everyone here looks. People either want to be models, were models once, or are currently models. Don't let it get you down. You're here to be somebody, too."

I'm not sure what Corrinne means by that, but I hope it's somehow a compliment. "We're early," Corrinne announces. "Let's go to the bar."

I start to sweat. I'm not wearing my own clothing, which makes me even more nervous. The only bar I've ever been to is a ballet bar back when we could afford my lessons. Besides, I'm four years away from being the legal drinking age. I know that Corrinne has some ID that says she's twenty-one and that her fake name is Mauve, who is actually some third cousin of hers.

"Okay," I say. "You know I don't have an ID, right? I'll just get a Shirley Temple. I'm totally fine with not drinking," I add because it's true.

"They don't ID. It's pretty alienating to ID your customers when you're charging eighteen dollars a drink," Corrine declares.

*Eighteen dollars?* You could order half of the Sonic menu for that.

Corrinne marches on into the bar, which is a long, narrow room. Gold drapery hangs from the windows, pink couches and striped armchairs line one wall, and a gold-and-navy mirrored bar takes over the other.

I make a move to find the remotest and darkest corner when I see Corrinne hop onto a barstool in the very front. Hesitantly, I push myself up onto the stool next to her.

"You ladies look nice tonight," the bartender, who also looks like he could strut a catwalk, says from his perch. He puts out two fancy, cloth napkins, one in front of each of us.

I'm nearly positive he's using the word *ladies* as a trick. It's probably a code word for *underage*. Soon, the cops will be called, I'll be exiled back to Texas, and everyone will say, "It figures. It's Amber's daughter, after all."

Corrinne doesn't bat a smoky eye and orders us two Tanqueray and tonics.

Without another word, the bartender starts making our drinks.

As Corrinne sets a speed typing record on her iPhone, I text Hands to make sure all is okay. He responds immediately:

Decided tonight's going to be a drinking night. It's off-season anyway. Bubby's driving, he's the DD. OOO.

Hands must be taking the whole there's-a-new-Tony-Romo-in-the-Spoke thing hard because he usually never drinks, no matter the season. I wonder if I should excuse myself and call him when a gaggle of girls enter the bar, throw open their arms, and embrace me.

"Kitsy!" a girl in a strapless cobalt blue dress that barely covers her bottom exclaims. "Corrinne has asked us to adopt you."

"Great," I say and nod uneasily since I already have a family. Maybe we're a semi-dysfunctional one, but it does include an irreplaceable and darling little brother.

"Make that disappear," Corrinne directs, motioning to my drink. "We're going to the suite."

I decide not to finish it because I don't want to look like Amber when she sucks one down. No one's paying attention anyway. Everyone's complimenting one another's clothes, which, if I'm hearing correctly, were all bought new for this event as if it were prom.

We cluster into the elevator, and I see more buttons than there are on one of those fancy algebra calculators. There are thirty-two floors. I want to press all the buttons and see them light up, but I hold myself back. We step out on seven.

A door flies open and Vladlena stands before us, surrounded by silver buckets on the floor. I wonder if her room has leaks before I realize the buckets are each holding ice and a bottle of champagne.

"Seventeen buckets for seventeen years!" Vladlena exclaims in the most exotic Russian accent.

All the girls squeal. I think if Vladlena can fit in from another country, I can fit in from another state . . . although I'm pretty sure Vladlena's from the same society as Corrinne, even if it is of the Russian variety.

Corrinne drags me over to Vladlena and introduces us.

"Kitsy," Vladlena says, "so good to finally meet you. I've been dying to ask you if you could find me a cowboy like Corrinne's Bubby."

I don't clarify to Vladlena that Bubby's way more into catching pigskin than roping a horse because I don't want to pop her Texan cowboy dream.

She gracefully bends down and hands me a bottle of champagne. Vladlena must be over six feet tall, and I feel small in more than one way.

Even though I've never had champagne, I brace myself for the cork flying, and the champagne spraying everywhere like it happens in New Year's Eve movies. But when Vladlena gently twists off her bottle's cap, there's just a soft pop. "A trick from Russia," she says and smiles.

I can especially appreciate Vladlena's trick because I'm currently admiring the expensive suite. It has a quilted ivory couch and the white-and-peach drapery perfectly matches the bedding. I have to resist my sudden urge to buy a plastic drop cloth and cover the suite with it. Cleaning falls under the things-that-won't-get-done-unless-I-do-them category at home, so I have become a bit Martha Stewart about housekeeping.

When someone slips an iPod into a docking station, the entire suite turns into a dance party. *This* I can do. To the ditty of the moment, Corrinne and I dance throughout the palatial suite.

For a few short minutes, I feel like I belong.

That feeling ends when seven popped-collar, pastel-Polo-wearing guys show up at the door. When the boys enter, the girls stop dancing, pick up their champagne glasses, and refill.

The flock of guys sit on a couch and start passing around a flask. Corrinne makes no motion to introduce me, and the girls huddle like an opposing football team on the other side of the room.

All the girls gather on the bed and drink more of the champagne. My head starts to feel lighter and lighter, so I decide to stop drinking.

Corrinne brings me over to talk to Blake and Breck, identical twin brothers, who apparently haven't gotten over wearing nearly the same outfits.

"You're from Texas?" Breck or Blake asks. "We know tons of Texans. Do you know the Bensons, the Heads, or the McLinns?"

All the names ring bells as rich oil families I've read about online in the *Dallas Morning News*. But I most certainly don't know any of them, nor do they live anywhere near Broken Spoke.

I shake my head. "No," I repeat again and again until they run out of names. And then there's a pause.

"Do you live on some sort of farm?" Blake, I think it's Blake, asks.

"No," I say, "farming has pretty much dried up. Unfortunately, crystal meth's the only crop that's selling well in my part."

Blake and Breck look at me as if I just said that I grew up in a jungle raised by benevolent wolves.

Corrinne immediately interjects to rescue me. "Kitsy's going to be an art student at Parsons's Foundation summer program," Corrinne says, redirecting the conversation like a captain steering a ship. I'll have to thank her later.

Usually, I can find something in common with anyone, but it isn't working with these twins.

"Really? Our cousin Iona is taking that course, too," Breck (I think) says and points to a girl sitting alone on the couch. She's dressed in a polka-dot shirtdress and red combat boots. While she's definitely pretty, with brown ringlets and a slim figure, she doesn't blend into this ripped-from-a-Polo-advertisement scene.

"Ah, I-ona," Corrinne groans. "As in I-don't-wanna-know-ya Iona. Looks like this party's no longer VIP. You know no one likes her since she cut off Waverly's pony-tail in fourth grade and called it art, right? Good thing Waverly had a work event tonight—she still blames having thin hair on Iona. She would go totally Lindsay Lohan on her."

Not that I'd ever say so to Corrinne, but I'm already taking to this Iona. Waverly is Corrinne's best friend from New York and boarding school, and let's just say we didn't see eye to eye (or cowboy hat to cowboy hat) when she visited Broken Spoke last year. She's a lot like Corrinne except minus all the redeeming qualities.

Blake—or Breck—rolls his eyes at Corrinne and beckons Iona over. Corrinne storms away in a huff, leaving me to fend for myself.

"Hey," he says to Iona, "this is Kitsy. She's attending the Parsons summer program."

Then the twins disappear to find more champagne. I vaguely hear in the distance, "We couldn't have drunk it all, there are seventeen bottles. Okay, order delivery. You only turn seventeen once!"

"Hello," Iona says. She inspects me as if she's a referee trying to determine something like whether a ball (the ball being me) was out of bounds. If this were football, I get the feeling she'd definitely throw a flag.

"I'm surprised I don't know you already," she says as she twirls a brunette ringlet around her finger and raises her hazel eyes. I notice that she has a reverse widow's peak; at the middle of her hairline, she's missing a tiny patch of hair.

"I'm from Texas," I explain for the fourteenth time that night. "I like your name." Smile and compliment is my routine for one reason: It works.

"Iona means island. Your friend Corrinne calls me I-don't-want-to-know-ya Iona. I'm not completely wowed by her creativity level, but I'm not surprised either. Look around: It's like looking at whitewashed walls. Even Vladlena blends in. We're the only ones that stick out," Iona says.

Great. So I *do* stick out, even in Corrinne's clothes. I want to go back to MoMA where it's the art, not the people, that's on exhibit.

"What medium do you usually work with?" Iona asks me.

"I mostly sketch," I answer. "I haven't had a lot of exposure to other media. Our school budget mainly goes to our football program, so the other programs, like art, get the scraps," I admit.

As much as I love football and what it brings to the Spoke, I do wish that the art facilities at least *somewhat* compared to our brand-new stadium, complete with a scoreboard that looks like it's out of the twenty-second century. The art room, on the other hand, is more nineteenth century. Calling it outdated is an understatement.

Iona scrunches her nose and says, "My school doesn't have a football team. I personally think it's a barbaric sport, but that's just my opinion."

Maybe if I lived in New York where there were a gazillion other activities to do on Friday night, I'd agree with Iona. But without football, Broken Spoke would be a scary place.

Iona continues without waiting for my opinion: "My medium is definitely painting. Like me, most students in our class are just taking this Foundation course to learn about other media to enhance their specialties—what they'll probably major in at art school. Some of the other students are ridiculously talented. I hear there's one guy who sold out his entire charcoal exhibit before his first show was even over."

The only exhibiting I've ever done was back on Amber's refrigerator when she still noticed my work. Cringing, I vividly remember the day she took my family portrait off the fridge after my dad had been gone about six months; I had spent an entire Saturday drawing it. Even though I was eleven, I knew not to try to stop her as she threw it in the trash.

As Iona goes on about specialties and exhibits, I suddenly feel out of my league. I didn't realize that most of the other students were already art prodigies. My only specialty is makeup, and I don't think that'll impress anyone here unless someone seriously needs a makeover.

"I'm hoping that I'll find my specialty over the next couple of weeks," I say cheerfully.

"You'll definitely *need* to if you want to go to art school. Nearly all of them require extensive portfolios," Iona warns, raising her dark eyebrows. I find myself wondering what she'd look like with makeup. Even though she's being an art snob, she's more refreshing than the other snobs I've been talking to. I guess it helps that we have a mutual interest.

So I decide to continue the conversation: "I'm not planning on going to art school," I say. "There aren't any near me in Texas."

I've spent hours researching art schools, but we're four hours from Dallas, where the closest one is. It's just too far. Most likely, I'll be a day student at the junior college about an hour away.

Iona stares out the window and still doesn't make eye contact.

"Of course you can't stay in Texas!" she exclaims with a snort. "You'll have to come back East. Right now, Yale is ranked at the top and there's Rizdee, of course. If you can't get into those, maybe you can stay in the South and go to SCAD. Do you *not* plan to be a professional artist?"

"I would love to," I answer dreamily and imagine myself living and working in a funky loft/studio. But then the image of Kiki growing up alone with Amber pushes it out of my mind. I hear myself blurt out, "I can't. I need to be close to my family. I have a younger brother."

"That's unfortunate," Iona says. "You must be really talented to get into the program with no previous formal art education."

"I guess," I say, worrying that Iona is now pitying me. I didn't come to New York to be pitied; I get enough of that back home.

Corrinne snatches my wrist and pulls me away.

I call over my shoulder, "See you at school, Iona," but she's already turned away.

"No champagne. All out," Corrinne slurs. Looking toward the door, she hiccups and says, "Let's get pizza. I've got to start packing."

We hug Vladlena. Corrinne stumbles and I walk out into the hallway and to the elevator. I'm upset that I didn't have a camera to take pictures, so I could tell someone about tonight: "I was there once. I was at a party in The Pierre Hotel when I was seventeen." I'm sure without a picture no one will ever believe me.

Corrinne directs our taxi to Bleecker Street Pizza, where she orders two slices of pizza. We eat them while sitting on the curb.

"I miss Texas, Kitsy," Corrinne mumbles as she finishes her slice. "I feel so over that scene at the hotel. It's all about outdoing everyone else. It just isn't fun anymore."

"That's only part of New York, Corrinne," I tell her as we walk back toward her apartment.

"Thanks, Kitsy. You're my best friend. You know that?" Corrinne says.

Of course I don't say it out loud, but I'm a tiny bit grateful that she'll be gone this summer so I can find my own corner of New York.

We wander down an empty, tree-lined Leroy Street.

"I'm so tired," she yawns.

The Corcorans are still out when we get home.

Corrinne collapses in her bed in her dress and shoes. I lie next to her, and I start to tell her about Hands, the new quarterback, and Peggy's crusade to dethrone me, but then I realize she's already asleep. I pull off Corrinne's shoes and put the comforter around her. I have a lot of practice doing that at home. Carefully, I take off the clothes that I borrowed from Corrinne and fold them neatly in a pile on a chair.

After slipping into my pj's, I walk over to the windows facing the Hudson River. Under a full moon, it glimmers from the reflected lights. The only sound is the lulling cadence of cars driving down the highway. It's hypnotizing. I find a scrap piece of paper in the kitchen, and I sit at the window and draw the river and night sky until I'm exhausted. Before retreating to the bed, I search for stars, but I don't see any.

"Good night, Kiki," I whisper. "I'm thinking of you. We're under the same stars, even if I can't find them."

# Chapter 5

## Dorothy, You Aren't on the Island Anymore

When Corrinne finally wakes up at noon, I've already been awake for more than an hour studying the river scene. It's now so full of activity that I can barely imagine it's the same serene place I sketched last night.

"Corrinne!" I start talking right away. "I saw a helicopter fly by; I think it was a coast guard one. I also saw a real protest march—with signs and everything. And, ohmigosh, people are in such good shape. Runners keep sprinting up and down the river path like someone's chasing them."

"My head feels like it got beat by the champagne demons," Corrinne groans and rubs her temples.

I walk to the kitchen and pour Corrinne a glass of water. "How about some fried eggs? I think grease helps a hangover."

"How about we order in and watch E!? There are a gazillion places that deliver. We could survive in this apartment without ever leaving." Corrinne turns on the TV to E!, where Kourtney and Khloe are yelling at Kim.

With New York City outside, why would anyone ever want to just order in and watch TV?

After fifteen minutes of being still, I get restless.

"Hey, Corrinne," I say. "Do you mind if I go to the Guggenheim?"

I know Corrinne's not going to be up for two days of museum-going. One day of it is definitely her max, but I can't bear to miss an opportunity. The Guggenheim is a lot smaller than MoMA, so it seems like the perfect museum for an afternoon visit.

"Don't you want to veg on the couch with me?" she begs. "And see what the Kardashians will do next?"

I could be okay *never* seeing what the Kardashians have done.

"How about you pack and I'll go on my own?" I ask.

"Fine," Corrinne concedes. "I do need to concentrate on my summer wardrobe. But hurry back, I want my Kitsy-time."

When I'm in the lobby, I realize that I forgot to ask Corrinne how to get to the Guggenheim on public transportation. I decide to take a cab, just this one time.

I catch one going east and climb in. After a while, I

can't help asking the driver's story. He tells me he's been driving New Yorkers in cabs for thirty years!

When the meter hits nearly fifteen dollars, I can feel my wallet shrinking.

"Sir, how much farther is it?" I ask.

Reaching toward the meter box, he says, "How about we turn this off? I'm going off-duty soon anyway, and we're almost there."

"Thank you," I say, both surprised and humbled by his kindness. It must've been obvious I was eyeing the meter.

"No, thank you. It's refreshing to get a passenger who actually wants to make conversation. So, this your first time at the Guggenheim?" he asks me as we drive up Central Park West.

"Yes, sir," I say. "First time in New York. First time out of Texas. I love it—it's fun to be anonymous," I add, feeling a certain distance from my former life, even though it's only been two days.

"I watched the Guggenheim being built way back when. They finished it the same year I got married—1959. People thought the architect, Frank Lloyd Wright, had missed the mark big-time. Nowadays, it's hard to imagine Museum Mile without it."

He pulls the cab over to the sidewalk.

In real life, the building looks as if a white, spiraling spaceship landed on the edge of Central Park. The museum itself looks like a piece of art. I can't wait to see what's inside if the outside is this incredible.

I hand my driver a twenty and he smiles at me in the rearview mirror. "Make sure to take the elevator to the top, then work your way down. You want gravity to go with you."

Entering the museum, I feel like I've found a secret castle filled with something better than treasure. All of the art hang on walls inside the spirals. Heeding the driver's advice, I pay for my admission and take an elevator straight up to the top.

When I get to the top, I look down and think about how Kiki would love to drop a penny just to see what would happen. As for me, I love looking down the spiral and seeing the art from the changing distance. With each step I descend, I see the artwork from a different angle. It's like seeing the same painting in ten different ways.

In one of the galleries, I stop and listen to a docent talking to a group of tourists. She's wearing a bohemian skirt and long, dangly beaded earrings. She moves her hands quickly as she describes a dark painting of a lively bar. I completely want the docent's life.

"This is the first work Picasso painted in Paris, a new city for him. He painted this at *only nineteen*. You can feel looking at this painting, he's *near* but not in, or part of, this party. Many people say that sometimes it takes an outsider to depict something as it is, not how people want it to be."

I think about my night at The Pierre. Although I never

thought I'd be able to compare myself with Picasso, I can relate to being an outsider in a strange new city. I never thought that being an outsider might work to my advantage in art, but maybe it will let me see New York in ways that others can't.

A little while later, the vibration of my phone interrupts my thoughts.

Corrinne: We're on borrowed time. I ordered us Chinese. I sent Ivan to pick you up out front in ten minutes.

Slowly, I make my way down the ramp. I figure Corrinne (and Chinese) can wait a few more moments. For Corrinne, New York's museums might be old news. But for me, this might be the beginning of the rest of my life.

After chowing down on lo mein and attempting to keep up with the Kardashians, Corrinne and I go to sleep.

I don't hear Corrinne's alarm. Waking me from a deep sleep, she shakes me to say good-bye. We hug tightly, and we promise to make big plans for when she sees me next in exactly twenty-six days, for my last weekend in New York.

"Remember, all my friends promised to take care of you," Corrinne says. "You're my Texan sister. Ask my mom about directions to school. It's only a few stops away on the subway."

Subway? Ohmigosh, I need to take the subway! How am I going to manage New York alone? I can't believe I put parties and an E! marathon before my education. My best friend is about to leave, I have class in three hours, and I don't even know where my school is. That's not like me, especially since opportunities like art school don't happen to me every day—or ever—until now.

I kiss Corrinne on the cheek. I don't say anything because I don't want her to worry. After all, she's letting me stay with her parents for the summer. She even told me to wear her clothes and hang out with her friends. She's done enough for me.

As soon as Corrinne leaves, I immediately hop in the shower and begin to get ready for my first day of school. Even though I'm apprehensive, I still feel that back-to-school rush. I've always been the student who buys her folders and pencils the first summer day they're displayed in Walmart. I'm also that girl—the one who plans exactly how she's going to decorate her locker. I always theme it with our school colors, red and gray. Hands would make big fun of me if he saw how giddy I am today, which reminds me that I need to call him. Maybe once I have a routine, I'll find more phone time.

When I'm finished getting dressed, I walk into the kitchen. No one is there, but a note lies on the granite kitchen countertop:

*Kitsy,*

*I had to run errands. Thank God you're here. I'd be lonely without any children. Good luck on your first day at school. To get there and avoid the heat, you can take the Christopher Street PATH to 14th Street and walk a few blocks. I drew you a map. Call my cell if you have any trouble. Love, J.J.*

I admire Mrs. Corcoran's perfect cursive. I find it nearly impossible to imagine that she and my mom knew each other. Any stranger would guess they are from different galaxies rather than the truth: They are both from the same no-stoplight town. I wonder if one day someone won't be able to believe that I grew up in a small town. I always think "no way" when I hear about a celebrity who grew up in Barely on the Map, Nebraska. Someday, I want Broken Spoke to just be the start of my life rather than my whole life. My experience in New York is a great first step toward that goal.

I head downstairs, say good-bye to Rudy (who tips his hat to me!), and head off to start my new life as an independent, metropolitan art student. Mrs. Corcoran's map looks simple enough, and I find the PATH station right away. Two cops guard the entrance, which freaks me out a bit, but I head down the stairs to find the train. A smell, which is more pungent than any from a farm, drifts into my nostrils. I want to plug my nose, but none of the other people on the stairs are reacting. They are just hustling down the steps in their polished business suits, so I figure this is a normal smell—something you deal with for living in the center of the universe.

I'm about a third of the way down the stairs when a wave of people starts running up the stairs. Trying not to panic, I get pushed into a small corner. I feel invisible as people shove past me. They resemble an angry mob and are coming up *both* sides of the stairs. Aren't there rules here like there are everywhere else? Right side goes up, left side goes down. I reckon this is what people mean when they say New Yorkers would steal your firstborn if it meant they'd catch a cab in the rain. Finally, the stairs clear and I'm able to make my way down.

I know I need to buy a ticket. ("There's no such thing as a free ride, especially in New York," Amber told me about five times before I left.) I see two giant computers, and I figure that's how I buy a ticket. I'm pretty proud of myself for being able to navigate the scene so far, especially since I've never been on a train above- or belowground before.

The computer asks me if I speak English or Spanish. Much to my teacher Señor Luiz's disappointment, my answer is only English, although I did get an A- since I tried hard. The directions seem simple enough: HOW

MANY TICKETS DO YOU WANT TO BUY? CREDIT OR CASH? A dollar seventy-five later, I'm in possession of a yellow-and-blue MetroCard. I thought about buying a monthly unlimited card, but it was really expensive and I just wasn't ready to put down that type of cash on my third day even if it might save me in the long run.

I insert my card into the turnstile and pass through the gate to the platform. Corrinne is totally correct: I can *do* this. Just then, a train comes barreling down the tracks. People get off, people get on, and I follow them. Since it's only two stops, I decide not to even sit down. I hold on to the metal rail, but I grasp lightly because I don't know whose hands last touched it. When the train roars off again, I find myself jolting back and gripping on to the rail as if it were a Sonic tray and I was Rollerblading over a pothole. After what I think is a pretty long time, the train halts at another station, and I hop off.

When I look up at the sign, it says HOBOKEN, not 14th Street. I don't panic: I imagine that some stops have two names, and one acts like a nickname, like how Times Square is also Forty-Second Street. It's probably like Hands: His name isn't actually Hands, of course, it's Clint. No one has called him Clint since his first one-handed catch in the PeeWee League. People still talk about that catch ten years later. It's part of Broken Spoke history.

I follow the crowds up the endless stairs. No wonder New

Yorkers are so skinny! The subway is more exercise than cheerleading practice. Only when I'm at the top of the stairs do I wonder if there's more than one train. What if I just went the wrong way? I look at my watch, and my pulse slows. I *do* have almost two hours. I can walk if I have to . . . and maybe this isn't even the wrong stop. I need to calm down.

At the top of the stairs, I ask a police officer which way Parsons is.

He blinks a few times. "No idea, pumpkin," he says.

Don't panic, Kitsy, I tell myself. There are a lot of schools in Manhattan. Start walking.

The area looks nothing like I've seen since coming to New York. There's the river, a sign for a bus terminal, and few outdoor cafés, but nothing looks familiar. I have no idea which way to walk. In the distance, I see a 2ND STREET sign, which makes me more confused since I'm looking for Fourteenth Street and Fifth Avenue.

You've never met a stranger, I remind myself. You're the Mockingbirdette cheerleading captain, I think. You just need to ask someone.

I walk up to a girl who looks about my age. She's wearing a tight black dress and red acrylic nails and has *big* hair (probably compliments of AquaNet). People say Texans have big hair, but it doesn't compare to what I'm seeing right now.

"Um, ma'am, can you tell me where Parsons is?"

"'Ma'am'?" the girl repeats and laughs. "No idea, I went to Rutgers," she says in an unfamiliar accent that grates on my eardrums.

I'm beginning to think Parsons is not as prestigious or well-known as the glossy catalogue led me to believe. I might as well be asking the way back to Broken Spoke. For a moment, I ponder calling Corrinne or Mrs. Corcoran, but I don't want them to worry about me or think that I can't do this. I wish I had one of those expensive GPS smartphones right about now, but there's not much use for them back home, where I can navigate my entire town with my eyes closed.

I stay standing at the top of the subway stairs, completely unsure which way I should turn. I hope that the third time is really a charm, and I ask a man in a tight, graphic T-shirt and jeans. He's wearing a big diamond medallion and at least seven gold chains. Men sure like jewelry in New York.

"Excuse me, sir. I'm looking for Parsons. To be honest, I'm lost," I finally admit.

"Parsons?" the guy says, after giving me a once-over. "Isn't that in Manhattan?"

"Yes," I answer and stare at him as if he's Captain Obvious.

"Where are *you* from?" he asks. "Girls 'round here don't call me 'sir.'"

"Texas," I answer. "I'm Kitsy Kidd, pleased to meet

you." I hold out my hand. I'm hoping my personal touch might help get me to my destination.

The guy raises his eyebrows at my hand and grips my fingers lightly. I'm surprised someone with "guns" like his has such a delicate handshake.

"Uh, I'm Kenny DeTito," he says. "And I'm pretty sure you should be looking for the Parsons over there." He points across the river to another town with skyscrapers.

"What's that?" I ask.

"Manhattan," Kenny answers.

"How's that possible?" I ask. "I was in Manhattan less than fifteen minutes ago, and I took the subway, not a boat."

"Oh, Dorothy," Kenny says, laughing. "You're not on the island anymore. The PATH goes under the Hudson River and to New Jersey. And, see, it's not as bad as people say."

"Ohmigosh," I gasp. "I've got to get back. How do I get back there?"

"The yellow brick road," Kenny says and laughs at his own joke. "No really, you take the PATH again and make sure you get on a train that says to Thirty-Third Street."

"Thank you," I say. I'm not sure how something like this could have happened. I'm not only in the wrong place, I'm also in the wrong state. I turn and start to run down the stairs.

"Hey, girl," Kenny calls out before I reach the bottom.

I look back as he yells, "Can I get your digits? Show you how Jersey guys do it better?"

I shake my head and yell back, "Got a boyfriend!" *A boyfriend I need to call.*

"All right, all right," I hear. "Say hi to Toto for me!"

I'm from Texas, not Kansas, I think as I hurry back down the rest of the stairs, put more money on my card, and go back through the turnstile.

My second-grade teacher, Miss Georgie, always told us, "If you find yourself in a hole, the first thing to do is stop digging." I reckon this is good advice for now. I ask a young man in a navy suit with a periwinkle tie how to get back to Manhattan just to make sure.

"This train," he says and points into the tunnel where I can see an incoming train's light in the distance. Talk about a light at the end of a tunnel.

"Thank you." Once I'm on the train, I start to breathe again.

After a couple of minutes, the subway comes to a halting, grinding stop in the dark tunnel. No one appears extremely surprised. Then, people start to groan and look at their watches. A couple more minutes pass, and people start muttering swearwords under their breath.

Just as I go to ask someone what's going on, the loudspeaker comes on: "Hello. We apologize for the inconvenience. Due to repair work at the Thirty-Third Street station, we're experiencing delays. An announcement will be made when we know more. Thank you for your patience."

Everyone groans and moans some more. I sigh and look at my watch. I still have some time, so I try not to have a conniption fit. I sit down between a kid with a skateboard and backpack and an elderly woman with a mini shopping cart, and I pull out my sketchbook. I came here to do art, so I'll do art.

I'm so absorbed by sketching the woman's beautiful red oriental-print purse that I forget that we're still not moving and that I'm getting closer to being late. Just as I look at my watch and realize that I now only have thirty minutes left before class, the subway takes off again. We pass Christopher Street, where I started, and two stops later we arrive at Fourteenth Street. I jump out of the subway car and race up the upstairs. Once I'm outside, it almost feels like coming home again and I take a breath of relief.

I pull out Mrs. Corcoran's map and start heading toward Parsons. When I arrive at the school, with its big glass windows, I smile. I no longer feel as skittish as a long-tailed cat in a room of rockers. Everything will be okay. I even have time to find a bathroom and reapply my makeup, which melted during what I've decided to call "The Subway Incident" when I tell the story.

I text Corrinne that I made it to school and that I miss her. I omit the going-to-New-Jersey part of my day.

I find room 302 easily. When I open the door, I find a

small classroom with stadium seating. There are four rows of desks, each one five across. They are all full except one seat in the center of the first row. The room's silent. Most of the kids look around my age, and all of them, particularly the two that are wearing toboggan hats in summer, would probably fit Corrinne's "artsy" description. There are definitely no preppy pastels here. The class is evenly divided between girls and boys.

Out of nowhere, I'm suddenly disappointed that I don't spot Art Boy. Until now, I didn't even realize that I'd be secretly hoping the boy I met at MoMA would be in my summer program. On top of being a little surprised at myself, I know that would be a ridiculous coincidence in a city of millions, but I'm a dreamer at my core.

Perhaps I'm surveying the crowd a little too closely because I then feel everyone's eyes on me—including Iona's, who I spot sitting in a middle row. I take my seat quickly.

Everyone's silent as we wait for class to begin. I find myself thinking how I got from Broken Spoke's art room, which is a converted faculty lounge, to this beautiful, modern space at one of the best art schools in the world. Only two months ago attending this school was just a card in my deck of dreams, and now it's my reality.

*"Guess what?" I ask Hands. It's early spring; we're at a field party, sitting in the bed of Yellow Submarine. The night cackles with laughter and the sparks from a bonfire.*

"Chicken butt?" Hands responds as he fingers his state championship ring. I don't laugh. Sometimes, I wonder if he and Kiki are on the same grade level for humor.

"No, listen," I demand. "This is important."

Hands puts his arm around me tightly. "I'm all yours," he declares and gives me a squeeze.

"I'm applying to art school in New York for this summer. Mrs. Corcoran heard about this program, and she told me that she'd sponsor me if I got in," I confess.

"That's great, Kitsy," Hands says. "I know you have talent. All the guys are still talking about how good the girls looked at the spring fling. I didn't tell them why, but I know it's because you did everyone's makeup. None of those girls usually look that good. Well, besides you, of course."

"It's not a school for makeup," I mutter defensively, pulling away from him. I love doing makeup, but I don't want to be the next Bobbi Brown. I want to be the next Georgia O'Keeffe.

"I didn't say it that it was beauty school," Hands says gently, and I relax. "You deserve a chance at real art school."

"I have to submit a recent work with my application, and I'm freaking out," I admit. "I can't exactly send in before-and-after headshots from prom for my portfolio. All of my sketches are either of the Spoke or are sketches of famous paintings. How am I going to compete with the kids who live in New York and attend real art classes?"

"You have no idea how good the competition is, Kitsy. All

*you can do is try your best with what you have. When you go into a cheer competition, are you worried about how you're going to do or how the other teams are going to do?"*

*Sometimes, I really think Hands should go into coaching. He's got that motivational-speaker thing down. It's a big part of why I love him. He's like inspiration in a can.*

*"I'm thinking about how well I can do," I answer.*

*"Because that's all you can control," he says, and I nod my head in agreement.*

*Before cheer competitions, we always chant: "Nobody can fly like a Mockingbird." I need to remember that no one can fly like Kitsy, either.*

*Bubby's voice booms toward us from near the campfire. "C'mon, lovebirds, you've dated since you were five. Why don't you two take a timeout from each other to be social with your friends?"*

*I motion for Hands to go, and reluctantly he does.*

*There's a little bit of daylight lingering, so I decide to pull out a sketchbook from my pocketbook, which is bursting with my pom-poms, a roll of toilet paper, and who knows what else. Looking around, I settle on sketching the outline of an old oak tree. Do the best with what you have.*

A sixty-something man with a long gray ponytail in a red-print Hawaiian T-shirt saunters into the room and brings me back to the present.

"Good morning. As you all must know," he says, and puts his briefcase on the front table, "I'm Professor Paul Picasso, your instructor. When your last name is Picasso, you're immediately destined to teach art rather than be a famous artist because there can be only one Picasso. My only hope for immortality is that one of you will make an important contribution to the art world. And by the art world, I don't mean commercials or Pixar but the *real art world*."

I look around the room to try to gauge other people's reactions, but everyone's eyes remain glued on Professor Picasso. What's so wrong with Pixar? I want to ask. And what does the real art world mean? Two minutes in, and I'm lost—for the second time today! But if I can find my way to New York City, I've got to believe I can navigate this class.

"*And*, we *won't* be doing introductions. This isn't summer camp. You're not here to make s'mores or friendship bracelets. You'll be making art—and not arts and crafts— or at least, that's the hope. You all submitted a piece of work with your application, and the admissions committee selected this class based on what they saw. Some of you have raw talent while others of you have clearly studied art. It doesn't matter who's who, all that matters is what you do with it from here on out. Come every day ready to learn, and try not to waste your time or your parents' money."

Or even worse, waste your best friend's parents' money. Suddenly, I feel self-conscious. Maybe I don't belong here. Maybe I belong back in the Spoke with Madame Williams, who tells everyone that his or her work is a masterpiece. It's cozy back there; it's like a cocoon of compliments. But the thing is, I don't want to be comfortable. I want to be challenged and that's why I'm here.

"And now, without further ado," Professor Picasso continues, "I'll explain the structure of our course. We have class every day from nine in the morning to four in the afternoon. There will be a break for lunch at noon. Just so you know, I think that punctuality is next to godliness. For the first three weeks, we'll work on developing skills in three separate disciplines. There will be a figurative drawing week, a clay week, and a photography week. The final week will be less structured, so you can work on portfolios. Children, it's now time to get started."

Professor Picasso opens the door. Another man, who's tall but very round in the middle, saunters in. He's wearing only a black terry cloth robe, and he casually takes it off to reveal he's wearing . . . absolutely nothing.

"Obviously, as you now see, we're starting figurative drawing today. Please begin to sketch our model. And remember, art feels no shame. Let's be mature about this."

I feel my face go completely white.

Next to me, there's a guy wearing black jeans, a white T-shirt, and coral-framed glasses. He looks over at me and mouths, "Hot."

I laugh on reflex, and then quickly cover my mouth before anyone realizes I'm the immature one in the room.

I'm exhausted after sketching the male naked form for two hours, and I've sweated through my top despite the fact that the AC was blasting the entire time. A front row seat is usually a good thing in my book, since teachers associate proximity to the front with a desire to learn. But today I would've preferred a seat a few rows back, so I wouldn't have a magnified view of our model *and* so I could figure out my classmates.

After our lunch break, while we wait for the model to return, Professor Picasso explains why he picked a "robust" model that carries twenty-five extra pounds at his waist.

"It's a lot harder to sketch fat people. Always choose *fuller* figurative drawing models because it will strengthen your skills. Anyone who can draw a stick figure can sketch a Kate Moss wannabe," he tells us. I see heads nodding in agreement.

When our model returns, I find myself wondering how he does it—how he is so okay with being so exposed. Alone in NYC (and Jersey) for only a few hours, I feel more than ever that vulnerability is a pretty scary thing. You can feel naked in a lot of different ways. With each line of my pencil, I feel as if I, too, am disrobing.

After a lesson from Professor Picasso on how to mark off different sections of the body, he dismisses us. "You can go for the day. But, first, give me your best attempt."

He quickly moves around the room collecting sketches. When he reaches me, I tear out what I think is my best sketch. I try not to make eye contact so he doesn't see how I was sweating like a hog at a 4-H competition. He hasn't said anything to anyone else when he collected their sketches, so I'm shocked when he says, "*Really?*" I look up to see him raise his furry, gray eyebrows, which resemble aging caterpillars.

"Yes, sir," I squeak, and I see my classmates start to whisper. His "really" was most certainly not a *really* with excitement.

Professor Picasso looks away without another word.

I quietly collect my belongings, and I walk out the door. Some of my classmates, including Iona, are gathering in the hall.

"Kitsy," Iona calls out. "What was your sketch like? Why did Picasso say *really* to you? Did you reinterpret his instructions?"

"No," I answer, "I drew only what I saw." I don't mention that it wasn't pretty, either.

"That's weird then," Iona says, looking confused. "We'll find out tomorrow. Apparently, Picasso gives critiques of everyone's work in front of the class. It's basically a roast. I think it's going to be *fantastic*. I love to watch people get skewered, especially kids with huge egos."

I can barely muster a "great, see you then," before I turn to scuttle down the hallway. New Jersey? A fat, naked model? A "really?" A roast that doesn't involve a pig or a cow? What have I gotten myself into?

I'm halfway down the hallway when I feel a hand on my shoulder. "I'm Ford," the jokester with glasses who sat next to me says.

"Kitsy," I introduce myself. "Kitsy Kidd. You almost got me in trouble in class for laughing."

"No one's ever been hurt from laughing. And, I wouldn't worry about Iona. I know her from school and she just likes to get into people's heads. By the way, I totally *heart* your clothes," he says, examining my outfit, a watercolor blue-and-green print skirt with a magenta top. "How did you think of putting those colors together?"

I hesitate for a second before speaking—then I remember why I'm here.

"Okay, I've never told this to anyone, but I get my inspiration from color palettes from artworks that I love. I figure artists, especially great ones, know color way better than any expensive designer does. Today, my outfit is based off of the colors from Monet's *Water Lilies*."

"That's *so* classy," Ford says and twirls me around. "Much cooler than ordering out of J.Crew like most of the *chicas* I've grown up with do. They all look like teenage clones."

I nod. Back home, I love being part of the Mockingbirdettes. But I don't like how we all dress alike for game days. We match everything down to our earrings, hairstyles, and socks. I personally think it'd be more fun if we showed our individual personalities, but I always got voted down on that one.

Ford breathes in and continues, "I would completely *die* to work in fashion, but my parents aren't so gung ho about it. I even took them to the Metropolitan Museum of Art to see the Alexander McQueen show, the amazing fashion designer's retrospective, which was AH-*mazing*. But it's, like, my parents are totally blind. On second thought, if you saw the way they dressed, you might think they're actually blind. They wouldn't let me take another fashion class this summer because they think it isn't *real art*. They're liberal art professors and are total academic snobs about any disciplines other than the classics. This summer course is our compromise."

"I think fashion is art. But *really*, what do I know?" I joke, mimicking Professor Picasso's *really*.

Ford bursts out laughing. Even though I made a joke of

it, remembering Professor Picasso's *really* feels like someone pricked me with a needle.

"I do understand the parent thing," I say and nod knowingly. "My mom wants me to do something practical even though she doesn't know the meaning of the word."

Ford smiles back. "I think it's practical to follow your dreams since that's what will make you happy. Isn't it actually *impractical* to do something we don't like? That'd be setting ourselves up for failure," he says and winks. "I've got to run, but I'll see you tomorrow."

"It was really nice to meet you, Ford!" I call out.

Even if Professor Picasso wasn't impressed with me, at least *someone* out there thinks I have an eye. And I can't forget I've met two people since I arrived here who can talk art, which is two more than I've ever met in Texas. It's been a nice turn of events from Broken Spoke, where most conversations play out like an episode of *BSFN, Broken Spoke Football Network*, with reruns from the last fifty years playing on a loop.

When I'm outside on the street, I turn my cell phone back on. Four texts.

Waverly: Big party tomorrow! Corrinne told me to invite you. Call me.
Kiki: Are you famous yet?

Hands: Coach wants to get breakfast tomorrow and "talk." Not good.

Corrinne: How'd it go? I can't believe I'm in the country at camp, and you are in the city. Talk about funny!

I'm shocked that Waverly actually invited me even if Corrinne did ask her to. And a party on a Tuesday? I mean, it's summer, but isn't it technically still a school night?

I should call Hands or Kiki to talk and catch up with them both about New York and home, but I need my thoughts for myself right now. I start walking back toward the Corcorans', figuring I'll save some money and skip the subway fiasco. I know that Hands especially needs Mockingbirdette Kitsy right now, but I'm feeling a little more like Struggling Artist Kitsy. I need my own personal cheerleader so Hands will have to wait.

As I walk down the streets of the West Village, I already feel calmer. I take a deep breath and try to think good thoughts. This is the place of dreams, even if today wasn't perfect. You can't expect to wake up and have your dreams come true instantly. You have to earn them, and if I'm good at anything, it's working hard.

To: corrinnec@gmail.com
From: kkidd@gmail.com
Date: Monday July 16
Subject: Missing you!

I'm not sure if you'll get this since you're at camp, but just wanted to say hi. It's hard navigating this place without you!

The first day of school went okay—not sure the professor likes me, but I'm planning on charming him into it. I also met a new friend—I think you'd love him because he has as many opinions as you. Maybe more. ☺ And I'm going to a party with Waverly soon. It was really nice of her to invite me. More later. Wish you were here.

# Chapter 6

# How High Have You Been?

"TIME'S UP FOR TODAY. HAND me your sketches," Professor Picasso announces and immediately starts circling the room like a vulture. Simultaneously, everyone tries to make frantic last-minute changes to the best figurative drawing from today's class before he collects them.

Ford pushes down his glasses. Today, they are candy-apple red. "You'd think we're on *Survivor*," he whispers seriously.

Like with most classes, where you sit on day one is most often where you'll always sit. Anything else would disrupt the order. Although at first I was uncomfortable with my close-up views of our model, I've decided I like my seat. Ford's entertaining, and I'd like to make a friend here.

Ford checks out my red skirt from the Proenza Schouler for Target collection, which I paired with Corrinne's Milly pink-and-yellow-striped top. Fashion magazines are always telling you to mix high and low, and it's easy to do when I mix and match Corrinne's clothing with mine.

"Who inspired today's outfit?" he asks. He gently touches the skirt's material.

"Georgia O'Keeffe's *Red Canna*," I whisper and smile. It's especially nice to have someone admire my artistic sense of dressing. Nervously, I finish my shading. "I'm freaking out because of what Iona said about Professor Picasso roasting us today."

"I think that's a rumor," Ford says, putting down his pencil and pointing to Professor Picasso. He continues to silently roam the room, collecting and stacking the sketches as he walks.

He makes his way to Ford, then to me. After taking my sketch, Professor Picasso pauses for a long minute, looking at it closely before he puts it on the top of the pile and walks to the front of the room.

I close my eyes and ask for anything other than a *really*. Maybe I prayed too hard because Professor Picasso launches into an entire speech.

"Kitsy," he says to the class, "is using a technique called chiaroscuro, which I hope most of you know is a strong contrast between dark and light."

Last night, after I studied Rembrandt's nudes online, I scoured art websites for information about the proper technique for chiaroscuro. I was determined to change Picasso's *really* into a *wow*. I smile, thinking I'm being complimented.

"While Kitsy has made a valiant attempt to use an incredibly advanced technique, it falls flat with her skill set. I want you people to draw what you see instead of focusing on reinterpretation, especially when using techniques above your skill level. Please remember this."

The class nods as one, and I use all my energy to retain my posture and quietly say, "Thank you for the advice, Professor Picasso."

Inside, I feel like I'm wilting.

Once we're outside the classroom, Ford puts his arm around me and says, "Hey, Kitsy, I think you made the model look *way* better than he did in real life. He needed a little bit of chiaroscuro if you ask me."

"Thanks," I say, looking at my watch, and remember that I need to be showered and ready for Waverly's party in the next hour. Something I definitely don't feel like going to anymore.

"Can't wait to see you tomorrow, especially to see what you're wearing. Want to start a fashion line someday? Ford and Kitsy? Or if you really want, Kitsy and Ford."

"Let me see how this art class goes," I say, wishing I

was going to hang with him, not Waverly. "I'm feeling a bit discouraged."

"It's only day two, Kitsy. Just yesterday, you were the one giving me a pep talk about art. You need to give yourself the same one right now. Besides, Professor Picasso did call it a valiant attempt. You have to hear the good stuff, too," he says, giving my shoulders a quick squeeze before heading the other direction.

As I walk toward the building's exit, I aim to try to take his advice, hoping that the Village streets can calm me down two days in a row.

I hear Iona calling my name from down the hall, but I pretend not to hear and keep going. I'm not exactly in the mood to give her ketchup to go with my roast.

*Hear the good stuff, too*, I remind myself.

*Ding-dong* goes the bell. I still can't believe I'm standing at the door of the Wicked Witch of Uptown, Miss Waverly Dotts.

But before I have time to change my mind about being there, Waverly opens her front door and pecks both of my cheeks with little kisses. I don't return the favor because I'm so knackered.

"Earth to Kitsy. I know Manhattan's, like, a new planet for you, but you're really spacing out." Waverly's looking me up and down, and I watch her mouth drop open. Honestly, it's not Waverly's best look.

"Closet, Kitsy. Now," she orders and beckons me to follow her. I had been hoping for a tour of her apartment, not her closet, but I'm not about to ask since I've never known what to expect from Waverly.

Looking down at my simple black dress from home that I've paired with Corrinne's accessories, I'm ready to protest. I look fine. I might not *feel* fine after my second day of art school, but I look totally acceptable.

"How are you, Waverly?" I ask, trying to renegotiate this encounter back into a normal human one versus Hurricane Waverly storms Kitsy once again.

"No time for chitchat, Kit-Kat," Waverly says before shrilly laughing at her own joke. Then she pulls four dresses out of the closet and hurls them onto her wrought-iron canopy bed. I let the Kit-Kat thing slide even though I only let Hands call me that and only in private.

Surveying Waverly's room, I decide the theme is Princess and the Pea in New York City. There must be a dozen pillows on her bed; her white-and-pink fluffy down comforter has her monogram stitched and stamped all over it like zebra spots. Money sure doesn't buy taste.

I try again with civil conversation. "What are your plans for the summer? What kind of job do you have? Corrinne mentioned you had a work event."

Waverly digs her hand into a jewelry box as if it were a

treasure chest. She tosses a few long chains on top of the dresses.

She looks at her mess and keeps walking. She probably has a maid to clean that for her. Waverly's perfectly manicured nails don't look like she's ever cleaned a day in her life. I'm not ashamed that I'm responsible for most of the cleaning back home. Like my grandma always said, "No one has ever drowned in their own sweat."

Waverly pulls out a black dress that looks nearly identical to the one I'm already wearing and a stack of bangles.

"This." It's as if I'm Waverly's own personal Barbie doll.

She looks down at my flip-flops. "Flip-flops are not city chic. They are daytime shoes, but only in resort locations like Bermuda and Bora Bora," she declares. Kicking off her own shoes, pink heels, she chirps, "These. On your feet."

I quickly change into my "new" outfit as Waverly goes back to her closet and puts on a pair of four-inch magenta high heels.

"I'm working for a stylist," she says. "If you couldn't tell. I totally should've taken before-and-afters of you to put in my portfolio. I work, like, what's the word . . . magic," Waverly finishes, looking at me as if I were a mannequin rather than a human being with ears to hear and feelings to be hurt.

Great. According to Miss Waverly Dotts, teen stylist, magic is required to make me look suitable for the city. I guess I'll need to invest in a fairy wand if I want to make it through my month here. I *totally* understand why Iona cut Waverly's ponytail off. I might need to write her a belated thank-you note for that.

Glancing down at her watch, Waverly perks up. "Time to go. And don't tell Corrinne, but I invited Rider. Always helps to have an inspiring musician and his band on the guest list even if he is from nowhere."

"Nowhere" echoes in my head. If you are from *nowhere*, I think, does that mean you're a *no one*, and that you'll always be a no one?

Waverly gracefully turns on her heels as if they were ballet flats and not monstrous stilettos. I fumble into my Waverly-approved outfit and stumble after her as I try to adjust to walking in someone else's shoes.

Arriving at another high-rise in the Upper East Side, we take an elevator up twenty-three floors and enter a party already in session. Music is playing but it's difficult to hear it over all of the many conversations.

Rider, who has already swapped his Broken-Spoke emo look for the hipster style, barely gives me a head nod when I spot him near the kitchen. No matter that we're from the same remote corner of earth. Now that Rider's in New York and part of a New York band, I reckon he's too cool for the girl who held paper towels to his bloody nose when he fell on the playground in fourth grade. Maybe that means I can reinvent myself, too. I'm off to a good start since I'm not even wearing my own clothes and I'm here with girls I don't even know.

Before running off to the bathroom with a girl named either Octavia or Ophelia, Waverly gives me a few introductions. I take some rosé wine, which tastes disgusting, and settle on the couch next to one of the twin brothers, Blake or Breck, from Vladlena's birthday party. I'm ready for take two. Hopefully, this time I'll find some common ground with them.

"So, Kitsy, as a Texan, where do you see the future of oil going?" he asks me earnestly, moving closer to me.

Was that some sort of a pickup line? And if it was, who in the world gets sweet on someone talking about *oil*? I set my glass on a side table and stand up. "As a Texan, I'm going to search for deeper wells," I say confidently.

I'm only in New York for four weeks, and I'm not spending four more *seconds* with either of those twins—or Waverly. I need to make my own friends, not tag along with Corrinne's crew. I have got to get out of this party. I'm here to forge my own path, so why not explore New York on my own? I'll text Waverly that something else came up. I maneuver my way through the party and out the door.

In the hallway, I notice a door marked ROOFTOP and decide to see if I can go up. I push it open, and start to climb a steep flight of grated metal stairs. After charging up the stairs, I rest near the top and take a deep breath. One advantage of my tiny house: no stairs. Summoning my energy, I move to tackle the last stair when my three-inch pink pump heel—or rather Waverly's pink pump heel—gets wedged into a crack in the stair. I want to leave it and keep going up, but then I'll be barefoot and have Waverly Dotts after me. I knew I shouldn't have listened to her and worn flip-flops like I wanted.

Slipping my foot out of the wedged high heel, I see that my toes have started to bleed into Waverly's Loubi-bottoms or whatever she called them. Oh, great. Please, God, I pray, don't let Waverly make me buy her a new pair. If she does, I'll have to become her indentured servant for life.

Bending down, I try to yank the heel up with two hands. No luck. Is it too soon in my friendship with Ford to ask for a rescue?

I sit on a narrow step of the dark, dank stairwell to ponder my options. I sort of want to cry, but I think the lack of fresh oxygen in this city has dried up my tear ducts because they don't come.

And then the door downstairs creaks open. I'm hoping it's not Waverly: I don't want to throw my one-shoe self off the roof.

"Hey there," an unfamiliar male voice calls from the bottom. "What are you doing up here?"

*Great!* Now this scene has added an additional character, a no-good city man who is ready to take my country innocence away. Amber, Hands, and every other Broken Spoker warned me this would happen in New York City, and I have no one to blame but me for not listening to them. What was I thinking?

"Um-m," I stutter, trying to make out the figure to discern what my assailant looks like. I'll probably have to do a sketch composite later.

"Don't worry," the voice calls out to me gently and I hear him start walking up the stairs. "I'm Tad. I think we were just at the same party. I saw you sneak out and I figured that you might be coming up here."

I sigh a huge breath of relief. I just might not end up as a victim on *Law & Order: SVU*, which I'm sure has filmed in this exact stairwell.

Tad climbs the stairs to me before he stops to look at my shoe that's being held hostage by the stair. He points and says, "I can honestly say that's the first time I've seen a high heel like that."

I soften up and laugh. "It's very urban Cinderella, isn't it?"

"It's only Cinderella if I'm a prince, and you end up running away. And I'm no prince"—and I can finally see his face. With full lips, jade-blue eyes, and a Roman nose, Tad looks fit to play a fairy-tale prince. Like many of Disney's leading men, he's tall (at least six feet), dark (his hair is chocolate brown), and definitely handsome. Strangely, he also looks familiar.

Pointing toward the roof, Tad adds, "I'm hoping that you don't run away. In fact, how about a smoke on the rooftop?"

"Only if you can retrieve my shoe," I say, smiling. "It's actually not mine. That's part of the problem."

With one hand, Tad bends down, yanks the heel, and frees it from the stair. "Not bad for a musician," he says and pats his own back before handing me the high heel.

At the very top of the stairs, there's another door that Tad pulls and holds open for me. This is the very first time in New York—minus doormen, who are paid to do it—that someone has opened a door for me. Light coming from the roof shines on Tad's face, and my heart races as I realize how I know him. I stop and don't move any closer.

"Something wrong?" Tad asks me, still holding the door.

"I know this may sound weird, but were you at MoMA on Saturday?" I ask.

I cross my fingers that I'm not going crazy.

Tad snaps his fingers and winks.

"That's it!" he exclaims, pointing at me. "When I saw

you at the party, I thought I knew you. Funny how New York isn't that big after all. And if I remember correctly, *you* ran away."

Smiling, I think how I'm here less than a week, and I'm already having a New York moment. Somehow I've met Art Boy not just once but twice in a city of millions.

"I didn't want to leave," I say, looking directly at him as I step through the door and out onto the rooftop.

Before I can tell him about why I didn't stay and talk at MoMA, I see it. Rather, I see all of it. I forgot that we're twenty-four floors up. The city looks like a jewel box, an urban landscape of twinkling skyscrapers. Who knew electricity could be so beautiful? Maybe Texas *isn't* the only place that's God's country.

I walk straight past Tad and go to the rooftop's edge. To the east, I see the river and the moonlight dancing on its smooth surface. From another angle, I see the park. The bright street lamps illuminate its greenery. I keep turning and see the Chrysler and the Empire State Building, rising high in the sky. It's like the movies. It's how I thought it would be.

"Whoa, girl," Tad says and comes up behind me, "you okay?"

I spin around and ask impulsively, "What's the highest you've ever been?"

Tad smiles and points to his pack of cigarettes. "This is about as high as I get these days. What are *you* on?"

"No, no, not like that," I say, laughing and shaking my head. "This, this right here is the highest I have ever been. Twenty-four floors. Before this, it was the top of our local bleachers. I was too scared to climb the water tower. There's also this spot to jump off a cliff into a deep pond, but I'm not crazy enough to do it on account of the swimming rats. So this is definitely the highest I've been."

"Pretty sick," Tad exclaims as he looks around to take in the view for the first real time since we got up here. "I forget how amazing it is. It takes stopping for a moment to remember. So where exactly are you from? Not here obviously. Thankfully, our rats don't swim."

"Broken Spoke, Texas," I respond softly.

Tad lights up his cigarette and blows the smoke into the night air. He hands one to me, and I wave it off. "You must know Rider then. He's the newest guy in my band, Hipster Hat Trick. We picked up Rider from some of his YouTube clips. We try to get him to tell us about Texas, but he's always saying how he doesn't want to talk about the past. What are you doing in the city?"

"I'm in art school," I say. I can feel my cheeks get rosé, the color of that gross wine downstairs.

"That's cool," Tad says and ashes off the building. I cross my fingers that he won't ignite the entire city. "I love art, too, but I'm the equivalent of tone deaf when it comes to drawing, painting, really any of it. I do love looking at it. It helps with my music, so that's why I'm always at MoMA. It inspires me to write. How's school coming?"

"It's been . . . ," I say, slowly taking a breath and figuring out how to summarize my first two days at Parsons. "Interesting. First week is nudes. The professor totally did it to freak us out. Of course, I got the most up-close and personal seat. So my nudes are more of a zoom lens than a figure sketch if you know what I mean. Am I talking too much? Sorry. I talk a lot when I'm comfortable, which hasn't happened much at this party," I say and force myself to stop running my mouth. I wish I at least had a piece of gum to pop. That usually slows me down.

Tad smiles really big and takes the two steps between us. He puts his hands on my shoulders. He leans toward me, and I don't lean away from him.

"I'm a native New Yorker, and I can assure you that we *all* talk a lot. We even speak with our hands. So never worry about talking too much here. And you," he says, "are adorable."

I step out of his grip. "My name is Kitsy, not adorable. I really can't believe how people don't use names in this city. 'Not important,' this girl Waverly said about her own doorman's name when I asked her what it was earlier tonight. I mean, his job is to guard your building from this city, yet his name is unimportant?" I manage to stop my tirade. "Sorry, I told you I talk a lot."

"Just makes you more adorable," Tad says and tilts his

head closer, just as I feel my pocket vibrate.

"Hold on a second." I pull back quickly as the image of Hands texting me from the Spoke pops into my head. If it is Hands, I'm not sure if I feel relieved or upset. And that in itself scares me.

I look at my new text, and it's not Hands. I exhale without realizing it.

Kiki: Call me . . . it's Mom.

I feel my shoulders go limp, I take one last look at Tad and the view, and then I turn back to the stairs.

Tad's in a band with Rider, who is Corrinne's number one enemy. I have a boyfriend. Yet there's something here making me want to stay.

But it doesn't matter because I have to talk to Kiki.

"Sorry," I call back over my shoulder. "I need to run."

"Wait, Kitsy!" Tad exclaims. "The highest I've ever gone is the World Trade Center. You know . . . before it all happened."

I have no idea how to respond, so I don't say anything at all. I half smile and move to shut the door.

"Good night, Cinderella. This is the *second* time you've run away from me," Tad calls out as I pull the door shut without a word.

I descend the stairs with one heel on and one heel in

hand. Figuring no one cares, I don't bother to say good-bye to anyone at the party and decide to just text Waverly that I had to leave early. Outside the building, I keep attempting to hail cabs that either already have passengers or whose drivers shout out "Off duty" through their windows as they speed by. Allegedly, there's a signal for on, occupied, and off duty, but it's basically impossible to determine which lights indicate what. They must teach Taxicab Light Systems in New York City schools. This is not intuitive.

When a doorman from a neighboring building notices my confusion, he walks over and helps me hail a cab. He looks down at my feet and asks, "Rough night?"

"It had some highlights," I say, recalling the view—and re-meeting Tad.

I shouldn't take a cab since they charge per second, but I can't afford to get lost on the subway instead of talking to Kiki right away. I climb into the cab, wave good-bye to the doorman in shining armor, and dial Kiki's number quickly.

"Kiki!" I exclaim before he even has time to say hello. "What's wrong, baby?"

Kiki's giggles erupt through the phone. "Nothing, I just wanted to let you know that I finished all my summer reading today. I think I'm a kid genius!"

"That's great, Kiki," I tell him because I do want to

encourage him with his reading. "But why did you say it was Mom?"

"Because I know that you worry about her and that you'd call right away," he answers and I slump back into the cushiony seat. Maybe Kiki *is* a prodigy. He sure is perceptive.

"Are you worried about her?" I ask, gripping the phone.

"Nope. She's the same as always," Kiki says.

Which is exactly what I was afraid of. I know you shouldn't expect people to just change, but I'll admit I sure was hoping for it.

"Come home soon," Kiki says with a yawn.

"Go to sleep now, Kiki," I instruct. "Remember we're looking at the same stars."

After putting away my phone, I rest my head on the window. Looking up, I only see buildings with tiny cracks of night sky. I still can't find any stars, and I feel farther from home than ever, which feels comforting and scary at the same time.

To: kkidd@gmail.com
From: corrinnec@gmail.com
Date: Wednesday July 18
Subject: I need an update!

So what's the story? My best friend is in the greatest city in the world and I haven't heard from her in days. Tell me about one of your NYC adventures! I'm nearing emotional and physical fatigue with nature. My nails don't do well with dirt. In good news, I was elected green team captain for our color war. In bad news, I need to wear head to toe kelly green. I look like a leprechaun-ette. Give me some gossip, Kits.

# Chapter 7

## Just a Small-Town Girl

THE REST OF MY FIRST week feels like déjà vu of my first two days. On Wednesday, Professor Picasso knocked the simplicity of my figurative sketch, so again I spent hours that night studying famous nude paintings just to have him say on Thursday: "This figurative drawing loses its focus on the subject; the model becomes secondary to Kitsy's style, which doesn't feel authentic."

On Friday, I go in with a new attitude: I'm just here to draw what I see. As Professor Picasso comes around to collect the day's sketches, Ford, who has striped navy frames on today, hums the theme from *The Twilight Zone* in my ear. I let myself laugh.

Professor Picasso looks at his figurative drawing. "Ford, you're exaggerating features in an attempt to get away from drawing the details. That's lazy. Don't do it."

Ford shrugs and then gives my knee a squeeze when Professor Picasso reaches for what I think is my best sketch.

After looking at it for a minute, he says, "I actually see a little bit of Kitsy here." My heart lifts like an air balloon. I feel the most encouraged I've been since starting art class.

I smile and feel a soft kick on the back of my chair. I turn around to see Iona giving me the thumbs-up. She sure is difficult to figure out.

As Professor Picasso stacks the sketches, he makes an announcement:

"We're having an end-of-the-term exhibition. I'll send out formal invitations to your local mailing address, but also bring your friends, bring your family . . . bring any warm bodies. Not to worry you, but there'll be art critics, art dealers, and art college representatives. No pressure though," he says with a snort.

I feel a tiny prick in my air balloon heart. Critics? What if I'm the sad, lonely girl standing by her "art" while the Important New York People say, "What happened to this program? I thought it was selective." Then again, I've had my share of critics, and I've always come out swinging. Here's to you, Peggy.

The upside to this is that I don't have to worry about

Amber being there. Not that I have ever been to a real art show, but the ones in movies usually have free wine. And a drunk Amber is the only thing that could make my future vision of the exhibition worse. She'd probably spill a drink on some girl like Iona.

When we're leaving class, Ford stops me and says, "Hey, Kitsy, want to go to the rooftop at the Metropolitan Museum of Art? Every summer, the Met's rooftop garden has a solo exhibition. My boyfriend and I always try to go as many times as we can while the weather's nice. I've been telling him all about Kitsy Kidd from Broken Spoke. He's dying to meet you!"

"I'd love to . . . ," I say and trail off. I promised myself that I'd spend tonight catching up with Kiki and Hands and working on my sketches. "I have another commitment, but let's hang out soon."

"For sure," Ford says with a wave.

When I get to the Corcorans', no one is home. The Corcorans went to Nantucket this weekend and invited me to join them, but I thought it would be too weird. Two parents plus their daughter's Texan best friend? It's been six years since I have been in a two-parent family, and I'm not sure I'm ready to be the plus one to the Corcorans. Besides, I don't want them to spend one more dime on me than they already are, so I told them that

I'm swamped with homework. Even though I insisted I'd be fine alone, Mrs. Corcoran asked Maria, their house-keeper, to sleep at the apartment. For the first time in about ten years, I have a babysitter. I'm relieved she's not there when I get home.

I download Skype on Corrinne's old computer, some-thing I've been promising Hands I'd do for a week. Since I planned on staying home tonight, I told him earlier to meet me online after his practice ended.

Dialing up QBSTATECHAMP, Hands's online moniker, I adjust my screen so Hands can't see into the Corcorans' apartment. I don't want our worlds to feel any farther away than they are.

Hands, wearing his practice jersey and sweaty from an afternoon practice, pops up in a window on Corrinne's Apple computer.

"You got even prettier," Hands says as I push some ringlets out of my face.

"Ohmigosh, Hands!" I exclaim. "Today, I think my professor almost complimented me, and this guy from class invited me to go to a show on the rooftop of a museum. Everything is so amazing here. I mean, there are moments that are hard but being here in general makes up for those."

"What?" Hands interrupts, his face falling. "What guy?"

"He's gay," I say. "But, Hands, that shouldn't matter.

The whole reason I came here was to study art and meet people who I have something in common with."

I see Hands wince and take a deep breath.

"Kitsy, are you saying . . . that we don't have anything in common? We've dated for six years. I know you better than anyone. We're a team—like a QB and center," Hands says.

Hands is right. In the Spoke, he does know me better than anyone. But there are people here, including me, who want to know Kitsy as an artist and that's something I've never experienced. How do I get Hands to understand that I want to grow?

The silence hangs in the air. Even though we're looking directly at each other's image, Hands seems farther away than he did on the phone. Maybe this whole Skyping thing was a bad idea.

His lips tighten, something I usually only see if he messes up a big play. "I should go. I guess this is interfering with your art schedule."

"Hands," I start to say, trying hard not to sound annoyed. "I didn't mean it like that. I stayed home to talk to you, didn't I?"

"I didn't mean to put you out," he says and he pushes the brim of his baseball cap over his eyes. "I stopped by your house today and tossed the ball with Kiki. I think he misses you almost as much as I do."

"Thanks, Hands," I say quietly. I do appreciate Hands and I don't want to forget that. "I wish I could give you a hug."

"Me too, Kitsy," he says. "I like virtual Kitsy but I miss the real thing. Why don't we talk later? I want you to have a good experience. Besides, all that's happening here is football practice. Nothing exciting like New York."

"Are you sure, Hands?" I ask. I do have a book of half-finished sketches.

"I'm sure," he says, looking somewhere away from the camera. "I love you. O O O."

"X X X," I say. "I love you, too. I wish you were here."

"No, you don't. This is your summer," he says and manages to give me a tiny smile.

I shake my head as if to say no, but he's right. This is my time. Maybe I should've gone to the museum. I don't think this conversation really made me or Hands feel any closer. I give a small wave and blow a kiss before I shut down the computer. Retreating to my room, I spend the night alternately sketching and making a list of all the museums and shows I still want to see in New York.

In the morning, I tie on Corrinne's pink robe and make my way to the kitchen. At the sink, Maria is gently placing two ice cubes in a pot with only a single tall, green stem growing from it. She's already dressed for the day, and there's a small duffel bag at her feet.

"I'm Maria," she says in perfect lightly accented English. "I got in late last night, and I didn't want to wake you. Can you believe what I found in the trash room?" she asks, pointing to a potted plant with two bare green stems growing from the soil.

"I'm Kitsy Kidd. It's so nice to meet you," I say and firmly shake her hand. "What kind of plant is that?"

"It's an orchid," she says, moving it to the windowsill. "Or it was an orchid before someone gave up on it after it stopped blooming. Not everyone knows that often orchids will not bloom for months, and then all of a sudden, they will come back to life. It's very important to always keep watering them. And remember, they like ice cubes better than water."

"You must have a green thumb," I say.

"I did live on a farm in Mexico," she explains, shifting the pot into direct sunlight. "Getting an orchid to bloom is easy compared to the field work I did growing up."

"Corrinne always talked about how she missed you when she was in Texas," I say, thumbing a photo of the Corcorans on the bookshelf.

"She is like my second daughter," Maria says and blows Corrinne's image a kiss. "Mrs. Corcoran said you're the big reason Corrinne came back from Texas with a whole lot less attitude than when she went. I'm looking forward to having you here. It's lonely without Corrinne and Tripp. I'm heading back home to Coney Island for the day. Do you want to come along?"

"No thanks. I'm going to work on some sketches. And just so you know, I think Corrinne did all of that transforming on her own," I say. I wonder if I'll come back from New York changed, too.

"Corrinne's lucky to have you as a friend. There's a casserole in the fridge. See you later, Kitsy," Maria says.

As I flip through the Corcorans' coffee table books over breakfast, I start to feel uneasy about last night's Skyping session with Hands. I reach for my phone to call him when it vibrates.

Hi, it's Tad. Got your number from Rider. What's a Texan doing on a gorgeous day like this?

Tad, as in the Tad who in a city of millions I've run into twice. Tad, the musician with an eye for art. It's not that I haven't thought of him because I have. I just never thought he'd bother to call. But I also never thought I'd make it to New York City to take real art classes either.

I text Tad back.

Reading.

My phone buzzes again.

Aren't you supposed to be doing all the touristy things? This is your first time in New York.

Without thinking about how Tad could interpret it, I type:

Taking the double-decker bus alone isn't fun.

Especially when you're saving every penny, I think. Milliseconds later, my phone buzzes again.

Send me your address. I can do better than a double-decker. They're too much $$.

Think this over, Kitsy: A hot New York rocker guy wants you to send him your address where you're currently staying alone. No way I can ask Hands or Amber if this is okay because I know their collective answer: No with a capital *N*. Even Courageous Corrinne would probably say no and I wouldn't tell her because I'm not supposed to be hanging out with Rider or his band mates on Best Friend Principle.

But my fingers text back. After all, he's one of the only people who I can discuss art with. How can I give up the opportunity? But I know that there's more than just that. In New York, I can finally be a yes person. In Texas, I'm always saying no on account of being busy with Kiki and Amber.

Me: Morton and Washington.

Tad: See you in 10. I'll text you when I'm there.

I fly to the bathroom. Do I have enough time to shower? Is showering too much? What if it looks like I'm trying too hard? Wait, I'm not even trying. I have a boyfriend. Tad's, like, a tour guide.

I throw on a cotton tangerine dress and a pair of old white Converses. Checking myself out, I think my clothes give the appropriate message that reads, "This is not a date. I could be your little sister."

Zipping my sketchbook into my purse pocket, I tell myself that I'll do some sketching while I'm out. I promise myself to spend more time on the phone with Hands and Kiki tomorrow. That reminds me I should ask Hands to pick up some more challenging novels for Kiki from the library.

After, I leave a note for Maria that I'm going out with a friend and not to worry if I'm not here when she gets back. I sit impatiently with my legs crossed and try not to watch my phone for Tad's text. I'm about to go out into New York with a real New Yorker, and I get to wear sneakers. Maybe this will be the summer of my life. Maybe this summer isn't just about me and my art. Maybe it should be about fun and surprises, too.

"Here, take this," Tad says, handing me a MetroCard. He's wearing orange New Balances, a Yankees T-shirt, and a loose-fitting pair of jeans.

"Oh," I say, its yellow and blue colors flashing me back to the New Jersey incident. "I don't like the subways much. Did you know they go underwater to other states?"

Tad laughs, shaking his brown hair.

"We're taking the bus. You just use the same card."

"The double-decker?" I ask enthusiastically.

"No, the city bus. Here's a secret, Kitsy. They follow pretty much the same route. We'll spend our money on other stuff, not buses that charge more because they have two levels and are painted red."

I turn double-decker red for suggesting it. Maybe Tad notices because he puts his hand on the small of my back. I try not to stiffen. Even though he's a New York native, he doesn't remind me of stylist/socialite Waverly. Or Corrinne.

"Kitsy, we're going to have fun. This is New York City, the Empire State, the Melting Pot, the Center of the Universe. So let's act like it."

The only nickname Broken Spoke has is the BS, so Tad has a point.

"Okay," I say, watching a bus lumber to a stop in front of us. Tad steps back so I can go on first. Maybe there are actually Yankee gentlemen willing to show a newbie around with no strings attached. Although I've never heard about it, there might be such a thing as northern hospitality.

Tad stands on the bus and holds on to the railing above my seat.

"I like standing," he says as I notice that his blue eyes have tiny flecks of hazel in them. "Besides, there's almost always someone that needs the seat more."

I won't lie. The view of looking up at Tad isn't bad.

As we pass through the different neighborhoods, Tad gives me a running commentary.

Approaching a small park with a pool and track near the FDR Drive, Tad gets all giddy. "That's Thomas Jefferson Park," Tads exclaims. "That's where I learned how to ride a two-wheeler and to do a cannonball. In the summer, my family had BBQs there every Sunday. It was like my personal park. People say it's not fair to raise a kid in the city because they need to be outside, but what they don't know is that something like fourteen percent of Manhattan is public parks for anyone to use."

"I didn't realize that," I say. "You should work for the city."

"Just want to make sure you enjoy your visit here," he says with a smile. "I want you to know what it's like to live here, not just be a tourist. Maybe I can even persuade you to buy a one-way ticket next time."

That sounds like heaven to my ears. But how could I ever make it work?

As we wind our way through the city, I keep my nose pressed to the glass. I'm pretty sure I see Tad smile every time I light up at seeing something new.

"Here's a little piece of national history," Tad says and nods toward a beige building with a gable roof and beautiful balconies that looks like it belongs more in France than it does in New York. "That's the Dakota, where John Lennon was shot. I wonder what music today would be like if he hadn't died."

I try not to swoon over the way Tad talks about art and music. I don't want it to be obvious that I haven't met many people like him.

Our bus cuts across the city, flies down the West Side Highway, and passes the financial district, where the World Trade Center towers once stood.

Pointing toward a nearly finished building, Tad says, "That's One World Trade Center. The mast is supposed to evoke the Statue of Liberty's torch. I can't wait for it to be done. The city's ready."

I think back to the first grade, when our teacher tried

her best to explain what was happening on that day. "Hopefully I can come back to see it when it's all finished."

"Of course you will," Tad says. "Once you visit New York, it gets in your blood. It'll draw you back."

I want to explain to Tad how I've felt drawn to New York my whole life. But how do you describe that to someone who's from here? How can you get them to understand that what they've always had is what other people have waited their whole lives for?

As we steer around the remaining wreckage and construction from 9/11, both Tad and I are quiet. Navigating our way through the financial district, we go uptown toward Union Square. I see in the distance the words TEXAN BBQ in neon lights even though it's still daylight.

"There!" I say. "Can we eat there?" I ask. Not only do I really miss barbeque, I also need to see New York's take on Texas.

"That's some cheesy tourist restaurant," Tad says. "It might as well be T.G.I. Friday's."

"Please," I beg. "I'm a Texan ambassador, after all."

I purposely neglect to mention that sometimes we drive an hour just to go to the nearest T.G.I. Friday's, which I love since I'm a sucker for their wings.

"Fine," Tad concedes, smiling. "It's your day."

I like how that sounds.

• • •

"I can't believe we're in New York, and you want to eat Texan food," Tad says, looking down at a pile of ribs. "It's a sin. We could eat Ethiopian. Vietnamese. Argentinean. We could eat countries that we've never heard of, and now we're in a cheesy chain."

The smells take me back to the tailgates in Broken Spoke. "You didn't have to say yes," I say, holding a rib to my mouth.

"Yes, I did," Tad says. "It's impossible to say no to that smile."

I try to frown, but it makes me just smile bigger. "It's just how my face goes."

"Don't apologize," Tad says, swallowing his first bite with trepidation. His face relaxes. "This really isn't bad after all."

Nope, none of this has been bad at all.

"So, when are you going to make it big?" I ask him. "I want to say I knew you when."

Tad pauses and puts down his forkful of mac 'n' cheese. "I already did," he says, "or . . . I almost did."

I don't say anything. I've learned that sometimes it's better just to wait. My nanny always said, "Let people narrate their own stories, Kitsy. Don't be thinkin' you're Oprah all the time."

Tad wipes BBQ sauce from his stubble. I don't know

if Hands could even grow a beard. He's a redhead, but he calls it "cinnamon" even though I've told him that's a spice, not a hair color.

"A few years ago, I signed a record deal, but then some stuff happened."

Tad looks down at his food. I want to know more, but I'm not going to push. And a few years ago? How old is Tad now? Maybe he was like a Bieber.

"I actually just started back up again," he says and smiles. "I was on pause for a long time."

I lick my fingers, purposefully trying not to be sloppy *or* sexual, which is harder than it sounds. I blurt out, "So what were you doing in between?"

"Absolutely nothing," Tad says after a long pause. "First, I lost my dad, then I lost my music . . . then I lost me. Hipster Hat Trick is a cover band. We don't write our own songs. We play pop hits and occasionally switch them up a bit."

You wouldn't realize that Tad's experienced that kind of loss. He seems so cheerful. But I guess the same could be said for me.

"Do you write any of your own songs?" I ask.

"Just for me," he answers, then he wags a finger at me. "But I don't want to talk about this, Kitsy. This is your day, not Confessions-of-an-Almost-Rock-Star day. Besides, my story is totally common. There are more musicians that almost made it than there are people in Manhattan."

In Texas, I mostly talk football with the boys. I'll brag that I know the difference between a Hail Mary pass and a Music Miracle City, and I can name the last twelve Heisman Trophy winners. However, I must say there's something heart-palpitatingly nice talking to a guy who has a passion for something other than football.

"So what do you really think of my city, Kitsy? I've lived here my entire life. We moved once, but it was just across the park from the Upper East Side to the Upper West Side. Even when I did a year of college, I went to NYU. The city's the only home I've ever known, so I like hearing what other people think," Tad says.

A year of college definitely answers my question that he's older. I don't ask how *much* older.

"Well, it's so not like the movies," I say. I watch through the window.

"What movie did you want it to be like?" Tad asks. He looks relieved to have ended his story. "Please don't say *Sex and the City*." He holds up both hands in the air and crosses his fingers. "There are way too many girls in this city who moved here thinking it'd be like that show. They all end up crushed, alone, and broke from buying too many expensive shoes. Instead of being cat ladies, they're shoe ladies."

I look down at my sneakers. I guess I'm in no need of

worrying about that fate. Maybe I'll end up in an apartment packed full of art supplies, but that sounds like a great destiny.

"I wanted it to be like *Home Alone Two*," I answer. "My brother and I watch all the *Home Alone* movies every Christmas. I want to meet the pigeons and the pigeon lady." Smiling, I think about Kiki mouthing the words of nearly every line from the movies. I hope one day he gets an opportunity like I'm having here. Maybe I can even be the one to make it happen.

Laughing, Tad says, "We call them feathered rats, but okay. We'll do the park next, and you can meet our city's animal, the pigeon." He extends his pinkie out to me, and I bring mine to meet his.

"By the way, Kitsy, I like seeing the city through your eyes," he says as we twist our pinkies.

That sounds like a big-brother comment. I surprise myself by wishing it didn't.

"Where are we going?" I ask as I follow Tad through Central Park.

"You'll see," he says.

I make quick steps trying to both keep up with Tad and take in all the people sunbathing, running, and meandering around the park. Eventually, we approach a lake near a restaurant called The Boathouse.

Tad points and says, "X marks the spot."

"We're eating again?" I peer into the elegant restaurant's windows and see white tablecloths and lakeside views.

"No, silly. We're going boating."

Within minutes, Tad and I are adrift in a green boat in Central Park's lake. I'm not sure how my life figured out how to get this good and I can't help but wonder what the diners in the restaurant think of us. I try to understand how I'm in a boat floating next to ducks on a lake surrounded by weeping willows, and yet I can see the vast skyline. New York really does have everything.

I try not to look back at Tad; I don't want to upset the boat's balance. But on a whim, I dip my hand into the lake and create a splash that sprays him across the face.

Tad doesn't retaliate, only laughs. "Hey, Kitsy," he says, "next time, you're getting soaked for that."

The way he says "next time" makes me think that my life really is just starting, and that here, anything is possible.

Walking through the streets in twilight, I wonder if you really need to go anywhere but New York to see the world.

Entering a crowded pedestrian street with hundreds of tricolored red, white, and green flags strung across the buildings, Tad blocks my path.

"Passport, signorina?" he asks. "We're now entering Little Italy."

"I don't have one," I answer honestly.

"Since you're beautiful, I believe Italian customs will let it slide. But Kitsy, I have a feeling one day you'll have a passport with so many stamps that you'll need extra pages."

I don't know whether to blush more about the beautiful comment or the fact Tad thinks I'll be a world traveler. Luckily, it's dark, so he can't see the rouge in my cheeks. I guess I didn't need to wear my CoverGirl Plumberry Glow 140 out tonight.

In front of the many outdoor cafés, waiters yell out, "*Bellissima, mangia qui,*" which Tad tells me means, "Pretty girl, eat here."

"I spent a summer in Florence studying art and music," he explains.

"Did you go to the Uffizi?" I ask. "Did you see *The Birth of Venus*?"

Venus coming out of her shell is probably my second-favorite painting after *The Starry Night*, of course. I feel a bit like Venus right now.

"I went to the Uffizi four times. Let's go in here," he says and points to a green-and-white sign that reads FERRARA BAKERY & CAFÉ. "This is the only bakery that remotely rivals Italy, where I gained eleven pounds in three weeks. It was totally worth it."

Tad orders us two cannolis in broken Italian.

I smile, still not believing that I'm in (fake) Italy with Art Boy.

The matriarch of the place puts them in a bag and asks, "*Lei è la tua ragazza?*" Tad shakes his head.

Outside, I ask him what she said.

"She thought you were my girlfriend," he says and laughs as if that were the most absurd thing he's heard. I laugh, too, because it should be ridiculous since I have a boyfriend and Tad is a cultured New Yorker, but part of me likes that she thought that. I chalk it up to me liking the possibility I could be with someone who's lived in New York forever even though I've only been here a week.

Next, we explore Chinatown and watch the street vendors pack up for the night. Young men approach us every few feet, trying to sell fake purses. "Gucci, Prada, Vuitton," they whisper in our ears in broken English.

"We're doing an around-the-world. First, Texas. Then Italy. Now China. Texas is like its own country, right?" Tad asks.

"Pretty much," I answer. And right now, Broken Spoke seems like its own galaxy compared to this place and this night.

"And there's one last stop," Tad says, pointing at the LUCKY'S KARAOKE sign.

"Karaoke?" I repeat, not wanting to believe this. "Tad,

I'm tone-deaf. Even though I'm Team Captain back home, I don't lead the cheers because I can't carry a tune. And you're like a rock star. This will be embarrassing."

"I'm a has-been-before-he-even-was rock star," he corrects. "Like I said, every other guy with a guitar has a story about how it almost happened to him. And Kitsy, you're singing. Everyone should be allowed to sing. It's our right as humans."

"How about I just watch you?" I ask hopefully. I reluctantly follow Tad through the front door and up a shaky, carpeted staircase. "It wouldn't be fair to the other people that have to listen to me sing."

At the top of the stairs, Tad briefly whispers with the lady at the front desk and hands her some cash. Then he opens door number seven and waits for me to walk in. "There are no other people. I rented out the whole room. No more excuses, kid."

Kid, there he goes with that kid thing. See, Kitsy? It's not a date. You might be about to enter a dark room with an older boy, but he thinks of you as a kid. He's the big brother you never had but always needed. This is totally okay to be doing.

Tad walks over to the TV screen and starts flipping through the songs.

"One song, Kitsy," he says. "That's all I ask. What will it be? We can do it together."

"Journey," I answer.

"Let me guess. 'Don't Stop Believin''?" he asks and raises one eyebrow. "That song has been on at least three TV shows and five commercials in the last week. Have you ever heard the saying that somewhere on any given night, drunk kids are singing this song?"

In the Spoke, it's a very popular song and gets played at the field all the time. That's not why I love it though. I like it because it's about getting away.

I shake my head at Tad. "You said it was lady's choice," I argue.

With a smile, Tad finds the song and hands me one of the microphones.

The classic piano beginning starts.

Glancing sideways at me, Tad belts out.

"Just a small-town girl, living in a lonely world, she took the midnight train going anywhere." He looks to me to sing the next lines.

Does he think of me as a small-town girl?

"Just a city boy, born and raised in South Detroit, he took the midnight train going anywhere," I sing. I hope I managed to hit at least one note.

Tad air guitars the instrumental before belting out the chorus. "For a smile, they can share the night. It goes on and on and on."

We finish the song and I find myself wishing this were

my reality, that I could do this every night with Tad, and the most magical day of my life wasn't almost over. I guess the best days are the ones you aren't expecting. Sometimes when you stop chasing something, it has a way of finding you.

"What does that song mean to you?" I ask, flopping down on a couch.

Tad comes and sits right next to me.

"Meeting someone who surprises you," Tad answers without a second thought.

I wonder if he thinks of me as that person.

He shifts to face me on the couch. "What do you think it's about?" he asks.

"I think it's about leaving somewhere and finding another place you belong . . . even if it's just for a night."

Tad pauses, stretches, lets out a big yawn, and looks down at his watch: "Three in the morning, you definitely shouldn't be out this late. Hell, I shouldn't be out this late."

"That's not fair," I argue. "You need to do a solo."

"Okay," he concedes. "But you pick it."

I get up and flip through the index. I stop dead on the word *Mockingbird*.

"That's my school mascot," I say. "We do a cheer to this. I want to hear your rendition."

"That's a nursery rhyme," Tad says, looking over my shoulder. "My dad used to sing it to me when I was little."

My dad sang it, too, I think. This song makes me ache every time I hear it. But unlike a lot of Dad memories, it's a happy one.

Tad doesn't protest anymore and presses Play.

"Hush, little baby, don't say a word, Mama's gonna buy you a mockingbird," he croons. And I'm sure that the writer never intended this song to sound so sexy. Tad probably doesn't either. But it does, and all the hairs on my arm stand straight up.

When he finishes, I realize I haven't checked my cell phone since this morning. But I make no move to get it from my purse.

"All right, kid," Tad says, opening the door. "Let's get you back to your apartment."

"No," I protest, a little too quickly. "What about going to a late-night diner? They *always* do that in the movies," I say, although I'm not hungry in the least.

"How about we walk back?" Tad says. "Slowly. The long way."

"Okay," I say, happy to extend the time before we have to say good-bye.

Standing with just Tad on a deserted street, I think about how amazing it is in a city of millions that you can be the only ones on a particular street. If you just stay awake long enough, you can have a bit of the city to yourself and it's completely worth the wait.

"I hope you know the way. In Broken Spoke, there's really only one main road. This place is totally catawampus," I say. If I'm being honest with myself, I'm partially hoping we get lost.

"Catawampus?" Tad repeats and laughs.

"It means crazy in Texan," I explain.

Looking up at the buildings, Tad says, "I always thought you country folk could read the stars like a map."

"No way," I say, looking up to the small cracks of starless sky peeking through the buildings. "I'm not an astronomer, but at least we actually have stars in Texas. Don't you miss them in the city?" I ask, thinking of Kiki and wondering if he's still sleeping in my bed under Van Gogh's stars.

"I've always lived here, Kitsy," he says. "You can't miss something you've never had."

I disagree one thousand percent because I have missed this—the incredible vastness and variety of a big city—my entire life. I just didn't know it until now.

Rounding the corner, I see a diner called the Manatus. It has big plastic booths, and the lights are still on. Sonic closes at eleven o'clock on weekends, and that's the latest *anywhere* stays open in Broken Spoke.

"It's still open," I exclaim, peering at a waitress refilling a drink. "Can we go in?"

"I have a better idea," Tad says, swinging open the

door for me. "You go. You have to get used to doing things alone but not feeling lonely. It's the best part of the city."

"But, it's three. How will I get back to the apartment?" I ask.

"It's five blocks, Kitsy," Tad says. "If you made it all the way from Broken Spoke to here, you can make it five hundred yards. If you're scared, you can call me and I'll stay on the phone the entire walk. Go order some ice cream and make a memory with just yourself."

So maybe he doesn't see me as a child. That gives me goose bumps all over.

I follow his instructions, but all I can think about is that I don't want to make a memory with only myself.

Sliding into a booth alone, I watch Tad leave and disappear down the street. It's almost light.

I order fries and a chocolate shake to go. While I wait, I look over the other customers: an old man drinking a cup of coffee through a straw, three British tourists slurping milkshakes, and a few college-age guys downing beers and an appetizer sampler. I know the other customers are watching me, too. They probably want to know who I am.

Before New York, everyone always thought they knew my story. Amber's daughter, what else was there to say? And, in Texas, it would be me on the other side of the counter serving the customer. But here, no one knows me, and they might be wondering who this independent and mysterious girl is alone at a diner at three in the morning.

After I get my to-go order, I leave the restaurant and glance at my phone. There are seven texts and four missed calls from Hands and Kiki. Briskly, I walk toward the Corcorans' apartment . . . but I feel someone in the distance watching me.

I spin around quickly and wish I had brought the Mace that Hands gave me. I think this really is the end of my life and I will be the newest example of why small-town girls shouldn't go hunting dreams in the big city.

I look up the street, and I suddenly realize it's Tad standing under a streetlight and watching me walk home. I turn back around and keep walking. When I'm finally at the gate, I turn my head to see Tad walking the other way.

That was by far one of the kindest things anyone's ever done for me. But I have no one to tell. I quietly sneak back into the Corcorans' apartment, where I hear Maria snoring soundly in Tripp's room. Sipping my shake and eating my fries in bed, I think maybe I found heaven.

# Chapter 8

# A Good Liar Needs a Good Memory

I WAKE UP TO MY phone ringing. I check the caller ID, hoping that it's Tad calling to tell me how he had a great time or Ford calling to hang out. But it's neither; it's Hands. I pick up.

"Kitsy," Hands gasps. "I thought you were dead. I almost called the cops, but then I remembered that in New York City, you would be just another missing small-town girl among hundreds of others who will never be seen again or found alive. Since I thought no one else would care, I was about to come there to find you myself. What's going on?"

"Hands," I say, "don't be so dramatic. New York's totally safe."

So safe that I went out until three in the morning with a stranger, I think. That doesn't sound as reasonable as it did in my head last night. And a musician, really? I'm acting like Corrinne. I should know better. I vow to be more responsible from now on. This summer is about art and I should be taking advantage of my opportunity.

Hands raises his voice a bit, which is something he does on the football field and only when the Mockingbirds are losing badly, which means it *rarely* happens. "It's two p.m. Sunday, your time, Kitsy. I repeat: two p.m. I haven't heard from you since *Friday* night. What am I supposed to think? I almost called Amber. Did you not see my missed calls, texts, and voice mails?"

Rolling onto my stomach, I confirm that it's actually two p.m. on the digital alarm clock. Yup, I guess that's what happens when you stay out all night. I never sleep this late; Kiki or Amber always wakes me up needing something. Of course, I saw Hands's calls/texts/voice mails last night; I just figured he could wait until morning! I didn't realize that I'd sleep until afternoon.

"I'm sorry," I say weakly. I debate whether or not I should make something up. I've never lied to Hands before, but I've also never been in the position of telling him that I didn't call because I was with some older and hot New Yorker musician during one of the best days of my life. Or at least the best day other than our football team winning state last fall, but that's everyone in the Spoke's best day. I want a personal best day that's all mine.

I decide to go for the lie because it's the only way I can think to make Hands less upset, right now. I repeat my story twice in my head. By the third time, it almost sounds true.

"My cell phone's reception has been weird. I was working on drawings until late last night, and I turned off my phone to get into the groove. Professor Picasso says that you can't multitask art—it's not like doing homework and Facebooking at the same time, Hands. You need to actually concentrate."

"Oh. I see. Calling your boyfriend comes after your *art*?" Hands asks slowly, and there's something about the way that he says *art* that grates on me. It's like he doesn't actually think it's important.

"That's what I'm here for," I say, sitting up in bed. "My art."

I say this even though I *know* my art wasn't the reason I didn't call last night. As an artist, don't you have to see things and not just spend all your time on the phone with your long-distance boyfriend?

"Haven't I been supportive of your football? Can't you support me now? Do I not bake brownies and wrap the Tupperware in red and gray ribbons every week during the season?" I ask.

That was low of me; I'm using how much Hands loves my brownies against him, but I'm desperate.

"Don't worry about baking brownies or supporting my

football anymore," Hands says harshly. "Coach talked to me after practice. The new guy will, in fact, be taking my starting spot. I might as well join you and the Mockingbirdettes on the sidelines. It'd be better than sitting on the bench."

I jump out of bed and land with a thud. "That's exactly it, Hands. I'm here so I don't have to spend my life on the sidelines. Art is my thing, or I want it to be my thing. As much as I love cheering for you, I'm trying to do something where *I'm* in the spotlight."

"I know that, but I needed you, Kitsy," Hands says. "You're the one person who I thought could make me feel better, although I think I was wrong about that."

Holding the phone away from my face, I take a quick breath. Hands has always been there when I needed him. The times I wanted to show him the new cheer for the sixteenth time, the times I called in the middle of the night about Amber's drinking, the times I brought Kiki on our dates without even asking. Hands deserves to need me once in a while, too.

"I'm so sorry—"

"Don't worry about it," Hands interrupts in a tone that makes me completely worry about it. "I sent you something, so make sure you check the mail for it. I'll let you go now; I wouldn't want you to have to *multitask*. Call me when you're done making *art*."

And then I hear it—rather, I don't hear *anything*. Hands

has hung up on me. This has never happened before. But we've never been apart and he's never lost his spot on the team. It's not like I'm going to get another summer in New York anytime soon. I might not ever get back to New York at all. I'm allowed to be selfish, just this once, right? It's not like I'm yachting in the Greek isles—I'm here for school!

I patter into the living room and slump on the couch. I try redialing Hands three times and each time it goes straight to voice mail. I don't leave any messages. *Are we breaking up?* I don't remember my life without Hands. He feels like family at this point . . . but maybe that's the problem.

Hush, I think. It's just the distance. I aim to try and put the thoughts out of my mind because bad thoughts, like chickens, come home to roost.

I slowly make my way to the lobby to get out of the apartment and out of my head. Rudy calls out my name and says, "You received a delivery from Cookies by Design yesterday. It looks beautiful *and* delicious." He pulls a box from underneath the front desk and opens it to reveal an artist's palette made out of cookies. "Someone back home must miss you," he says with a wink.

"Thanks, Rudy," I say, taking a quick peek at the card. It says, "I'm so proud of you. O O O. Hands." Each O shoots a dagger at my heart.

I run back upstairs. I find some construction paper scraps and decide to make Hands a card, too. I cut out a football shape from the brown paper and glue on tiny white strips for laces. With a black Sharpie, I write: "I'm sorry about what I said. I just miss you. Thank you for my gift. X X X."

I take a picture of it with my cell phone and text it to Hands. After twenty minutes of waiting for him to call, or at least text back, I panic. What if we are really breaking up?

I decide to email Corrinne. She knows how to both get into situations and how to get out of them.

> To: corrinnec@gmail.com
> From: kkidd@gmail.com
> Date: Sunday July 22
> Subject: Howdy, Cowgirl!
>
> I know you're busy at camp, but I've got a quick question and need your help. How do you know when a relationship isn't working? How did you know it was over with Bubby?
>
> FYI: I'm having the best time ever, NYC is amazing. I hope you aren't missing civilization too much. I can't imagine camp can be any more rural than the Spoke. Wish I could send you some Sonic in the mail.
>
> Kisses.

My email isn't completely forthcoming, but I don't want Corrinne to think I've gone totally crazy. She'd be just as likely to believe that I went out until three in the morning and that Hands was ignoring my calls, as she would to hear that I was on *Girls Gone Wild: Big Apple Edition.*

I'm surprised when an email from her pops up a few minutes later.

> To: kkidd@gmail.com
> From: corrinnec@gmail.com
> Date: Sunday July 22
> Subject: Re: Howdy, Cowgirl!
>
> Ohmigosh, Kitsy. We get only 10 minutes of internet every three days and somehow you emailed me during my window. I know, that's totally barbaric, but it's part of the "camp experience," so I'm told. I'm having a great time though, which shocks even me. I know a relationship isn't working when it isn't fun anymore or when I meet someone else. As for Bubby, it was too much effort and not enough reward. Why, is he asking about me again? I have 5 seconds, so just know I love you! I'll try to check my email again soon.

I'm impressed by this camp being so low-tech. Corrinne and her iPhone are rarely seen apart. I should've explained that I needed advice because of course Corrinne assumed the Bubby question had to do with her, not me. It's true that Corrinne has had high school boyfriends and will have college boyfriends *and* post-college boyfriends, but I have only had exactly one boyfriend and thought that may be it. I can't relate to her gain-loss analogy because she neglected the love part of the equation. That's what I feel for Hands, right? Love?

Now I just feel more confused about everything. Maybe these Tad tingles are side effects from yesterday and this whirlwind week. My inner compass must be a bit off. It's not used to being orientated anywhere but Broken Spoke, after all.

Nibbling away at Hands's cookie bouquet, I sketch works of art from the Corcorans' coffee table books until the sun finally sets in the summer night sky.

When the alarm wakes me up bright and early, I hear the pitter-patter of rain against the panoramic windows. Looking out, I see that it's not just drizzling but *pouring*. In Texas, we call this type of rain "a frog strangler." The rain almost distracts me from remembering about yesterday's fight with Hands.

Grabbing my cell phone off of the nightstand, I take a deep breath when I see that I have a text from Hands. I open it and there's no message, but an aerial view of our football field with the words I'M SORRY. O O O written out in shaving cream. I smile. I knew that we couldn't stay mad long. We have too much history. I text Hands that I love him. While I'm glad that he's forgiven me, something is still nagging at me. Then, out of nowhere, I find myself wondering why Tad hasn't texted me. Is it wrong for me to even care? But I don't have time to mull it over. I have to get to school early today and I've got to scramble.

I find a note from Maria on the kitchen counter.

Dear Kitsy,
I saw you were in bed early last night! You must have been tired from your late Saturday night☺ Let me know if you need anything. I'm off to get the dry cleaning before the Corcorans return from Nantucket. Left some egg chilaquiles. They're made from leftover tortilla chips! Enjoy!
Besos, Maria

Opening the fridge, I find a covered dish with soggy tortilla chips, chilies, and eggs. I microwave it, gobble it up, and leave Maria a note.

Maria,
Best food I've had in NY. Seriously.
You should open a restaurant.
Thanks, Kitsy

I search the front hall closet for an umbrella. Even though I pride myself on being prepared on account of constantly juggling my three duties—carhop/cheerleading captain/part-time mom—I did forget to pack an umbrella for New York. I find a large one with a wooden handle in the back corner that looks like it could cover the entire West Village.

I figure the rain will have to be my shower today. I'm out the door less than ten minutes after waking up. Walking up the eclectic Christopher Street, which is filled with gay bars, tiny ethnic restaurants, and smoke shops, I try to focus on not poking out anyone's eyes with my huge umbrella as we cross paths.

As I wait for the light at Seventh Avenue, I admire how all the girls in New York coordinate their Hunter rain boots with their umbrellas. The girl next to me sports black Hunter rain boots to her knee, a chic yellow rain jacket, and a chic black umbrella. She looks like a beautiful and expensive bumblebee.

With my flip-flops and a golf umbrella, I feel like a total tomboy at a *Little Miss Sunshine* pageant. When a gust of wind swoops by, I almost fly away like Mary Poppins and get blown back to Jersey. Luckily, I end up at school and *not* in New Jersey. Field goal for Kitsy! Got to appreciate the little things.

As I walk down the hallway, my flip-flops make squeaking noises with every step, and I'm soaked from head to toe minus my sketchbook, which I had hidden in the waist of my pants.

Even though I'm an hour early, I find Iona sitting in her usual seat when I open the door. She gives my appearance her all-knowing look.

"Hi, Iona." For once, I definitely don't sound chipper, not even a little bit.

She stares at me as if I were a piece of art and she's decoding me. "I thought you were the she-must-be-on-Red-Bull type."

I did, too, but my pep meter is on empty.

"What's wrong?" Iona asks. Strangely, it looks like she might actually care.

"The rain," I answer.

But I'm also wondering what happened to no-one-can-get-a-word-in-edgewise Kitsy. I must've left her in Texas. Despite all of that well-meaning advice, you can't just "be yourself" two thousand miles away. It's just not that easy. At home, I'm a caretaker, a girlfriend, and a cheerleader. But here, I'm an aspiring artist—who goes out with a strange boy until three in the morning and then lies about it. Who you are depends on *where* you are. Why doesn't anyone ever tell you that? *That* would have been a great piece of advice.

"You know what we say in New York? Or rather, what the gangsters say?" Iona asks.

I raise my eyebrows to show the faintest interest.

"We say *fuhgeddaboudit*," Iona says, laughing. And when she laughs, her eyes get all squinty, and she doesn't seem so intimidating.

I laugh along with her because it is sort of funny. I didn't expect Iona to have a sense of humor, especially after our first introduction, when she grilled me on my (nonexistent) art school credentials.

"Can I see your sketchbook?" Without waiting for an answer, Iona gets up and walks across the room to me.

I don't even have time to cover up the sketch I'm working on with my hand.

"Wow," Iona says, picking my book off my desk. "You're as good as the very best kids in this class, even the ones who've been taking classes since nursery school. But . . ."

"But what?" I ask.

"Artists who have perfect technique or who can replicate are not the ones that get noticed. Besides, technique you can learn. In person, Kitsy, you have all this energy, but your art doesn't reflect it. If you really want to do this, you need your art to have a *je ne sais quoi*, a less-studied element to it." She drops my sketch and it flutters back onto my desk.

"I'm from Texas, Iona. The Middle of Nowhere." I hold up my index finger next to my thumb to make a point. "My entire city could fit on one city block. Work with me in

English, and I'll try to translate it into my native tongue."

"*Je ne sais quoi* is French for 'I don't know what,'" Iona says and smiles. "It's used to describe an intangible quality. Think about your favorite piece of art in the world. I'm willing to bet you don't love it because of its technique. It makes you feel something even if you can't exactly describe what it is. That's *je ne sais quoi* to me."

I think of *The Starry Night*, and I know that Iona's right. While Van Gogh did have amazing technique and developed methods and a new style for painting, it's been my favorite painting since before I knew *anything* about art. It made me feel something just by looking at it. The little village in the middle of nowhere reminds me of Broken Spoke, and the night sky reminds me of the world that's bigger than Broken Spoke.

"Thanks, Iona," I say. "It's really kind of you to help me. And I think I know what you mean. It's just I'm new to art as serious business. In Texas, I only sketch for myself. The only kind of public art I do is makeup for my cheerleading team. I'm still getting used to being critiqued."

That is, being critiqued about something that I've created.

"New Yorkers have a lot of opinions, Kitsy. Professor P. will just be one of them. Make sure you get some thick skin, but don't lose your sensitivity. I think that will play an important role in your art." Then Iona leaves me to draw, her Doc Martens boots stomping as she walks away.

"By the way, you should apply for the scholarship," Iona says as she trots up the stairs to her seat.

Wait, scholarship?

"What scholarship?" I ask. "I didn't see anything about that in the orientation packet."

I turn around and watch Iona sit back down, put on her glasses, and lean back. "That's because it's not in the orientation packet, it's a separate application. Every year, one summer student is picked for a ten-thousand-dollar scholarship donated by an anonymous patron of the arts."

"Ten thousand dollars?" I stammer to make sure I heard it right. That's roughly 1,600 hours at Sonic, not including tips. Ten thousand dollars would be the difference between everything for me and my art. Not to mention my life.

"Yes," she says. "And I'm predicting that you'll get it. A lot of these other kids are just here because they got in, and it looks good on their already-bloated résumés," Iona says. "None of them flew across the country to be here. I think that says something about you."

New York keeps surprising me. Monday might've started with rain, but it's getting sunnier by the second.

Professor Picasso begins Monday's class at exactly nine a.m. "Enough with nudes, which I know must disappoint your hormones, but this week is pottery week."

Broken Spoke High's budget, particularly the art budget, gets slashed every year, so we definitely don't have any art supplies other than charcoal and antique (read ancient) paint. So when our class goes into the pottery room, I almost faint when I see it. Inside, there are twenty stations, each with its own pottery wheel. This is like the new Dallas Cowboy football stadium of art rooms. (Not that I've been to a game there—it costs sixty dollars just to park!)

My heart starts pumping again, and I get the same rush that I did when I first came to New York, the same one I got from singing "Don't Stop Believin'" with Tad, and the same rush I got when I realized Iona wanted to help me, because she thinks I'm a good artist.

Professor Picasso explains the terminology for, as he puts it, "those of you who might not have had the pleasures of working with clay." I'm so excited that I find myself barely able to listen. I've always wanted to try throwing clay ever since I saw the classic movie *Ghost* with Amber on late-night TV. Amber just kept commenting on how hot Patrick Swayze was, but all I could think was *I wonder if one day I'll get to try pottery*. The closest I've ever been to *really* working with clay is Kiki's Play-Doh.

Professor Picasso stops lecturing for a moment and sits down at the wheel right next to where I'm standing.

Splashing water on the clay, he slowly begins to press

the foot pedal. He explains that working with clay on a wheel is called "throwing." As Professor Picasso gradually opens, centers, and grounds the clay from a heap into a vase, I decide that *throwing* is totally an inappropriate term. Watching someone work with clay on the wheel is like watching a transformation. A caterpillar to a butterfly. Michelangelo once said that he could see the object inside a block of marble, and that he'd chip and chip away until it became free. I wonder if I'll be able to see something in this clay and figure out how to let it escape—or better yet, find the artist in me and let her be free.

As we all sit down at our individual stations, I start to forget the other stuff: Hands, Amber, Kiki, and Tad. Maybe Professor Picasso is right. You can't multitask with art. I need to figure out how to concentrate. Maybe then I'll find my *je ne* . . . whatever it's called.

As a class, we start slowly together. We lather our clay blocks with water as if we were baptizing them. Then, Professor Picasso instructs us to put our feet on the pedal and slowly start spinning our wheels.

"Slower, slower," he urges us. "Now press your thumbs into the center but hold on to the edges. Keep your foot on the pedal."

Instead of looking at my own clay mound, I find myself watching the other students in the class. I see most students' clay start to effortlessly mold into shapes. They don't even seem nervous. Meanwhile, I can't figure out how to concentrate on the pedal and the clay at the same time. I feel like those kids who can't rub their tummies and pat their heads at the same time except I'm the cheer-leading captain and I'm actually very coordinated. It's a requirement for being the top on a pyramid.

Peeking out of the corner of my eye, I notice Professor Picasso watching me. You can do this, Kitsy, I say to myself. You wanted to do this, Kitsy. As Professor Picasso hovers over me, I press as hard as I can and barely push my thumbs into the clay. I didn't know that throwing clay required hands of steel!

"Kitsy . . . ," Professor Picasso says calmly. "Slow the wheel, Kitsy."

I should probably mention that I don't have my driver's license. You need a parent to drive with you for a hundred hours before you qualify. No way Amber's up for that. So maybe because I'm not used to a pedal or because I'm ner-vous, when I hear Professor Picasso say *slow*, I just press down harder. Like a firecracker exploding, the clay flies *everywhere*. Most of it hits me, but I see one kid across the room blocking his face and I'm pretty sure a glob smacks the ceiling.

An epic flame-out. Worse than the time I crashed into a trash can and spilled a tray of milkshakes at Sonic because I was busy thinking too much about bills and not enough about Rollerblading. My cheeks go redder than the clay, my mouth drops open, and I'm totally speechless. Most of the other students stop their wheels, and it seems time is frozen. The room is silent.

Putting his hand on my shoulder, Professor Picasso explodes into laughter and the other students join him. Is this happening? Aren't teachers supposed to keep other kids from laughing at students, not be the ones that *start* it? Are manners really an exclusively Southern thing?

Briefly, I envision my escape out the door, out the building, off Manhattan, and back to Broken Spoke, but I stay firmly seated. After all, Kitsy Kidd is not a quitter. And the only thing worse than staying here is running home.

"Kitsy," Professor Picasso says, not unkindly, "this happens *every* year. It wouldn't be the pottery unit if it didn't happen *at least* once. Go clean up and start again."

And just like that, everyone goes back to work, and the snickers stop.

When I pass by Iona and her almost perfect vase on the way to the bathroom, she asks me, "Do you need any help?"

"I'm good, but thanks for asking." I really need to tell Corrinne to be nicer to her.

In the bathroom (luckily, the empty bathroom), I spend a lot of time picking the clay out of my ear, my shirt, and yes, my bra. Once I'm all cleaned up, I stare at myself in the mirror.

"What do you want, Kitsy? Why are you here?" I ask my freshly washed face.

"To be somebody. Or try to be somebody," I reply to myself. "And remember, this is supposed to be fun, so loosen up."

I remind myself that nothing—not fixing a leaky pipe or holding your head high as you pay with coupons at the Piggy Wiggly—flusters me, so why should this? They were laughing at the situation, not me.

Back in the classroom, I take my seat and Ford calls out to me.

"Still looking fabulous somehow, Kitsy."

I smile until I see Professor Picasso walking over and stroking his reddish beard. "Ready for round two?" he asks and drops another slab of clay on my wheel.

"Never been so ready for anything in my life," I lie.

Looking down at the hunk of clay, I try to remember exactly what Professor Picasso explained earlier, but all I can remember is flying clay and yelps of laughter.

I see Professor Picasso step to move around the room, and I breathe in and do something I've never been good at doing: asking for help.

"Professor Picasso," I say quietly, "can you help me this time?"

With a surprised look, he smiles and says, "But of course."

Sometimes it actually helps not to act like your usual self.

. . .

Two hours and thirty minutes (and two tries plus help from Professor Picasso) later, I'm looking at my *very own* clay vase. It definitely tilts a little to the left, but I have to trust myself with clay, and I find that I like that.

When Professor Picasso asks the class to put our work on a table so it can be fired in the kiln, I hesitate. I'm having total separation anxiety from my masterpiece . . . okay, from my *novice-piece*. Gently, I place it next to my other classmates' work, most of which are far more advanced than mine. I'm okay with that though.

"Class, there's more to this announcement than how to fire vases. In one hour, we're going to have a meeting in our classroom about applying for the scholarship that our anonymous benefactor has kindly donated again. The student who has the best portfolio showing will be awarded a ten-thousand-dollar scholarship to be used toward an art education. I'll discuss the rest of the details at the meeting. Remember, this is not for a Girl Scout patch, so only come and apply if you have serious intentions about applying to art school and furthering your art education with the goal of becoming a working artist."

The words *working artist* ring in my ears like a favorite Christmas hymn. Working artist definition: someone who gets paid to do art. It almost sounds impossible that it exists—that some folks make a living from it, and even crazier, that some artists get rich doing it. Of course, that's not why I want to be an artist. It would be amazing to work somewhere where perks include being emotionally and spiritually fulfilled. At Sonic, my only real benefits are free Frito Chili Cheese Wraps.

I figure I have enough time to go and get a snack from one of those stores that Corrinne called bodegas. They just seem like mini convenience stores to me except they don't sell gas, which makes me realize I haven't seen a single gas station in New York. All the cars must run just on the city's energy. I'm going to try to channel that energy more and figure out how to infuse it into my art, not let it distract me from my art.

I pull out my cell phone as I walk into the sticky-like-a-Popsicle-wrapper summer air. I breathe a sigh of relief that the rain's stopped, so I don't need to open the world's largest umbrella. Pausing, I smile as I realize that I haven't thought about Hands, Amber, or Kiki for almost three hours. It's not that I don't love them, but it's that I didn't come here to think about them. And no thoughts about Tad or the fact that he didn't call either. A minor victory in the Chronicles of Kitsy.

I turn on my cell phone and feel it vibrate in my hand. I brace myself for the Texts from the Spoke, and I say a silent prayer that the home front's forecast is calm and calamity free. It'd be nice to get away from my Broken Spoke worries physically—and mentally—for at least a day.

It's not a 580 number that pops up though; instead, a

917 number reads across my screen.

> Want to play hooky? I'm in Union Square Park, watching a rousing game of chess. Find me.

I look at my watch. Tad sent me the text at two, it's almost three, and the scholarship meeting is at four. Breathe deep, Kitsy, and pray to Cupid that he will make the pitter-pattering of your heart stop. I don't want to have a heart attack on the sidewalk. Besides, Tad's probably not even there anymore, I shouldn't go anyway, and I have a devoted boyfriend writing *I love you* in shaving cream on the BSHS football field. But I decide that I can easily walk to Union Square, say hi to Tad if he's still there, and make it back in time for the four o'clock meeting.

As I approach Union Square I realize why everybody falls in love with New York City. On one block alone, there are two Mister Softee ice cream trucks and a cupcake truck. A bunch of little kids are shrieking and splashing around in the fountain and a group of break-dancers perform a routine to the sounds of a boom box that's blasting Michael Jackson.

For a second (and I'll confess that it was barely even a full second), I take in the scene, forgetting that I came here to find Tad. I remember why I'm here when I see a cluster of people huddled around a giant chess table. A mixture of relief and disappointment washes over me when I don't spot Tad among them.

He's not there. Back to class, back to life, back to reality. Pivoting, I decide to skip the snack at the bodega and go for a cupcake from the Cupcake Stop truck. The name is telling me "Red light!" but this is probably my one and only chance to eat cupcakes out of a truck. Maybe it's something I can bring back with me. It'd definitely make tailgating a lot more fun and would finally add some estrogen to the menu.

Waiting in line, I listen in on two friends' lively debate over what cupcake to split. I think it's a pretty great day when the biggest decision you have to make is choosing between baked goods. As much as I try, though, I can't put Tad's text out of my mind. Why would he text me on a *Monday* if he didn't *like* me? And more important, why should I care if he does? I have less than three weeks left here, and then I go back to the last seventeen years of my life in Texas. If I'm calculating my math right, I'll have spent less than one percent of my life here. Zero isn't even a real number according to my algebra teacher, Mrs. DeBord.

"Next!" the lady in the truck calls out from the tiny window.

Confronted with a rainbow of mini-cupcake options, I suddenly freeze with indecision—then quickly overcome it when I see a mound of frosting topped with a giant Oreo cookie.

"Can I get one Oreo?" I ask.

As she wraps up the cupcake in pink tissue paper, my eyes stay glued to a Funfetti mini cupcake.

"Would you like the Funfetti mini, too?" the lady asks.

I nod sheepishly.

"It's on the house, or on the truck," she says, laughing. "It's one of those days I feel like being nice."

"Thank you," I tell her, beaming. I balance in one hand two cupcakes and in the other hand, a giant umbrella.

Backing away from the truck, I start off toward school when I hear from behind me snapping to a beat I recognize:

"*Do wah diddy diddy dum diddy do. She looked good. She looked fine.*"

I refuse to turn around. Don't be offended, Kitsy. It's a New York thing; men are more forward here. If anything, be complimented. Picking up the pace a bit, I use my umbrella to propel me away from the serenade.

"Kitsy!" the voice calls.

I spin around to find Tad at my heels.

"A cupcake!" he exclaims and reaches out for it. "For *moi*? That's so nice."

"Hi, Tad," I say, instinctively clutching my cupcakes close to my chest. "I tried to find you, but I couldn't, so I settled on something sweeter instead." I don't know where those last words come from. I know that they don't sound like me.

Tad pauses for a second. Did I cross the line?

Putting his arm around me in a big-brother type of way, Tad says, "I just got back from MoMA. Jealous much? How was school? Didn't anyone ever tell you that only the dorks and burnouts go to summer school? Okay, to be fair, I went to summer school, too."

"Well, somebody did warn me to stay away from musicians who try to get you to play hooky," I say, ducking out from underneath his arm.

Not to mention, my boyfriend, Hands, instructed me to stay away from all boys in New York. Actually, all *people* in New York.

I pop the entire mini Funfetti into my mouth and chew it slowly to buy myself time.

"So how about coming to see *the* Hipster Hat Trick practice in Brooklyn?" Tad reaches toward my Oreo cupcake and swipes some frosting off with his finger.

"Can't," I say, looking at my watch. "I have a meeting."

Tad looks at the frosting as if he's debating whether he should lick it off his finger or not. Finally, he does, and then he casually licks the side of his mouth with his tongue. Holy Holly Golightly, it doesn't make me feel casual at all.

"A meeting or a band rehearsal? Do you even need to think about that decision? Do you think the artists hanging in MoMA learned to do art by going to meetings?"

Tad doesn't wait for my answer; he continues on. "Besides, you have to see art to make art. Not that I'm calling Hipster Hat Trick art. Don't get me wrong. I'm not that conceited or delusional. But c'mon, Kitsy, live a little."

Tad spins me then dips me. I cling tightly to my cupcakes and umbrella.

"Sing with me!" Looking up at the clouds where the sun is trying its hardest to peek out, Tad dances in a little circle around me and snaps out the rhythm and sings: *"I've got sunshine on a cloudy day. When it's cold outside, I've got the month of May."*

Before Tad can get to the "My Girl" chorus where things will get even that much more confusing, I stop him and surprise myself by saying, "Okay, okay, I'll go."

I'm not getting the scholarship anyway, and I definitely need to learn to live a little. It's just a band practice, after all. The whole group will be there, including a kid from home, and absolutely nothing will happen.

And that's how I end up on a subway Brooklyn-bound despite Corrinne's warning that everything I need is in Manhattan.

# Chapter 9

# The Thing About Good Girls

THE THING ABOUT GOOD GIRLS is that just because they are good, it doesn't mean they don't ever consider being bad. On account of having a mother who isn't exactly *Nick at Nite* material and having a father who hasn't been spotted in six years, I pay plenty of attention to how people perceive me. All my life, I have sat in front rows, led cheers, and dated the nicest boy in school so that people would know, without a doubt, that I'm good. But now that I'm out of my area code, I find myself thinking what it would be like to be different. Not to be bad, necessarily, just to be different.

Sitting next to Tad on the L train heading toward Williamsburg, I realize I don't even know if Tad has a girlfriend or what his last name is. I just know it feels exciting to do something that surprises even me.

"So then," I say, recounting, "there was, like, clay *everywhere*. Like, even on the ceiling fan." New Yorkers love exaggeration.

Tad laughs and shakes his brown hair. I try not to pay attention to how cute he looks when he does it.

Tad jumps up as the subway lurches to a halt, grabs my hand firmly, and pulls me up from my orange bucket seat.

"This is us," he says. I love the way "us" rolls off his tongue. Even though the only us I'm supposed to belong to is Hands and Kitsy.

When we make it up onto street level, Tad takes my hand and we walk a few blocks east past restaurants, dingy bars already full with customers, and bodegas. There are entire blocks void of people, and there just seems to be more room to breathe. This is totally not Corrinne's scene with its rough edges, and lack of department stores and chic cafés, but I love it here.

He doesn't need to tell me why because I see it: a spectacular view of Manhattan.

"Wow, I can't believe the best view of Manhattan is *here*," I say, glancing around the much less glamorous Brooklyn.

"I think sometimes you've got to get out of a place to be able to take the whole thing in. When you're in it, you only see what's in front of you. You should come back and sketch it from this view," he says. "I'm jealous that you can make a memory or an experience into something tangible."

"I love how you think about art," I say, half to myself because Tad's already heading back away from Kent Avenue and the river. I'm not sure he even hears me.

When we reach a building with a marquee reading MUSIC HALL OF WILLIAMSBURG, Tad extends his hand and says, "After you, Kitsy."

"You practice here?" I ask, walking in and admiring a large stage where I notice Rider and another guitarist tuning up their instruments. I'm used to people practicing in their parents' garages, not at actual venues with a stage and a stocked bar.

"Yeah, a guy I know owns the place, and lets us practice here on random afternoons. It's got great acoustics, and some pretty amazing bands have played here," he says.

Rider, wearing a cut-off jersey tank, sees me approaching and stops fiddling with his guitar.

"You're a long way from home, Kitsy Kidd," he says. I see him do a double take from me to Tad, back to me.

"I could say the same to you. A little different from playing at the Broken Spoke High gym, huh?" I tease, being bolder than the Kitsy I know, the good one.

"Let's just agree to not mention the words *Broken Spoke* for a while," he says before turning back to his guitar. "There's a reason we're both in New York for the summer: It's called 'getting away.'"

"Fine by me," I say loud enough for only me to hear over the stringing of the guitars. I'm glad that Rider isn't part of Hands's huddle in the Spoke. It's nice to have a little divide between here and there, which is pretty easy since it seems that everything in the world divides the two.

"You okay hanging by the bar?" Tad asks before he climbs onto the stage. "I know the bartender, Cooper, over there. He'll hook you up." Tad gives a nod toward the tall, bearded guy pouring out a shot. Actually, now that I look around and think back to our walk here, it seems almost everyone is bearded in Williamsburg. Well, at least the guys.

Did I come all the way here to hang out at a bar alone?

"No problem," I manage to choke out even though I feel totally deflated. It's not like Tad misled me though; he invited me to his band rehearsal and I accepted. My only question is why I did, especially since Tad admitted that his own band is lame. I can't believe I skipped a meeting for a ten-thousand-dollar scholarship, however far-fetched my chances were, for this. I'm well acquainted with being disappointed, but it's a new feeling to be so disappointed with *myself*. Maybe being different isn't so great after all.

I take a spot at the bar, one stool away from the only other girl there, a leggy blonde in a green romper. She definitely fits into Corrinne's categories of a person who wants to be a model, who was a model, or who is currently a model. If I had to sketch her, I would have to shade her cheekbones in for about ten minutes to accurately show how defined they are.

"What'll you have?" asks the bartender, Cooper, and I rip my stare away from the maybe-model next to me.

Looking down at my watch, I notice it's four thirty p.m. The scholarship meeting is over, so I guess I'm officially here. Might as well settle in. Who knows, maybe this isn't a mistake. I need to wait it out and see.

"I'll have a Coke," I answer. I don't want to be any more uninhibited than I already am acting, so I stick to my signature drink.

"In *that* case, all your drinks are on the house. And even if you do decide to go stronger, they are still on me. Tad and I go back."

"Thanks a lot," I say, wondering about Tad and his life a little too intently.

I text my brother, figuring I should do something that Good Kitsy would do.

Can't wait to see you, Kikster. Bringing you home tons of stuff.

The bartender places a large Coke with a straw in it for me. I'm disappointed when I quickly taste that it's actually Pepsi.

The beautiful blond looker peers over at me with curious eyes.

"Taking it easy?" she says. "Don't worry, I had a big weekend myself. I should be taking it slow, too."

I'm flattered that this Bright Young Thing thinks that I'm the type of girl who could have a big weekend in NYC. And I guess, in a way, I did.

I recall each detail from Saturday in my mind as if it were a movie rather than my actual life. I almost forget that I'm upset with Tad for abandoning me at the bar and upset with myself for being here.

"Late night on Saturday," I say.

She raises her shoulders. "What night isn't in New York."

Especially when you are modelesque, I add mentally, and I imagine her at a club surrounded by champagne on ice and adoring men. I wonder what she's doing here and not posing in couture for some glossy magazine cover.

I think that our little conversation is over, so I look toward the stage, where the band's started practicing a rendition of the eighties song "Jessie's Girl." Tad gives me a wink and my palms sweat.

My phone vibrates and I almost drop it because my hands are so slippery.

Hands: You are my favorite. Call me tomorrow. I know that you are there to do your art.

The word *art* runs guilt through my veins, and I sip my Pepsi to get the taste of lies out of my mouth.

The blond girl looks back over at me as I check my phone and try to remember if I ever felt sweaty about Hands. I'm hot all the time in Texas, which makes it difficult to figure if I'm sweaty because of Hands or the humidity.

"Aren't phones annoying? It's like you can't spend a few moments enjoying music. It's pretty sad," she says before motioning to the bartender for another as she sucks down the last of her clear drink.

Quickly, I tuck my phone away in my purse, realizing at the same time that I forgot the Corcorans' umbrella on the subway. I get angry with myself for being so irresponsible. I'll have to try to figure out where to buy another giant umbrella and how to afford it with my dwindling Sonic savings.

I pull out a dollar for the bartender. I'd never stiff anyone after all my time working at Sonic.

Setting the money on the table, I swivel my stool to face her.

"Yeah, phones are annoying," I agree. "People expect you to be in constant contact even when you're trying to get away. It's like everywhere you are, you aren't just there; you have to be somewhere else electronically as well. It's especially hard when you're just trying to enjoy being somewhere amazing like this. I'm Kitsy Kidd, by the way."

I reach out to shake her hand when she says, "Not from around here." It's not said like a question.

"The handshake gave it away?" I ask as she reaches her long, manicured fingers to meet my chipped canary-yellow nails.

"No, it's just that all I hear is accent. I got asked the same question when I first moved here. It always embarrassed me. I'm Annika."

Apparently, last names aren't required in New York, even in Brooklyn. I think I know most people's middle names in the Spoke *and* I could draw their family trees for generations back.

Smiling, I say, "Pleased to meet you. Where *are* you from then?" I imagine she'll answer Sweden, Russia, maybe even Brazil like Gisele Bündchen.

"Let me see if you can guess." Annika pauses and takes a breath.

Changing her voice from her soft Marilyn Monroesque tone, she says in a nasal octave, "Gee, Kitsy. Pleased to meet you. Dontcha know where I'm from?"

My mind flashes to that weird movie *Fargo* about that small town in the Midwest. . . . Where was it again?

"Minnesota?" I guess on a long shot.

"You betcha," she answers. "But up north, it's pronounced Minn-Ah-So-Ta." Switching back to her first airy, whisperlike voice, she says: "Land of ten thousand lakes. The home of the Vikings, the Twins, and the Wild. And of course, Paul Bunyan."

"It was the blonde that gave it away. Plus, I saw the movie *Fargo*. Are you from St. Paul?" I ask, recalling my state capital knowledge from elementary school.

"Gawd, no," Annika answers as she reaches for a fresh drink. "That's an actual city with buildings, even though they're teeny-tiny compared with the ones here. I'm from Fergus Falls, population ten thousand. Home of the largest otter statue. And Kitsy, I'm not a real blonde. We're not all blondes back home. I'm not sure who started that rumor. Maybe the Chamber of Commerce trying to attract more male visitors?"

I laugh. I reckon every state gets stereotyped, for better or for worse.

"You're joking about the otter, right?" I ask.

"I'm negative-forty-degrees-below-with-wind-chill serious. We have the largest otter statue in the country. Otters were my school mascot, too. They built the statue with some hopes for tourism, but the thing is people are more interested in visiting the largest twine ball, which is in Darwin, Minnesota, and two hours away. Basically, no one visits, so now it's where local kids take prom pictures and get drunk.

"Evidence: Exhibit A," she says, pulls out her iPhone,

and scrolls to a photo of her and the otter statue. Not to be mean, but it's pretty cheesy.

"Oh," I manage, still in disbelief that this girl hails from a town as small as Broken Spoke. "My town doesn't even have a statue. That's a way cooler mascot than the one at my school. We're the Mockingbirds."

I don't even know why I say "Mockingbirds" like that. I've always liked the Mockingbirds as our school mascot because it's original. Most other schools are the Tigers, the Wildcats, or the Mustangs.

"Where are you from?" Annika asks and sounds genuinely interested, unlike most people.

"Broken Spoke, Texas," I answer. "It's kind of like *Friday Night Lights*."

Annika's eyes light up. "I loved that show. I'm a Tim Riggins fan all the way. Somehow, he pulls off long hair unlike anybody else."

I fiddle with my straw. "Yeah, it's a great TV show, but it's a little less fun if it's your life, if you know what I mean."

Annika shrugs. "They always make places look better on TV, even New York. In movies, small-town girls come here and get swept off their feet and have amazing adventures. That doesn't happen. If you want anything here, you've got to work for it. The small-town act doesn't get you anywhere."

I nod, wondering if I've been naïve all this time. If I really want to make it, should I be acting differently? Less like myself? But aren't I already doing that by skipping a scholarship meeting and following Tad around Brooklyn?

Pointing to the stage, Annika says, "That's Erik. He plays the drums. He's from Fergus Falls, too. We met in the hospital the day we were born. We're seven hours apart."

Erik, Rider, and Tad are standing together looking over some line notes.

"So is he your boyfriend?" I ask. Although Erik is okay-looking in his plaid shirt and unusually-tight-for-a-male jeans, I really can't imagine him and Annika as a pair.

"Gawd, no," she says, a bit of her Minnesotan accent slipping through. "Erik and I just go way back. We both feel the same way about Fergus Falls, so it's good to have each other to lean on since we don't relate to anyone back home anymore."

Tad, Rider, and Erik disperse back to their old spots onstage.

"Do you go back often?" I ask.

Annika pauses. "No," she says and shrinks a little. "I did a couple of times, but things change."

Then she grins as if she can change her mood with the press of a button. "The weather in New York is tropical compared to Minnesota, so this is home now. So what about you and Tad, little missy? Are you two an item?"

"Gawd, no," I say, mimicking Annika's expression, and she laughs.

"I like you," she says. "I think you have what the French call a certain *je ne sais quoi*."

My faces flushes, and I hold back the urge to tell her my life story from birth to my conversation with Iona this very morning about *je ne sais quoi*. Then I remind myself what Amber always says: "Folks only know what you tell them." And in this case, if some glamorous girl thinks I have a certain something, there's no need for me to be yakking about my insecurities, art related or otherwise.

"Erik told me that Tad's working on something new that's really great and original. I'm sure you know, but Tad was almost famous until everything that happened . . . happened."

With every pore of my body, I want to implore her to tell me what "everything that happened happened" was, but I don't. Sometimes the past doesn't need to enter the present. It's not as if Tad knows everything about *me*.

"Nobody thought that Tad would start writing again. Apparently just last night, he called a practice to work on something new he wrote. Erik told me to come today because it might be something big, although everyone in New York is always saying that." Annika stands up and watches the boys.

It seems like something big is always happening in New York, which is amazing. In Broken Spoke, it seems like the same things just happen again and again.

"Let's go stand closer and play the part of a 'groupie,'" she says, putting quotation marks in the air and swaying to the beat. "Every band has to have some hot groupies, right?"

Being a groupie doesn't sound all that terrible. Remember, Kitsy, if you are somewhere else, you can become somebody different if just for a moment. Just look at Annika, I bet no one even asks her anymore where she's from. She acts *so* New York.

With Rider on guitar and Erik on the drums, Tad edges forward, dragging his microphone. "This one . . . this one's for the girls."

Annika and I are the only girls in the hall, so I know that this song is at least 50 percent dedicated to me. I silence my phone. It's like Annika said. It's sad if you can't just listen to some music sometimes.

Tad starts out with a similar tune to the "Mockingbird," the song he sang at my request at karaoke.

Annika squeezes my hand, and I close my eyes to just listen.

> *I was floating*
> *I was sinking*

*I was drowning.*
*I was an anchor.*
*Pull me up*
*Raise me up*
*My buoy*
*Float me through the waves*
*Hold me against the current*
*My buoy*

I open my eyes to see Rider and Erik smiling at Tad, who looks down from the stage at me. I close my eyes again.

*Let me hold on here*
*I want to hold on here*
*Let me rest here*
*I want to rest here*
*Let me float here*
*I want to float here*
*You are my buoy*
*You fight the waves for me*
*You resist the current for me*
*You save me*
*Untie me*
*I want to be untied*
*Release me*
*I want to be free*

*Let me go*
*I want to swim*

When Tad finishes singing, Erik and Rider play a short instrumental ending. When I open my eyes again, everything seems clearer, as if I'm wearing contacts for the first time. Even the dark, dingy music hall seems much brighter.

Annika starts a steady slow clap, and I join her. I'm pretty sure being a groupie is somewhat like being a music cheerleader; it fills me with that . . . *je ne sais quoi.* All my anxiety about skipping the scholarship meeting to watch Tad sing cover songs dissipates. I don't think it was just a *coincidence* he asked me come listen today, the day he performed his first original song in, like, forever. Maybe nothing, including our two fateful first meetings, that's happened between us has been just *coincidence.* I wonder if coincidence and fate are actually the same thing.

Tad clears his throat and looks around. "I still need to finish the last verse, but what do you guys think?"

"Y'all were wonderful," I say loudly enough for him to hear me bright and clear over the feedback.

"Yeah, y'all were wonderful," Annika says, imitating my drawl perfectly. "So what's it about?"

And I swear this happens: Tad looks down, winks at me, and says, "It's private."

Back in Broken Spoke, Corrinne went totally nuts when Rider wrote a song about how good she looked in her Levi's. It ranged from slightly to moderately annoying every time she started singing "her song," but for just a moment, I want to imagine that I had something to do with Tad's song. That maybe somehow that song was not only for me, but also about me.

"Okay, enough of that," Tad says. "Let's go back to practicing our bread and butter. Other people's songs."

Erik and Rider fake moan and start tuning up to "Jack & Diane."

"Very cool," Annika says to me appreciatively. "A long way from Broken Spoke, huh?"

A long way from anywhere I've ever been or anything I've ever felt, I think. All I can do is nod.

I realize that I need to go when I happen to glance at my watch. I have spent enough time being different, and I need to spend some time being good and get back to the Corcorans.

"Will you tell everyone that I said good-bye?" I ask Annika, who's found her way back to the bar.

"Sure," she says. "We should hang out sometime soon. I don't even know what brought you to New York or what sent you away from Texas. Although I'm philosophically against telephones I'll ask Tad to text me your number. I know what it's like to have to fight the small-town-girl thing. I can show you how to leave that behind you." She gives me a hug.

"That'd be nice," I say. But am I really ready to abandon everything that's always defined me?

I people-watch on my subway ride home and I realize that the *underground train* no longer makes me anxious. Score! Back at the apartment, I walk in and find Mrs. Corcoran watching *The Real Housewives of O.C.* I know now where Corrinne gets her love of TV.

"Kitsy!" Mrs. Corcoran exclaims as she pauses the TV. "I feel like we're ships passing in the night. I'm so busy this summer. I can't tell you how great it is to just sit back and watch someone else's life," she says jokingly and points toward the screen.

I smile and relax. I'm happy to see someone who knows the "real" Kitsy even if she isn't around often.

"I want to thank you again, Mrs. Corcoran," I tell her earnestly. "We started pottery week, and the whole experience has been incredible."

Hopefully, she wouldn't be disappointed to find out that I've been exploring more than just art since I've been here.

"Stop thanking me. I'm just so happy to have you here. And, oh! I just remembered today we received an invitation to your exhibition, and I had a great idea. Why don't you invite your mom to come? Mr. Corcoran has a ton of airline reward miles. Wouldn't it be nice to show your mom where you've been going to school and what you've been working on?"

My heart stops—and not in the way that it did with Tad.

"Of course," I say feebly.

When I first told Amber that I wanted be an artist, she laughed. "If you want to pick an impossible career, why not just want to be an actress? Nobody cares about artists anyway. I can't even name a single one. All the good ones are long dead."

That was the last time I seriously talked to Amber about art. Whenever she mentions my art, she calls it "that adorable hobby," as if it were a phase, like playing with dolls.

"Okay, just have her call me," Mrs. Corcoran says and unfreezes the *Housewives*. "And Kitsy, I'm here if you need anything," she calls out above the TV noise.

Even though I have no desire to invite Amber, I nod. Sometimes no matter how hard you try, you still can't really get away.

To: corrinnec@gmail.com
From: kkidd@gmail.com
Date: Tuesday July 24
Subject: Re: I need an update.

I don't know about you, but it feels nice to get away from everything for a while. In New York, my time is all about me—a new experience but I'm digging it. I'm mostly busy doing my art but I've also had some really cool New York experiences with random people who live here.

I went to Bagel Bob's. I'm confused—how can they be so crunchy on the outside and gooey in the inside? Those bagels should be illegal—they're too good. And why do so many places here only sell Pepsi? Majorly gross.

Did they take your makeup away, too? That'd be a travesty!

Can't wait to see you!

# Chapter 10

## How to Make It in New York

*I DROP THE ENVELOPE AND my backpack at the mailbox and run inside. Amber's watching Mariah Carey hawk items on QVC and Kiki's playing with Legos.*

*I hold the letter up in the air. "I got in!"*

*Amber doesn't look up from the TV.*

*Kiki snaps the last piece into his skyscraper Lego. "Got in where?" he asks.*

*"There!" I say, pointing to his sculpture. "I got into art school in New York City!"*

*Amber turns around from her spot at the couch. "Do you think those crystal hoops would look good on me?"*

*I barely glance at the TV. "I do," I mumble. "But I don't think we can fit them into the budget. . . . Amber, did you hear me?"*

*"Mom, can we all go to New York?" Kiki asks. "I want to see real skyscrapers."*

*Amber flips the channel to the Home Shopping Network. "Kitsy isn't going to New York," Amber announces. "We can't even afford hoop earrings."*

*"Mrs. Corcoran said she'd pay for me to go. I told you about this—" I say, reading the letter to myself again. I can't help smiling even if Amber's being difficult.*

*"You really want to go to New York? It isn't easy to go away and come back here," she says and refills her drink. "Trust me on that. And you're happy here. You're popular, you have a job, and a nice boyfriend. Why would you want to mess that up for some silly adventure?"*

*"Because it isn't silly to me."*

After I stay late at school Wednesday to practice on the pottery wheel, I head uptown to meet Ford at the International Center for Photography.

Once I'm there, I spot him, standing near the ICP, a large glass building with huge photographs blown up three times larger than life hanging in the windows. Ford is waving at me with both hands.

"Kitsy," he says breathlessly, "on my way here, I saw them film *Project Runway* on this pier, near South Ferry. I saw Heidi Klum *and* Tim Gunn. All the models were on stilts. I totally could've done a better job than some of the designers. I would've used taffeta but, like, in a classy way. *And* I saw Eli Manning at the Five Guys on Seventh Avenue; he's always one of my top picks for fantasy football."

"You like football?" I ask. "Why didn't you tell me? I'm Texan after all."

"I *love* football," Ford says. "Maybe we'll do a fantasy league together this fall."

"I think I have enough football in my life," I say. "But I definitely want to stay in touch, and if you want to see some amazing high school football, you're always welcome to visit."

We walk in and Ford pushes ahead of me in line and announces: "I'm buying your ticket. I'm very old-fashioned."

"Do you know a lot about photography?" I ask.

"Not really, only fashion photography," Ford says. "But I figured it'd be good to check out some exhibits before we start our photography unit. My parents would be *so* happy if I became a photographer and worked at the *New York Times*. They're so not on board for me being a designer. They think it's frivolous. Screw it though. I'm definitely trying out for *Project Runway* once I'm legal."

"Will your family come to the exhibition?" I ask, thinking about Mrs. Corcoran's offer to fly out Amber. I still haven't called her about it.

Ford pulls out his wallet and pays for our admission.

"Of course, and I'm sure they'll give me their very honest opinion. They always do," he says.

"At least they're involved," I say. There are worse things, I think. For instance, not even being sure you want your mother involved.

After showing the guard our tickets, we walk into the main exhibit: a retrospective on photographer Stephen Shore's work. Along the white walls hang poster-size color photographs.

Ford reads the brochure to me: "Stephen Shore is known for his color work of banal American scenes and objects. Blah, blah, blah. He lived in New York City until he was twenty-three when he went on a road trip photographing less well-documented landscapes."

Ford gestures toward a photograph of a Chevron gas station. "Why would someone from New York City go traveling to photograph places like *this*?" he asks.

"I'm not sure," I say. I've spent a lot of time thinking about how to get away from places like that and get *here*. "Look at this one. It's a picture of Presidio, Texas," I say and point to a photograph of a dusty strip of stores.

"These aren't really my thing. They make America look depressing," he says and nods toward a shot of a plate of steak at a cheap restaurant.

"Parts of it can be depressing," I say. "Some parts can be even depressing and beautiful at the same time."

"I only like beautiful things," Ford declares and points down the stairs to another exhibit. "That's why I'm going to work in fashion. Let's keep going."

Something pulls me back. It's a photograph of a small-town strip that looks very similar to Broken Spoke. "I think these are beautiful in their own right because they're authentic," I argue.

"Who wants authentic?" Ford asks. "Art should be fantastical and breathtaking, just like fashion. Stores like Eddie Bauer and Cold Water Creek should be sued for selling fashion that's anything less than glamorous. Now let's speed our way through this museum and then go window-shopping because that's *my* favorite type of art-gazing."

"Sure, sure," I say, happy to have a friend, even if our opinions of art are very different.

After another night of avoiding Mrs. Corcoran's questions about Amber visiting, I buck up and call home on my way to class on Thursday morning. The phone rings nearly four times before Amber picks up.

"Kitsy," she says groggily. "What are you doing up so early?"

"It's almost nine here, Amber," I say as I weave through the morning foot traffic toward school. "The city's buzzing already. My class starts in a few minutes, and I've been up for hours. Where's Kiki?" I ask.

"Probably watching TV," she answers in the same tired voice.

I sigh. "Maybe take him to the park after sunset or something," I say as I pass by Carrie's stoop from *Sex and the City*. There are already a bunch of tourists lined up, taking photos. "Everyone walks everywhere here. It's amazing. I think it's important for Kiki to be outside even if it's hot."

"He doesn't like doing anything with me," Amber grumbles. "Every other word is Kitsy. You'd think *you* were his mother."

"I'm almost at school, so I only have a minute," I say as I wait for the light to turn. "But Mrs. Corcoran wants to fly you out to see my exhibition. That's where I show all my art—"

"I know what an exhibition is, Kitsy," Amber interrupts. "You know, I had a life before you."

I avoid her trap and say quickly, "I talked to Hands and he said his mom could babysit Kiki. It'd be nice to have family here for my show."

"You know I would come," Amber says and pauses. "It's just I've got some good job leads, and I think it'd be better if I stayed. I promise I'll make it to the first game to see you cheer."

I know that she's lying about the job leads. As much

as I didn't want Amber in New York, I suddenly realize now that I desperately wanted *her* to want to visit and see my art. Amber has made it to only two of my cheerleading events. I stopped inviting her because I don't want to get my hopes up. Even if she promises to show, she doesn't.

"This is not a halftime cheerleading performance; this is a real art event. This is what I want to do. This is what I wake up thinking about," I argue.

"Kitsy, it's one thing to let the Corcorans pay for your summer classes and whatnot, but I don't want people thinking I can't take care of my own family. There's no way I'm coming. Here's your brother," she says.

"Kitsy!" Kiki squeals, and I silently pray that he didn't overhear us. I try as hard as I can to shield him from these types of conversations.

"Kiki!" I say as cheerfully as I can. "Guess what? I'm going to call Hands and see if you and him can have a Sonic date tonight. How does that sound?"

"Amazing!" Kiki shouts. "They have a new foot-long hot dog! But I miss you, Kitsy. Have you found any real stars there yet?"

"Not yet," I say as I round the corner before I get to school. "I've got to go to class now, Kiki, but I love you."

"Love you, too," Kiki says. "Wait, how about *I* come visit you in New York since Mom can't make it?"

His words feel like punches to my stomach.

"I promise you that someday I'll take you to New York," I say and hang up before Kiki can ask when.

I'm not in a great mood as I walk into class. I'm bummed about Amber and I'm annoyed that Tad hasn't called since he performed his original song, which means it definitely wasn't about me. I also know that I completely messed up by skipping the scholarship meeting. I'm here for *my* art. I didn't leave Kiki at home for me to swoon over a guy that isn't my boyfriend.

"Hi, Ford," I say as I flop into my seat.

"What's wrong, Kitsy?" he asks, giving me an intent look. "You don't seem like yourself."

I like Ford a lot, but I'm not ready to unload Amber and Kiki onto him. Back home, everyone knows my family situation. It's nice that I can shed that here—at least on the surface.

"Nothing," I answer quickly and give him a huge grin. "So tell me more about how your fashion dream started."

Lighting up, Ford takes off his violet frames and launches into the story about how he used to sew outfits for his sister's Barbie dolls using his mother's old clothes.

It's pretty nice to get to escape from my own thoughts for a while and learn more about my new friend.

While I'm glazing my vase near the end of the class, Iona approaches me. "I didn't see you at the scholarship meeting on Monday," she says in an accusing tone.

I look at her and shrug. "Something came up," I say honestly and start another coat of glaze.

Iona raises just one eyebrow. "Something more important than a ten-thousand-dollar scholarship?"

My first thought: *No.*

"It's not that big of a deal," I say without looking up. "Besides, it's not like I'd win."

"That's a *great* way of looking at life," Iona says sarcastically just as Ford walks up.

Ford rolls his eyes at Iona. "How about another museum date this weekend?" Ford asks me.

"Kitsy probably doesn't think museums are important," Iona says to Ford, who gives her a confused look.

Picking up my vase, I sigh and say, "I've had enough for today." Without a good-bye, I walk across the room, set my vase down to be fired, and leave.

At my school, if you're a cheerleader and you date the quarterback, you're popular. But being popular only means you get invited to all the parties and no one bugs you at school. It doesn't mean that kids don't talk behind your back. And just because you're always around people, it doesn't mean that you have a lot of real friends. I never even had a best girlfriend until Corrinne.

Walking back home after the Iona-scholarship incident,

I dial Corrinne. If I've ever needed a friend, now's the time.

"Hey, Kitsy!" Corrinne says, whispering. "I'm hiding in the camp's shower house. I'm not supposed to have my phone, but I was in Facebook withdrawal. Of course, I picked up when you called because I'd break *any* rule for you."

"Thanks, Corrinne," I say and ready myself to confess everything I haven't told her about New York.

But then Corrinne squeals, "Holy Holly Golightly, Kitsy, I've had a personal life revelation. One of my cocounselors, Cory, is the hottest guy ever and I'm pretty sure he's going to have a *big* influence on my life."

I swear I'd be a millionaire if I had a dollar for every time Corrinne called a male *the hottest guy ever.*

"Of course, he barely knows that I'm alive, but that'll change," she says. "How's the art-making? Have you moved into MoMA and pitched a tent?"

Looking down at the cement, I wonder if I should tell Corrinne about everything that's going on. After all, she's been beyond kind to give me this whole experience. It'd be completely rude of me to tell her how I squandered my chances for a scholarship and I haven't even been back to MoMA.

All of a sudden, I'm so overwhelmed that I can't ask Corrinne what I really need to talk to someone about. So I lie: "I've visited lots. You were so kind to get me the membership. I'm just calling to say that I can't wait to see you at my show."

"Thanks, Kitsy," she says. "I love you, but I gotta go—my cabin needs to practice our lip sync. I can't believe I'm at some rugged camp, and you're in the city. Talk about total role reversal. It's like a Miley Cyrus movie. Love ya."

"Love you, too," I say and I hang up. I still think that Corrinne's "rugged camp" is probably still pretty luxurious. After all, exaggeration is Corrinne's favorite accessory. A big emergency there is probably deciding which pair of riding pants to wear to dinner. I don't want to weigh her down by making her deal with my drama.

I walk into the front door and drop all my things in a defeated heap when I realize Maria is there.

"Hello, Kitsy!" Maria says as she wipes down the counter.

I carefully pick up my things off the floor. "Hi, Maria," I say. "How are you doing? I loved the chilaquiles. You'll have to give me the recipe. I do most of the cooking at my house."

"Your mother doesn't cook?" Maria asks.

"No," I say, hoping Kiki has had at least a few meals that didn't come out of the freezer since I've been gone.

"She's just like Mrs. Corcoran," Maria says. "She doesn't cook either. Kitsy, did you notice that the orchid is starting to bud?" she asks, pointing to the plant on the windowsill.

"Wow," I say, admiring it. "I hope that I'm here to see it bloom."

"If not, you'll be back and that plant will still be here. It's a survivor. Oh, Kitsy, I have an invitation to my daughter Esperanza's *quinceañera* for you and the Corcorans," she says and places a beautiful, handmade invitation on the counter.

I only know a little about *quinceañeras*, a special tradition for many Spanish-speaking girls' fifteenth birthdays. A few of my classmates in Broken Spoke had them, but I've never been invited to one.

"I'm finished for the day," Maria says, heading for the door. "I hope that both you and the Corcorans will come."

"I'd love to," I call out after her. I doubt with the Corcorans' busy schedule that they'll be able to make it.

I guess there is more than one way for parents to be absent. Maybe Corrinne and I have that in common.

I fumble through my bag and pull out my cell phone to call Ford to see if there's any way he's up for another museum date right now. I need to get out. Good Kitsy is back in the driver's seat. I see one new text.

Hey, Texas! It's Annika. I have an event. Do you want to go for an hour then do something fun?

Maybe a date with Annika is *exactly* what I need. If

anyone knows how to make it in New York from a small town, it's her.

Me: Sure. What should I wear?

Museums will be here tomorrow.

Annika: Just look hot. Be at 42nd and 5th at 8.

I rush to Corrinne's closet and pick out a yellow jersey tank and a pair of black silk shorts. Quickly, I heat and eat a prepared supper, a chicken potpie from the fridge, and give myself a once-over before I head out. I'm not sure I look *hot*, but I know I don't look like myself, a feeling that I'm getting used to.

One hot and sweaty subway ride and a transfer later, I'm standing at Forty-Second Street and Fifth Avenue in front of a library. But it doesn't look anything like Broken Spoke's public library, which is a one-story brick building with the word READ painted in large bubble letters.

The New York Public Library is a white stone building that looks like it should house jewels, not books. Three huge archways, flanked by six columns, lead into the library. Above each column is a statue representing a "useful knowledge." Two marble lions guard the entranceway.

I recognize it as where Big and Carrie almost got married in the *Sex and the City* movie and from the opening scene of *Ghostbusters*. Quickly, I snap a few pictures and text them to Kiki. He's going to freak.

Feeling a hard slap on my butt, I spin around and find Annika. Her "hot" constitutes a dress the color of her skin that nearly makes her look naked, and a blowout that only a professional could do. She doesn't look small-town at all. I hope someone will say that about me one day.

"Love your makeup," Annika says.

Well, if all fails, I can always go back to blushing and bronzing.

"So what's your event?" I ask.

"It's a party hosted by a magazine to highlight young people in the arts."

"You work at a magazine?" I ask, having a hard time even imagining Annika behind any desk, even one at a fashion magazine.

"Gawd, no. That would probably require a college degree, and I gave up that when I, well, technically dropped out of high school."

"You dropped out of high school?" I try not to wear my shock on my face, but isn't high school necessary for most everything?

As we get closer, I notice a zillion cameramen lined up

on the library's steps, and there's a red carpet in front of the entrance.

Annika turns to me and says, "Hey, Kitsy, do you want the short or the long story about me?"

"I think we only have time for the short," I say as she loops her arm into mine.

Breathing in, Annika begins to speak. "Okay. Here it goes: I went to Mall of America last summer before my senior year. A talent scout was hanging out by the food court where I was eating at a Dairy Queen, an establishment this city is sadly lacking. Blizzards are mad good. Blah, blah, blah, blah, he was looking for an unknown to star on this new show. And, tada, I'm now that girl. The pilot got picked up a month ago, and we start filming next week. The show's totally unrealistic. It's supposed to take place in Wisconsin, and the plot is how all the girls spend their days chasing hockey players. Except it's stupid because in real life, girls in the Midwest play hockey, too. Basically, I have to swoon over pretty boys pretending to be hockey players when at twelve I could've outskated even the stunt players."

"Wow," I say. "You played hockey?"

Annika smiles. "And that is why I like you, Kitsy. After all of that, you just want to know if I actually played hockey. You're so not *New York*."

I smile and eat the ten million questions I have for her

about what it's like to be an actress.

"I don't even know how to ice-skate. We don't have a rink in Broken Spoke. Hands"—I hesitate, realizing I've never mentioned him to Annika—"he's my friend in Texas," I lie coolly. "He skated once when he visited his second cousins in Houston, and says it kills your ankles. My brother, Kiki, would die to do it because he's obsessed with the Mighty Ducks movies. I'd love to try, too, and I think I'd be good because Rollerblading seems similar, and that's how I serve my customers at Sonic."

I stop the Kitsy Monologue when I become pretty sure that Annika isn't listening. She's scoping out the scene.

"People will take our picture up there because I'm starting to get recognized. Everyone wants to be the one who finds the new 'it girl.' All the new 'it girl' actually means is that you aren't anyone yet." Annika uses huge quotation gestures each time she says "it girl."

We get in line behind other people, who are way more dressed up than either Annika or me.

"Let's put in some face time and find something better than this," she says.

I'm standing on a red carpet with an almost celebrity, and there's allegedly something *better* than this?

When we walk near the entrance, I hear someone ask, "Isn't that the girl on that new *Iced* show?" and another yells out, "ANNABELLE!"

Annika turns her head around, puts a hand on her hip, tilts her knees together, and pops her butt. She opens her mouth, not so much in a smile as a pout. Her pose immediately drops ten pounds off her already slender figure. Freezing like an ice sculpture, she holds her pose while a rapid series of lights flash. Only when it finally becomes dark again does she relax and drop the pose.

"How did you learn that?" I ask her once we're inside. "And how come that guy screamed 'Annabelle'?"

"The pose is a variation of the sorority squat that my sister taught me. As for the name, my agent thought Annika was too ethnic or too small-town or not enough of something. I like Annabelle way better but sometimes I just forget to introduce myself that way. Try to call me Annabelle if you can remember."

I think of my own name, and I wonder if I'd have to change it to make it in New York. Would anyone want to buy a Kitsy original? Even though I was named after my mom's first doll, I like my name.

"That's kind of how it is at the salons here," I say, thinking back to Corrinne and me at Spa Belles my first day here. "I told the nail tech that I liked her name, Joy, but that's actually her fake name. Her real name is Phung, but they all take American names to make it easier."

Annika/Annabelle laughs. "Nothing here is authentic. You can be anything here since nothing's genuine."

I'm not exactly sure that's a good thing, but I guess Annika knows a lot more about it than I do.

When Annika approaches the bar, a sea of boys and men getting drinks part to let her through.

"I'll have a vodka soda," she says. "Do you know what I miss from Minnesota?"

"What?" I ask.

"Nothing," she says with a shrill laugh.

As much as I love New York, I can't imagine not missing at least parts of Broken Spoke. But if you want to make it, maybe that's how it has to be.

A lady in a fuchsia skirt with a tangerine blouse taps Annika.

"I'm with *W* magazine. We're taking some sound bites from this party for our magazine. Can I ask you a few questions?"

"Sure," Annika says politely and motions for me to stand by her.

"What's it like for people to say that you are the next big thing?"

"Flattering," Annika says and gives a smile I haven't seen before. It's more controlled, as if she's hiding something.

"How's it having to hang out with hot guys all day?"

"Well, luckily, we spend most of our time in an ice arena, so that helps me keep my cool."

The lady laughs a little too hard. I imagine that's not the first or last time Annika will use that line.

"I read that you were discovered at a mall. You must be a natural since you've never studied acting."

Annika immediately freezes up and bites the corner of her lip. "I believe the scout saw potential. I have been taking acting classes with Stella Adler Studio for over a year, so I feel pretty confident in my abilities. Thank you so much for interviewing me."

The lady finishes writing down her notes, her photographer snaps a picture, and they both walk away.

Annika faces back toward the bar and finishes her drink in three big pulls through a tiny straw. "That's the thing about being an actress—you never stop acting. You always have to maintain that persona. Annabelle is Annika now," she says. "Acting's really the only way to get through New York. Trust me, I used to be just like you."

I try not to take that as an insult. After all, of everyone I've met in New York, Annika and I probably have the most in common. If she knows the road to success here, I'm ready to listen.

I look around at the waiters passing around fancy, unidentifiable appetizers (or hors d'oeuvres in NYC speak) and a marble staircase that must lead to levels of the party that we haven't even seen yet. By the time I turn back around, Annika's heading out the door. With one more glimpse, I reluctantly follow her outside.

Annika lights up a cigarette, and I'm glad that she smokes a different brand from Amber.

"Kitsy," I hear someone cry out and turn around to see Waverly, dressed like it's prom, albeit a *Gossip Girl*–style prom, waiting in the line to get in.

Annika raises her eyebrows at me.

"Hi, Waverly," I say and walk the distance to meet her.

"What are *you* doing here?" The *you* is definitely accented; perhaps Waverly didn't mean to do it—although I'd wager she did.

"With a friend," I say, pointing toward Annika, who waves her cigarette.

Waverly gives her a look of recognition and judgment.

"What are *you* doing here?" I ask, purposely accenting the *you*.

"My mom's magazine had extra tickets, so she gave me some."

"Great," I say. "Gotta go, we've got another event. Crazy night," I lie, taking Annika's advice about acting. This Kitsy persona is not intimidated by Waverly, who is currently looking at me with a shocked face.

I turn away from Waverly and ask Annika, "Where to?"

"Anywhere but here," she answers as she stubs out her cigarette with her stiletto.

"Do you care if I text Erik and Tad to meet up?" Annika asks in the cab. Her only direction to the cabdriver was

"Take me downtown and quickly."

I'm saved from answering when my phone vibrates in my purse. Annika watches me closely. "Is that home calling?" she asks, and I know, without checking, that it's probably Hands, Kiki, or Amber calling.

"I'm sure it probably is," I admit.

"Don't answer it," she says. "Give yourself a break for the night."

I do feel like I need a rest tonight. I'll check my phone later just to make sure nothing's *really* wrong. "Annika—I mean Annabelle—can I ask you something? If you don't miss anything about home, why do you hang out with Erik?"

"Because he thinks home sucks, too," she says. "We're the only two people from there who know that life didn't begin and end in high school. We never talk about Minnesota. I only told you about it because I could tell that you're new to this whole New York thing. I wanted you to trust me. I promise I'll help you blend in here."

Mrs. Corcoran rarely mentions the Spoke either. Maybe the best way to move forward is to not look back.

Leaning into the front seat, she says with confidence to the cabdriver, "Bleecker and Thompson."

Hard to imagine she ever lived in a small town where a large otter was the main attraction.

"Okay, here's the deal. They're at a bar called The Back Fence," she says.

"That sounds great, except I don't have an ID. I'm not exactly legal," I say, remembering that Annika knows even less about me than I do about her.

Annika slides her French-manicured hand into her clutch and pulls out an ID. "Duh, I'm not legal either. Good thing that we're not playing ourselves tonight.

"Here, you'll be Kirsten Fox. She's my older sister. She's away at University of Minnesota–Duluth becoming a nurse like my mom. I was planning on going there, too, before I got saved."

If being saved means leaving a small town, will I be doomed if I stay in Texas?

Examining the ID, I see a slight resemblance between Annika and Kirsten. Or, rather, I catch a slight glimpse of what Annika must have looked like before she became Annabelle, future "it girl," star of *Iced*. I wonder if the bouncer is going to notice that I'm not a brunette like Kirsten, and that I'm five foot five, not five nine.

Maybe Annika notices my concern because she says, "Just watch the 'y'alls' when you talk to the bouncer and maybe throw in a 'yabetcha' or two. By the way, Erik is with Tad, so I hope you meant it when you said you didn't care."

I shouldn't care since I do have a boyfriend, I think. But I can't bring myself to say that out loud. The guilt of calling Hands "my friend" earlier tonight makes me feel like I ate mud.

When we reach the bar, there's a line out the door. The whole bar seems only about the size of the Corcorans' kitchen and live music booms into the street from inside.

"They have a table," Annika says, shimmying through the crowd to the front.

For some reason, nobody stops us from cutting in the line. Maybe everyone's too drunk, or maybe this is just how it is for people like Annika. The bouncer quickly looks at our IDs before he lets us in. Maybe it's easier to be someone else than I thought.

Once we're inside, we spot Tad and Erik sitting at a table. Luckily, with the music, no one can hear my heart, which I can feel pounding at the sight of Tad, who is smiling and waving me over.

Tad's sitting on a bench and Erik is across from him on a wooden chair. There definitely doesn't seem to be room for two more. Annika drapes herself over Erik's lap, and I act casual and give Tad a small wave. Like Annika said, New York is about acting.

"Kitsy Kidd," Tad says, standing to greet me, "I didn't think I'd see you after you pulled another Cinderella at the Music Hall."

I laugh and say, "It's not Cinderella since you're clearly no prince."

The band starts playing "The Weight."

Tad laughs and asks, "Do you want to go outside for a

smoke? It's getting hot in here."

He doesn't wait for my answer but grabs a handful of peanuts from the red basket on the table.

"Free nuts," he says to me. "Who said there's nothing cheap in New York? And this place has history. Bob Dylan was allegedly discovered here. Pretty slamming, right?"

Erik says, "Bob Dylan's from Minnesota."

"He's from Hibbing," Annika says. "But everyone knows that it's New York that makes anyone famous."

"And once upon a time," Tad says, "it was talent."

I follow Tad out as he weaves a path through the crowd. He leans up against an ATM to light his cigarette.

"So how did pottery week go? Any more clay explosions?"

I smile. It's really nice to have someone interested in me—and my art. "Nope," I say. "Clay's like New York; you get used to it, and eventually it starts to work with you, not against you."

"That's a good way of looking at it, Kitsy," he says.

As I'm staring at Tad's cigarette, he catches my gaze. "I hope these don't bother you. I started after I stopped drinking, but my therapist tells me that's just habit transference."

I think how happy I'd be for Amber to transfer any of her bad habits for new ones. I'm so exhausted by her current ones.

"Not at all," I say, even though I hate the smell of smoke.

Tad nods. "I didn't know you were friends with Annika," he says through a cloud of smoke.

"We just met, but she's been really sweet to me. She just took me to a fancy event at the library. She's showing me the ropes. Did you know that she's going to be on a TV show?"

"It was the first thing she told me," Tad says and not jokingly. "You don't need to hitch on to her—or anyone's—star, Kitsy. You're doing great on your own. Besides, she's very into the scene, very different from you."

"What am I like?" I ask impulsively. For some reason, I suddenly want Tad to show me who I am when I'm not in Broken Spoke.

"You're special," he answers without missing a beat. "You're here because you have a passion."

My heart thumps like horse hooves on pavement.

"I really loved your song, by the way," I say, ignoring his compliment. "You're very talented at writing."

I smile, still holding out on a prayer that it was me who he was singing about. I want to be his buoy.

"It's just nice to not have to sing somebody else's songs for once. I probably wouldn't have gotten to write my own stuff if my record deal had gone through, so maybe everything falling apart was a blessing in disguise," Tad says as if he's realizing this for the first time.

He reaches out and brushes a hair from my face, and I don't pull away.

I wonder if sometimes life-as-you-know-it falling apart can be a good thing. I feel my old life unraveling like a spool of yarn, and I don't move to catch it. Maybe Annika is right to let her old life go and move on. Maybe I'm letting everything that's going on in Broken Spoke hold me back from having my best New York experience.

"What *did* happen?" I finally ask, unable to hold back.

Tad steps closer. "Nothing really interesting. My dad died the month after I signed with my label, and I spent all my time drinking instead of working. My label dropped me because I started acting like a rock star," he says, smirking. "Which is only allowed if you're actually already a rock star. It was stupid, but I was really young."

For a moment, I think about how I'm spending my time swooning when I'm supposed to be figuring out what to do for my portfolio. I wonder if I'm being stupid and young, too.

Then I have a terrific idea. "Do you think for my final project that I could do a photo portfolio on you and the band? I like the idea of it being about New York and making something of yourself here."

Tad steps back and looks at me as if he's not sure what to say, so instead he just lights another cigarette. Amber does that, too, when she wants to avoid something.

"Are you that into music?" he asks without looking at me.

"Not really," I admit. "I just want to tell the story of people trying to make it in New York. I think it's a really universal narrative."

Tad sighs. "That's true, Kitsy," he says encouragingly. "But we're a band that covers other bands' songs. We're not creating anything new. I saw your face at MoMA and how passionate you were about that place. I don't see that in your eyes when I sing. Besides, don't you want the project to be about something more personal to you?"

"Let me just try it. I think I can do a good job," I argue. "And maybe the band's just doing covers right now, but you're writing again. Don't sell yourself short."

Tad stubs out his cigarette with the toe of his shoe. "I wouldn't want to sell you short either. But if that's what you think your best project would be, then great."

The door swings open, and Annika and Erik stumble out of the bar.

"Smoking without me?" Annika asks Tad. It almost sounds like she's flirting, but I think that it's just an Annika thing.

"Never," Tad says sarcastically. "Are you all ready for the next place?"

My phone vibrates in my purse.

I check it and notice I have three new texts from Kiki.

Miss you.

Really miss you.

Bedtime story?

Reluctantly, I explain that I should end my night now.
I don't really want to, but I know that I'll see Tad and
Annika again soon, and I want to end the night still feeling
like I'm walking on air.

As I hail a taxi, Tad calls, "Careful, Cinderella, your
taxi might turn into a pumpkin if you aren't quick."

He's right; pretty soon, all of this will turn into just a
memory and I'll be back in Broken Spoke. But who will I
be when I get there?

To: kkidd@gmail.com
From: corrinnec@gmail.com
Date: Friday July 27
Subject: News!

We kissed! See, determination always gets you want you want! I have the guy and you're in the Big Apple. We. Are. Awesome.

Winning,

CC

To: corrinnec@gmail.com
From: kkidd@gmail.com
Date: Friday July 27
Subject: Re: News!

You kissed? Were you cozying up by the campfire? Did it remind you of being back at the field? I have no new kisses to report (obviously)—but I think I have finally figured out my portfolio project. Here's hoping I can prove that I'm talented at more than blending eye shadows and drawing killer winged eyeliner.

# Chapter 11

## In Your Own Backyard

I WAKE UP ON FRIDAY morning, our last day of pottery, feeling refreshed. Knowing that I'm going to do my portfolio on Hipster Hat Trick answers a big question that had been looming in my head. There are still a few others, too, of course. Luckily, working with clay all day provides a good distraction from everything. It's as if when I'm doing art, my brain shuts off all of my anxieties, and I can just focus on what I'm doing. My best vase ends up looking pretty professional.

Iona walks up to me after class as I'm finishing up glazing and pushes a folder to my chest. Today, her boots are painted zebra-print and she's wearing a leopard T-shirt dress. Somehow it works, although I'd never tell her that after the Kitsy-doesn't-care-about-museums lecture.

"What's this?" I ask her, taking the folder.

"It's the scholarship application. I took the liberty of scanning and printing you a copy. If you want, I can tell you what Professor P. said at the meeting."

I have only thought about the scholarship a thousand times.

Iona looks uncomfortable, something I never thought I'd see.

"Listen, Kitsy, I'm sorry about what I said yesterday," she says. "I have this problem of getting too nosy and thinking I know what's best for everyone. It's your business if you apply for the scholarship, but . . . I wanted you to have the chance to change your mind."

"You didn't need to do this, but I really appreciate it," I say.

It's strange because I've been confronted with a lot of generosity in my life, especially with my New York trip this summer. Why am I always afraid that someone's going to jump out from behind the barrels and take it away from me? I need to remember that life, and most people, are good. I'm glad that Iona's reminding me of that.

Without asking, Iona pulls a stool up next to my wheel and gives me the scoop:

"Here's the deal. The scholarship is judged only on the portfolio, which will be shown at the exhibition in two weeks. Professor P. said that he'd get more into it next week when we start our last unit on photography. But basically you get to choose your medium. Last year, someone did graffiti on clay pots and won. I imagine that's some sort of political statement, but I can't wrap my head around it."

"We need to make a political statement?" I close my eyes and think again that this scholarship is out of my grasp.

"All art makes political statements," Iona says matter-of-factly.

I thumb through the application. "So do you know what you're going to do for your portfolio?"

"I'm doing figurative drawing, but I'm not applying for the scholarship," she answers and stands up. "I'm fourth-generation legacy at Cornell. Most likely, I'll go there and do premed. I'll take an art class or two, but just to get a relief from classes like Organic Chemistry. Both my parents are psychiatrists and they have a practice on the Upper East Side. I want to work with them. Not that it'll surprise you, but there are a ton of people in New York who need therapy. I love to psychoanalyze as much as you like to make art."

I smile, thinking how that solves a huge puzzle of who Iona is in my head.

"Anyway, I overheard everything that was said at the scholarship meeting while I was working on a sketch. Just so you know, I don't have a lot of friends. My parents call it social anxiety, but I think it's because I'm selective. And you're one of the only people I can stand here, so I noticed when you weren't there."

Iona points at my best vase, which doesn't lean like the Tower of Pisa. In fact, it doesn't tilt at all. "That looks like a replica of the vase Professor P. made on the first day."

I start to thank her, since that had been the idea—to see if I could match his, but then I realize that it wasn't meant as a compliment.

Iona leans in. "Hey, Kitsy," she says. "I've taken a class with Professor P. before. If I had to analyze him, I'd say he's hard on people he thinks have talent. He's not the type to waste his time."

I pause and try to absorb what she's saying. "I hope you're right," I whisper back.

"Just be yourself."

And with that, Iona leaves. I hear her combat boots stomping down the hall. She definitely is someone to run down the river with, even if she doesn't quite get how hard it is to be yourself away from everything that makes you you.

Professor Picasso walks into the room from the kiln and I see the way he's looking at my vase, and I'm just waiting for his tirade. I try to keep Iona's advice in my mind.

"Is yours ready, Kitsy?" he says, approaching me. "It always scares me putting students' work in the kiln. We always have a few blowups, but that's okay. The second try is usually better. They relax and it's more genuine."

"Yes, sir," I answer, picking my vase up gently.

"Texas, right?" he asks me.

"All you hear is accent?" I ask, thinking back to Annika.

"Well, the accent, the 'sir,' and the fact that I taught art restoration for a semester at University of Texas in Austin. Love that city. And I'm also on the admissions committee here, and I remember your application, Kitsy."

"My sketch of the oak tree?" I ask, feeling my cheeks get red. After seeing art here from around the world, my sketch seems silly and insignificant.

"I remember how much passion it had."

"How can you see that in a sketch?" I ask.

"You can't see it," Professor Picasso says, surprising me. "You feel it."

He takes my vase and moves toward the kiln.

"Why do you focus so much on technique in class then?" I call out. "Why are you so concerned with that?"

Professor Picasso stops walking and turns around. "I'm a teacher," he says, looking across the room at me. "My job is to teach the basics of the discipline, but what I look for in art on the street, in a museum, or anywhere, is the feeling of the artist. Nothing else makes me look twice."

"How do you purposefully put passion into your work?" I ask.

"If I knew that," Professor Picasso says with a smirk,

"I wouldn't be teaching this class because my work would be hanging in museums. I know you have it because I've felt it from your work. You just need to find it again."

On Saturday, I'm walking around the city when I feel my phone vibrate. It's Hands. After our first mini-fight, I have tried to be better about talking to him more often. But it's like we're having the same conversation over and over again. I get the feeling he doesn't want to hear about my art any more than I want to hear the latest football scrimmage recap. Back in the Spoke, we have everything in common. But here it feels like we're two totally different people.

I almost answer the phone, but then I pause. The people on the street are just making their way. Nobody else seems to be talking to a long-distance boyfriend. I'll be home soon enough to talk, so I silence it.

For homework, Professor Picasso instructed us to visit a museum, so I figure it's about time I go to MoMA again. After all, I'm a member. Switching directions, I head for the subway. I'll be with Hands all year, but my time here is slipping away.

I first head to *The Starry Night* to get a photograph to send Kiki. You can take pictures here as long as you don't use a flash, which is perfect since my flip phone definitely doesn't have one.

I edge closer to the painting and read the description plate next to it.

It says, which I already knew, that Van Gogh painted the night scene from memory during the day.

I try to imagine drawing a scene only from memory. I could draw Broken Spoke, but that's the only place. And who would want a picture of our football field?

I feel a tap on my shoulder. An Asian man points first to the painting and then to me.

I raise my shoulders in confusion just as I realize he's offering to take a photograph of the painting and me.

How cool. People in New York are definitely friendlier than anyone gives them credit for. I beam, thinking how Kiki will love this.

Posing in front of my favorite painting of all time, I give my best smile. This will totally be my Facebook profile picture.

Then I drift into another room, and I'm flabbergasted when I see one of Claude Monet's *Water Lilies* paintings. I never realized it could take up nearly an entire wall. It's almost the size of a real-life pond.

Just as I'm standing and gazing at it, as if I were Monet on a bridge looking at my subject, a little girl about seven years old with auburn pigtails and pink denim overalls comes and stands beside me. Seeing her makes me miss Kiki.

"Hi!" she says cheerfully while I look around for her parents. I spot them watching her from the bench.

"Hi!" I say back, thinking how lucky she is to get to visit this museum at her age.

"Why are there so many water lilies?" she asks, pointing at the picture. "It's *boring*."

"Monet, the artist, is famous for water lilies," I explain. "He did over two hundred and fifty paintings of them."

"But why water lilies? *Bo-ring!* They're just weeds," the young girl says. "Why not a castle or a dragon? That'd be way more exciting!"

"That's a great question," I say, wondering why Monet, with all of his talent, kept painting the same subject: his own garden.

"Some of *my* pictures are better than these," the girl says confidently. "I do great unicorn drawings. Maybe they'll hang them here someday. They'd be way more interesting than water lilies."

"That's great," I say, admiring her confidence. At what age do we start to doubt ourselves?

"I think I know why Monet painted water lilies," I say, putting it together in my head. "Monet painted what was in his backyard because that's what he knew best. You can see the intimacy in the paintings."

The little girl shrugs at me and quickly patters off to her parents.

Looking at the water lilies one last time, I think about

how when you make art of the familiar, it helps you see it again. There are a thousand ways to see the same view, which reminds me of the Spoke. While my life has had the same backdrop since I was born, with each year, I see it differently. It changes as I change.

I linger awhile longer, wondering what it would be like to paint the same scene for thirty years like Monet. I guess it wouldn't be all that different from growing up in the same town for seventeen. It probably would get boring, but there's something comforting in the familiar.

On the Monday of our third week, Professor Picasso begins photography week with a lecture:

"Of all the artistic media, photography has changed the most over the last fifteen years. This might give away my age, but I'll say it anyway: When I first started teaching this class, we developed all of our film in the *dark*room."

Ford looks over at me then scribbles a note.

*See, I told you. Professor Picasso is from the Dark Ages.*

I stifle a laugh and scoot my chair away from his so I can concentrate.

Professor Picasso continues, "Even after digital photography became very popular, I initially resisted teaching it. Finally, I switched. In some ways, now there is lots of room for mistakes in photography. In other ways, it's still just as hard to get the one shot that makes people stop and stare as if they've never seen anything like it although they probably see it every day. Photography makes us see the beauty in the ordinary."

When Professor Picasso shows us the school's high-tech cameras and explains that we can borrow them until the end of our course, I get *major* goose bumps. The only camera I've ever owned is the cheap one on my cell phone. Amber used to have a nice camera and she snapped photos at every big event when I was little. But since my dad left, her camera has remained in the closet along with all of the clothes he left behind. Maybe she just couldn't figure out how to adjust to a family of three.

Professor Picasso goes on explaining to us about aperture, focal length, and shutter speed. I take copious, detailed notes because if there's anything I'm good at, it's studying and replicating something. He runs a slide show with some basic rules of photography like the rule of thirds and the rule of not letting the backdrop overwhelm the subject.

"For those of you doing portraits, be careful that your subjects aren't always performing or in character because that makes it nearly impossible to get a genuine emotion," he says.

After what seems like endless lecturing, Professor Picasso turns us loose on the streets with our cameras.

"Please don't go searching for a particular subject. Let the subject find you."

I'm sure that's really good advice, but I already have my project planned. And if I want to do my project on Hipster Hat Trick, there's no time like the present.

Once we're outside, Ford asks: "Do you want to go walk around? We could take some photos and check out some of the summer sales along the way."

"I'd love to," I say. "But there's somewhere I need to go. Can I take a rain check?"

Ford snaps my photo. "Sure," he says. Looking through the viewfinder, he nods: "You look gorgeous. I have *such* a good eye."

I laugh with Ford. Then I pull out my phone to text Tad to figure out where the band's practicing today. Once he responds, I take the L train to meet up with him and Hipster Hat Trick. They are practicing in Erik's cramped fourth-floor walk-up three blocks away from the Music Hall of Williamsburg. It's not the ritziest of backdrops, but the apartment has good light.

"Hi, Kitsy," the guys shout in a chorus as I walk in.

"Hey, dorks," Tad says, facing toward Erik and Rider. "I'm pretty sure I already mentioned it, but Kitsy is going to take some photos for her summer-school project."

I don't like how he says "summer school" as if it were a school for dropouts rather than a selective art program.

Maybe Tad's one of those guys who acts different around his friends. Maybe he's worried that they'll tease him for liking art—or me.

"Awesome, Kitsy," Erik says. "We really need to get some pictures up on our website. If people knew how good-looking we were, then we'd totally get more gigs. Well, I mean if they knew how good-looking *I* was."

Everyone laughs, including me. I want him to know that these aren't supposed to be glamour shots like the ones you get at the mall; these photographs are going to be art. Or at least I hope so.

The band begins to warm up, and I start looking through the viewfinder, trying to find the right angles. It's *way* different from using a point-and-click camera to get a shot of you and your prom date.

Finding the right setting is fairly easy, but getting the guys to act natural is impossible.

"Pretend I'm not here!" I yell at Erik when he makes kissy faces for the camera.

"You're too hot to be invisible," he says with a wink.

Tad turns around and gives him a look.

"I need to get shots that make it look like I'm a fly on the wall. I'm not supposed to be part of the scene," I say.

Tad gives me an encouraging nod and says, "Okay, guys, let's ignore Kitsy. Besides, we've got a lot of work to do before our gig Wednesday."

They continue their practice with the occasional argument over who's doing what part of what song, but they still can't help grinning every time I turn the lens on them.

After an hour or so, I carefully pack up the school's camera and ask Tad if I can come to their next gig. I think there the guys will relax and seem less self-conscious performing onstage. There will probably be a ton of other people, so they'll barely notice me.

"Sure, Kitsy," Tad says. "We're opening for a headlining band this Wednesday in the Lower East Side at a bar called Mercury Lounge. I'll send you directions. But if we aren't the best subjects for you, that's okay. We won't be mad. Well, we won't be as long as you take a headshot for Erik to give to his adoring fans."

Erik nods and winks. "That'd be cool," he says.

"Are you kidding me?" I say. "Y'all are the best subjects I can imagine. I just want to shoot y'all in a few different locations to show your depth."

"Depth?" Tad repeats and rolls his eyes. "See you at the gig, Kitsy."

Maybe Tad's skeptical about this project, but I'm not. Like he said, sometimes you can't see something when it's right in front of you.

On the train heading to the apartment, I look through my viewfinder at the other passengers: the lady with her head

233

buried in a romance novel, the guy punching on his Black-Berry keys even though there's no way that there's service, and the middle-school kids wearing basketball jerseys and selling candy for their team. I even get enough courage to snap a few shots.

Scrolling through these subway photos, I try not to see what's obvious: They are way better than any of the photos I took of Hipster Hat Trick. I ignore it and tell myself that I'll get better shots at their gig on Wednesday.

# Chapter 12

# Home Sweet Home

I HAVE SPENT ALL MY free time exploring with my camera: I have shot a thousand photos in the last two days and had to delete my memory card twice. My camera's becoming an extension of my body.

On my way to the Hipster Hat Trick gig on Wednesday night, I'm all worked up. After tonight I think I'll have all the shots I need for my portfolio, and then I can move into the editing phase. Although I've been wrapped up in Photo Land, I'm excited to see Tad tonight even if he'll be behind the microphone and I'll be behind the camera.

As I walk, I play a game where I see everything not as it is, but as a photo. Then I force myself to think of it from yet another angle and shoot that, too. Even though I walk around here every day, when I snap a photo it seems like

I'm seeing it all for the first time. Being behind the camera in New York makes me feel more comfortable somehow. When I first cheered at a varsity game, I felt amazing because I knew *why* everyone was watching me—because I was performing. Behind the camera, I feel like I do with my pom-poms—in control. Lately, I'm feeling particularly out of control in terms of the Amber situation. She keeps calling to ask simple questions and Kiki's voice sounds a bit sadder each time we talk. I'm glad to get lost behind the lens for a while.

As I'm walking east across Seventh Avenue, I see a small crowd gathered around the sidewalk. I edge closer and see a man lying on the ground in the center of the group of people. He's holding a piece of chalk in his hand and all around him is a beautiful, colorful drawing of a beach at sunset. In large capital letters, he's written HOME, SWEET HOME.

"That's amazing," a kid on a skateboard tells him as he flies by.

An older woman, accompanied by a white toy poodle, says to no one in particular: "It's going to wash away. It's supposed to rain later today. Why is he doing this?"

"I don't care," the artist says without looking up. "It's about the experience."

"That's no way to make a living," she says before putting some spare change into his hat.

No, but it'd be a cool way to live.

Most people continue on their way, but I linger and watch. Choosing carefully from his selection of chalk, he blends reds and pinks into the pavement.

"Where's home?" I ask quietly.

"Jamaica," he says, without looking up.

"Why chalk?" I ask, snapping a few pictures with the school's camera.

"It's the only tool I had growing up," he says. "I've tried oils for a while, but this is what I love even though it means I'm never going to make a living at it."

"It's incredible," I say and find a dollar bill in my purse.

"Thank you," he says. "I'm just trying to make the city brighter. Do my part."

I hope that my art will do that someday, too, I think.

Once I'm in the Lower East Side, I spot a green-and-black sign with the words MERCURY LOUNGE. I smile at how easily I'm now finding my way around. Entering the dark space I spot Annika, already parked at the bar. Even though I'm anxious to start shooting, I walk over and sit down by her. She did let me in on her VIP status last weekend. Sure made for an interesting look at New York.

"Dontcha know?" she says. "It's Kitsy Kidd," Annika says in her best Minnesotan accent, which I guess is actually her normal voice.

"Hi, Annika," I say. "I didn't know that you'd be here."

Holding up my camera, I say, "I'm working on my final art project for summer school. It's due next week."

"You're in *school*?" she asks. "That's one thing I *don't* miss: homework. My only homework as an actress is to get myself photographed and refrain from eating."

I snap Annika's photo without even looking through the viewfinder. "There," I say with a smile. "We both just did our homework."

"So how old are you?" Annika asks. "I mean, I know you aren't legal, but how young?"

"I'm seventeen, and I'll be a senior in the fall. I'm going back to Texas in just one week," I say, but I'm not really paying attention. I'm looking for angles and light. Now, as a photographer, I have a hard time seeing like I used to. I'm always looking for the best shots.

"I'm nineteen, so I'm only two years older than you. Weird, it seems like way more, but this place makes you grow up fast. Hey, you never told me what you were running away from in Texas."

*Running away?* I've thought about my trip here in a lot of terms, but I've never thought of it as me running away.

"I'm not running away," I answer, holding up my camera. "I just came here for the opportunities."

"Everyone who comes to New York is running away from something, Kitsy. Don't try to fool yourself. I'm running away from Annika," she says. "I'm leaving her back in Minnesota to freeze. Here's how to tell if you're running away: Is there stuff at home that you left unsettled? Are you worried about going back?"

I look at Annika and say nothing.

She raises the corners of her mouth in a sad smile. "There's your answer, Kitsy," she says softly.

Is she right? I always thought that by coming here I'm moving toward something, but am I actually just running?

Tad and the other guys come onstage from outside, and they start warming up.

"I've got to go take some shots," I tell Annika.

"Me too," she jokes, pointing to the row of bottles. "I'm jealous of you," she says. I look straight into the lens as I focus the camera on Annika to take her picture.

"Why?" I ask after snapping her picture.

"Because you still don't realize how life makes you choose," she says and releases her pose.

The gig at Mercury Lounge ended up awesome. While Hipster Hat Trick doesn't have die-hard fans like our football team does, the band playing after them has brought in a good crowd. The guys worked really well together, and they didn't stare back at me and smile every time I tried to take their picture. My best shot turned out to be the one of Annika though. She's even more beautiful in photographs than she is in person, but something else about her develops on film: She looks lonely.

Even though I want to stay and hear the next band, I decide to go home early to edit my photos. My portfolio is my priority. As I'm getting ready to leave, Rider saunters up all sweaty and out of breath.

"Y'all were great," I tell him, really meaning it. "Will you tell everyone thanks and that I had to leave?"

"Sure," Rider says, wiping his brow with a handkerchief.

"So when are you heading back? Maybe we'll be on the same flight."

Rider shakes his head. "I'm not."

"Not what? Not on the same flight?" I ask.

Rider grins broadly, and I can see why Corrinne fell for him. He's handsome, in the opposite way than the guys on the football team. His features are delicate and his body lanky.

"No, I'm not going back," he declares. "I don't know if Tad told you, but we might get to go on tour and open for this wildly successful college band. I turned eighteen last month, so it's up to me."

"Oh, wow. That's great." I wonder where I'd be if anything was just up to me. Could I ever leave the Spoke behind forever like Rider if there weren't people holding me back?

Looking at my watch, I realize I should head back to the apartment. "This is probably my last time photographing you guys, Rider. Next week, I'll be editing. So I guess this is good-bye."

I wonder if I ever will see Rider again, which isn't a common feeling to have with a fellow Spoker. We're used to saying good-bye in the see-you-later sense, not in the I-don't-know-when-I'll-see-you-later sense. It also makes me think about saying good-bye to Tad, and my stomach sinks in a bit. Is Hipster Hat Trick such a great photo project? Or am I just trying to take Tad with me when I leave?

"I'm sure the whole Hat Trick would love to see you back in New York. By the way, it's been really nice seeing a whole other side of you in New York. I never even knew you liked art," Rider says and reaches out for a hug. "Don't be a stranger," he adds.

Before I turn to leave, I say, "We grew up together— we could never feel like strangers."

From her perch at the bar, Annika whispers to the both of us, "You would be totally surprised about that."

Neither Rider nor I say anything in response.

Winking, Annika says, "Can't wait to see how I look in the photos. See you later, Sexy Texy."

I decide to take the subway home and on my walk there, I think about what Annika said. Did she mean that Rider and I will change so much that we'll feel like strangers to each other? Or did she mean that one day I'll feel like a stranger to the person I am now?

I'm on the F train one stop away from West 4th Street, where I need to get off, when I realize I forgot my camera, which belongs technically to Parsons, at the bar. I begin to sweat, knowing there would be no way I could replace it, not to mention that all my photos are on the memory card. My being careless tonight could ruin the whole summer. Frantically, I run off my train and head back to the Mercury Lounge. I cross my fingers and pray my camera will be there. I can't afford to lose it.

A small crowd is still there, but I don't see guys from the band or Annika anywhere. The bartender spots me and waves me over.

"Your friends are in the green room," he says. "I gave them your camera. Got to be careful, darling. This is New York."

"Thank you," I say breathlessly and ignore the fact that he's pointing out how, after three weeks, I still don't blend in here.

I knock and then walk into the green room and see Annika with her long legs wrapped around a lanky, shaggy-haired guy on a dingy couch.

"Ohmigod," I say, turning around to face the door. "I'm so sorry, y'all. I didn't mean to interrupt anything. Just forgot my camera." I'm talking quickly because I can't bear to think about who the shaggy-haired guy with Annika could be.

"Kitsy, calm down. No big deal. It could have been a lot worse if you came ten minutes later," Annika says lazily.

I turn around and meet Tad's eyes.

"I just need my camera," I say softly, trying to keep my voice calm and unaffected. Annika's not the only one who can act.

Tad quickly unwinds himself from Annika and brings the camera to me. His fingers briefly touching mine before I pull away.

Didn't either of them *think* I'd come looking for it?

"You okay, kid?" he asks me. Then, "Hey, I never realized how I call you *kid* and your last name is Kidd. That's funny," he mumbles but no one laughs.

I just stand there for a second staring at a smear of Annika's too-red lipstick on the corner of Tad's top lip. I want to wipe it off just like I want to erase what just happened. A part of me wants to forget New York and go back to how everything was before, when nothing was uncertain and I was safe.

"I've never been better," I say and snatch my camera from Tad.

Heading for the door like the dogs are after me, I hear Tad say to Annika, "Maybe one of us should go after her." I realize just how wrong I've been. I'm a kid to him. Just a tourist kid.

Once I'm outside in the hall, I stop holding the tears in my eyes. It's too hard. They fall quickly and smear my makeup.

"Kitsy. Wait!" I hear Annika call from the doorway. The pack of smokers turn to look at her. Their eyes fixate on her like wolves on prey. She ignores them and walks up to me.

"Annika, I thought there was something called Minnesotan nice," I say impulsively. "Isn't, like, everyone from Minnesota supposed to be nice?"

"No, they aren't, Kitsy," she says slowly and keeps some distance between us. "Just like not everyone in New York is an asshole."

"You *knew* I liked him," I manage to spit out.

Annika shakes her head and takes the last cigarette out of her pack. "Nope, you *never* said you liked him. And even if you had, that doesn't matter. You have to look out for yourself because no one else is going to, Kitsy. Besides, you're going home in a week. You're not here for some boy," she says, speaking more softly than before. She gestures to my camera.

"So you did me a *favor*? Where I'm from, we don't call that a favor. I don't know how they say it in Minnesota, but in Texas, we'd call you as crooked as a barrel of snakes."

Annika rolls her crystal-blue eyes. "You're *on vacation*, Kitsy," Annika says, looking back toward the lounge.

"This is a temporary break from your life. You get to go back. Why don't you go home and confront whatever you're running away from?"

"I thought you told me to *never* go back," I say. "You kept telling me to look forward, not look backward."

All of a sudden I don't even care about Tad or Annika anymore. I'm just really, really confused.

"We're different, Kitsy. I see that now. I can tell that Tad cares about you, but he thinks of you as a kid. Because in the grand scheme of everything, you are. I can't remember any guy liking me without thinking he's going to get something for it."

It's time to go home. I turn around, and say, "Maybe you should go back to being a brunette. I bet you had gorgeous brown hair."

"My hair color isn't up to me anymore . . . and Kitsy, if I had to do it all over again, maybe I would've never come here."

When I start walking toward the subway, I hear Annika call after me. But I think she's talking more to herself than she is to me.

# Chapter 13

# Taking Care of Baggage

WHEN I RETURN TO THE Corcorans', I'm ready for a long bath in Corrinne's giant bathtub. I need to be alone and spend some time reflecting on what just happened. I expect the apartment to be empty, so I'm startled when I see Mrs. Corcoran in the kitchen sitting on a counter stool and sipping a glass of wine.

"There you are!" Mrs. Corcoran exclaims. "I've been hoping you'd come home because I wanted to know if you'd like to go to the *quinceañera* with me tomorrow."

If Mrs. Corcoran notices my smeared, definitely-not-waterproof eyeliner, she doesn't mention it.

I stiffen my back and give the biggest smile I can muster. "I thought you couldn't go," I say, remembering the disappointment on Maria's face when she read a note from Mrs. Corcoran saying just that.

"I couldn't," Mrs. Corcoran says. "We had a company dinner to attend, but I backed out at the last minute. You're able to juggle so many balls and always have your priorities straight, so I thought I should take a page from you."

Normally, I'd agree with Mrs. Corcoran, but the scene back at the Mercury Lounge is making me think that I wasted a lot of my precious time and energy on a project—and a person.

"I'm not sure that's true," I admit. "But thank you for thinking that."

"So you'll come?" Mrs. Corcoran asks hopefully.

Although I would much rather crawl up into a ball and stay there, I nod. It would mean a lot to Maria and Mrs. Corcoran if I did attend.

When I get home from school on Thursday, Mrs. Corcoran is waiting for me and shoos me with her hands. "Go ahead and change quickly. We're already running late!"

When I change and return to the kitchen, Mrs. Corcoran has some of my older photographs of Hipster Hat Trick lying out in front of her on the counter. I wish she'd put them away. I hate seeing Tad looking up from his guitar at me. The photographs look even worse than the first time I saw them. Professor Picasso was right—it really is hard to take pictures of people performing. They look like they're playing rockers in a low-budget movie. No emotion looks genuine.

Mrs. Corcoran sees me looking and stops flipping through the photos. "I hope you don't mind, but I saw these on the desk. They're really good. When I modeled a million years ago, half the photographers I worked with didn't have half the sense of light that you already do."

"Thanks, but it was a stupid project," I say. I know that it didn't come close to anything original. Tad was totally right; taking photographs of an almost band is nearly as much of a cliché as *being* an almost band.

"I'm going to find something new," I say out loud. I thought about it all last night and today. Saying it to someone out loud feels like a relief.

"Well, you're very talented. I'm sure whatever project you pick next will reflect that, and, ideally, you, too." Mrs. Corcoran rummages through her purse and pulls out eyeliner and shakes the tube. "It's been a while since I've worn any fun makeup. And since you are Miss Estee Lauder, I wanted to get your help."

"Sure!" Even after a bad night, something about doing makeup feels cathartic. I apply my dotting trick to give Mrs. Corcoran a serious feline eye.

"I used to wear this all the time as a teenager," she says, admiring herself in the entryway mirror. "This is going to be fun."

Before we leave, I grab my camera off the counter. Maybe I'll find my new project tonight!

• • •

We take a cab to Coney Island and, after a long trip, we're dropped off in front of the Shrine Church of Our Lady of Solace.

"First, we'll attend a Mass, then go to the party. *Quinceañeras* are not just parties to celebrate turning fifteen, but they are also a religious event," Mrs. Corcoran explains.

"This is way different from that MTV show *My Super Sweet Sixteen*. I don't imagine Esperanza will land via helicopter at the church."

"Thank God for that," Mrs. Corcoran says. "Some of Corrinne's classmates' parties were sickening in their excess. One boy received a Hummer even though he lives in Manhattan and doesn't have his driver's license. It all becomes a total competition between the parents to see who can throw the best party."

"A little different from parties at the field?" I ask.

Mrs. Corcoran smiles. "I loved hanging out at the field. I still miss it."

"I miss it, too. I'm actually looking forward to parties there this fall," I add. As exciting as New York nightlife is, there's something special about partying with green grass under your feet.

After Mass, Maria finds us on the church's steps. "Fiesta time!" Looking at Mrs. Corcoran with a smile, she adds, "Thanks for coming. It was such a wonderful *sorpresa*. I think of you as family. I still remember Corrinne crawling all over while I cleaned. It's too bad that she couldn't come, but she sent a great replacement in Kitsy."

We walk behind the giant group of Maria's family and friends a few blocks to a large banquet hall called Manny's. Inside, a small mariachi band plays and a DJ is setting up. Hanging from the ceilings are beautiful pink and blue paper lanterns, in the same tones as Esperanza's blue taffeta dress. The smell of Mexican food wafts through the hall, and my stomach audibly growls.

Mrs. Corcoran takes my hand and says, "Let me introduce you to Esperanza."

We walk over to where Maria, her husband, and Esperanza are greeting guests. Mrs. Corcoran hands Esperanza a thick envelope, and I feel embarrassed that I don't have a gift.

"Kitsy," Mrs. Corcoran says, "meet Esperanza."

Politely, we shake hands. "I love your dress and tiara," I say because I really do, not just because it's part of some routine of mine.

"Thank you! I hope you'll take a lot of photos of my party. My mom keeps telling me how good you are at photography. She wants me to get a hobby. All I hear is Kitsy this, Kitsy that," she says with a laugh.

"I'd love to photograph it. It'll be my gift. This is all so beautiful, I've never been to anything like it."

"Don't worry, J.J.," Maria says, looking at Mrs. Corcoran. "The whole family pays for the party, so I'm not bankrupt. The godmother pays for the dress and cake, my family pays for the band and alcohol, and we pay for the food, but I cooked most of it. Of course, I'm always up for a raise."

Mrs. Corcoran blushes. "You know that I just gave you one, Maria."

They both laugh.

I think it's really cool how the whole family chips in; it reminds me of community (usually football-centric) events in the Spoke.

The DJ announces that the dancing will begin, and the guests gather around the perimeter of the dance floor.

Esperanza, along with eight boys around her age dressed in tuxedos, perform three original dances. It's like *High School Musical* but with way cooler outfits and Hispanic Zac Efrons.

Then the boys leave the dance floor and Esperanza dances to a final song with her best-loved doll, a very worn Raggedy Ann Doll.

Maria comes over to Mrs. Corcoran and me and whispers, "This is the symbolic moment where she crosses over, leaves her toys behind, and becomes a woman."

During that very sweet last song, I see both Maria and

Mrs. Corcoran wipe away tears. I wonder if Esperanza feels any more grown-up tonight than she did before. I know I'm starting to feel different after my summer in New York; it's definitely made me realize a lot. Even though I've always considered myself mature, this summer has pushed me to grow up even more.

After everyone applauds Esperanza's performance, the song "Empire State of Mind" comes on and everyone rushes the dance floor. In less than a second, the party begins to resemble the typical party I'm used to. I guess our worlds aren't that different after all.

Mrs. Corcoran laughs and goes to get a glass of sangria, and I start taking some photographs of the dance-floor scene.

Maria comes up and puts her hand on my shoulder. "I'm going to miss having you around."

"And I'm going to miss your cooking!" I joke, snapping a photo of her laughing. I have a feeling that my photos are turning out really well tonight. Nobody's performing—including me.

"That better be a good picture. I'll miss you, Kitsy—and your art. I saw some of it when I was cleaning up. You have a gift," Maria says. "You seem so very grown-up, Kitsy. You already know what you want to do. That's unusual. Sometimes, you remind me of me. Keep following your dreams even if you get off course."

"What was your dream?" I ask and wonder how many years it can take someone to finally catch it.

"I wanted to come to the United States, and now here I am—an American woman with an American daughter. Just listen to this music that my daughter picked out. My childhood dream to live, raise, and educate my family here in America is complete. The best dreams are the ones we have as children because they're most pure."

I nod, thinking about how my dream has always been to be an artist and how I need to always remember that, even when I'm older.

"Thanks for everything," I say to Maria. "But quit entertaining me. Go dance with your daughter. She's growing up right in front of you."

As Mrs. Corcoran and I are preparing to leave the party, a cousin brings in hot White Castle cheeseburgers, which I have never had.

"Let's get some and eat them in the cab!" Mrs. Corcoran says giddily. She seems so much more relaxed here than she does in Manhattan.

Maria comes up to us and gives us hugs.

"White Castle?" Maria shakes her head and laughs. "Maybe Esperanza's becoming too American. What's wrong with churros?"

In the cab, Mrs. Corcoran and I are both wearing

huge smiles and clutching Mexican candy from the piñata. Tonight turned out to be a whole lot better than I thought it could be after last night. I'm so glad I came. Moping doesn't help anything.

"That was so much fun," Mrs. Corcoran says. "It's sad, but I rarely ever have fun at parties anymore. These days, they're more like obligations. You looked like you were having fun, too. I saw you dancing with that boy."

"José? He's Esperanza's cousin. He told me it was a pity dance for the Texan. He said Mexico and Texas are neighbors, so he should be hospitable."

"You can charm anyone," Mrs. Corcoran says, laughing. "Some people come to New York to find themselves and end up losing who they are. You're still the same sweet Kitsy."

I'm glad that she thinks this. While I wanted to grow in New York, I didn't want to change too much. After walking in on Tad and Annika, I started to seriously doubt some of my decisions this summer.

"Want to know a secret?" Mrs. Corcoran asks.

"Sure," I answer, resting my head on the window.

"Dusty, my high-school boyfriend, visited me after I moved out to New York. That's when we broke up. Everyone thinks I dumped him, but that's not true."

"What do you mean?" I say, sitting up straight. Mrs. Corcoran, or Jenny Jo as she was known back then, dumped

Dusty, Bubby's dad, after moving to New York City. It's a Broken Spoke fact.

"That's what people assumed, and Dusty was too nice to set them straight. He dumped me."

"He hated New York?" I ask.

"No, he loved New York. He didn't love Jenny Jo, New York–style. I left Texas to be a model, but somehow, over time, I lost me. I don't think that'll ever happen to you, Kitsy. You should be impressed with yourself for staying you and growing at the same time. I'm still learning how to do that."

"Thanks," I say. We spend the rest of the cab ride in silence, but my brain is running full speed. If I grew up as much as I feel like I did this summer, then there's something I have to do.

When we're back up in the apartment, Mrs. Corcoran and I kick off our heels seconds after entering.

I look at Mrs. Corcoran and realize that I need to tell her now.

"Mrs. Corcoran. Can you change my airline ticket? I need to go home tomorrow night. I've been running from something, but it's not right. I'll go pack up my things. I'm sorry about this," I apologize, feeling my eyes start to well.

"Are you sure it can't wait, Kitsy?" she asks, putting her hand on my shoulder. "You're going home in a week."

"Maybe it can wait," I say. Then I shake my head. "But it shouldn't. It's too important."

"Okay, Kitsy. If there's an emergency, I can get you on a plane to Dallas. But I want you to try to come back here as soon as possible and finish what you've started. I've already cleared my schedule for your portfolio show next week, and it would break Corrinne's heart not to see you."

"Thank you so much," I say. "It's not an emergency, but . . . it's been going on too long and I finally need to deal with it. I just can't go into it right now. Do you think I could leave tomorrow night and come back late Sunday night? That way I won't miss any school. I promise I'll pay you back, a little bit each month."

"If that's what you need," Mrs. Corcoran says, "I'll call the airline right away. But I'm not letting you pay for the ticket. We have plenty of miles to use, so there will be no reason to pay us back. But first, let me apologize to you."

"For what?" I ask. I feel like I'm the one that needs to apologize for wasting the Corcorans' money and picking such a silly project.

"I haven't been here for you as much as I thought I would be. When I was in the Spoke last fall, I was convinced that I had changed and that I wouldn't ever get so wrapped up in New York again. But then I came back, little by little . . . I guess what I'm trying to say is—"

"That it's possible to be two different people in two different places?"

Mrs. Corcoran stops and looks at me appreciatively. "I guess you understand what I mean, Kitsy. It's okay to just be your best self though. Change doesn't always mean growth."

She gives me a big hug. "Will you take some pictures of my Spoke? I want to make sure that I always have a bit of home with me. The things that matter the most in life."

"Of course," I tell her.

I wish Mrs. Corcoran good night and go back to my room to pack. It's time for me to finally deal with some of the baggage I've been carrying around since I got here.

To: kkidd@gmail.com
From: corrinnec@gmail.com
Date: Friday August 3
Subject: Where are you?

Have you gotten my last few emails? Have you abandoned me for cooler New Yorkers? (You know that's a trick, right? There isn't anyone cooler than me. Please don't tell me you've been spending time in Brooklyn. Not now.) Stuff with Cory's going well but . . . he's a bit serious. I mean, what happens at camp stays at camp, right?

# Chapter 14

## Can You Never Go Home Again?

CINDERELLA HAS ALWAYS BEEN MY favorite fairy-tale hero-
ine. As a child, I dressed up as her for three Halloweens
straight. Many nights, I dreamt that my life could also
change with the swish of a magic wand or a kiss from a
prince, just like Cinderella's did.

By coming to New York, I got to realize my fantasy:
to escape and end up someplace magical. But after living
my own fairy tale, I don't think of Cinderella as a hero.
Instead of confronting her evil stepsisters and stepmother,
she hightailed it to the palace and left her father and
friends behind. In a sense, she left Cinderella behind, just
like Annabelle did with Annika. What's so heroic about
running away?

In my new fairy tale, the girl is brave. Not because

she figures out how to get away, but because she realizes that she needs to return home. There's no sense in spending your life running from yourself—or the truth. Happily ever after is not a place: It's a state of being, and you have to work at it every day.

Boarding the plane to Dallas late Friday night, I think back to Annika telling me how it's not easy to go home again. But I'm not Annika. If I were her, I would have five more inches, a TV show, and Tad. Now I know that those aren't things I want.

I text Hands *I've got a surprise for you!* before the flight takes off. I know that I should be more excited to see my boyfriend, especially after three weeks, but I feel like I'm wearing three barrels on my back.

During the flight, I sleep like I've been awake for weeks. There must be something like New-York-City-induced fatigue that occurs once you are off the island. But I'm glad for the rest because it keeps me from obsessing over why I'm heading home.

As the plane approaches Dallas, I'm relieved to see huge pastures of grass and a skyline that seems tiny in comparison to New York's. I don't think I realized how much I missed the palette of Texas, where there's every shade of Mother Earth. New York definitely has the monopoly on a lot of things, but Texas owns the rainbow.

Corrinne's grandparents pick me up from the airport early Saturday morning. They are the Grandparents of the Century. Mr. Houston even taught Corrinne how to drive a pickup with a stick shift, which must've required the bravery of a cowboy and the patience of a saint. It's funny to imagine that they are glamorous Mrs. Corcoran's parents, but families don't always match up like you think they would.

When I climb into the cab of Billie Jean the Third, Mrs. Houston turns around in the front seat and brushes a hair out of my face.

"You must be beyond exhausted, Kitsy. I sure know that we are always bushed after a few days in New York. Even the dogs seem to walk faster there."

I nod. It's not just New York that can be exhausting. Broken Spoke and family can be, too. Ditto for high school.

"Well, honey," Mr. Houston says, pushing his cowboy hat down to block the sun and shifting gears as we're getting onto the highway. "Tell us about your favorite New York experience, and something about your art class."

"I made a clay vase that exploded on my class," I tell them, laughing. "And my favorite New York adventure is . . . well, I had the best time when Corrinne was there."

Mrs. Houston shakes her long, silver hair and says, "I just hope she didn't get a good girl like you in too much trouble."

Oh, I did plenty of that on my own, Mrs. Houston. Out loud, I say, "My favorite memory by myself was definitely when I went to a diner at three *in the morning*!"

"Mercy," Mr. Houston says. "Out at three a.m. *and* alone? The twenty-first century terrifies me."

Mrs. Houston surprises me by smiling and nodding. "I think that's wonderful, Kitsy. Sometimes, we forget to reflect back on all the great times we had by just ourselves. You can be your own best friend, you know."

And your own worst enemy, too, I think. I really wasted my time on that Hipster Hat Trick "project" and now I have no idea what to do for my portfolio that's due next week.

"Rest, child," Mrs. Houston says. "I know you're tired. Before we go to your house, we're going to stop by the scrimmage. Kiki is watching Hands play. Did you hear about that new quarterback who moved to town? I think Hands will pull through, though. He plays with a lot of heart."

She's right. He does. I was way too dismissive of Hands and what he cares about when I was in New York. He's just as passionate as me even if it is about other stuff.

As Mr. Houston talks about Hands fighting for his spot, I think about how when you live in a small town, your struggles and your triumphs are everyone's business. Right now, I'm thinking that's a good thing. It's comforting to have people on the sidelines rooting for you when you're winning and there when you fall down.

When I wake up, we're driving down Broken Spoke's strip. There's not much to see—a Chinese restaurant called Chin's, a Sonic, a grocery store, and a hardware store. Rumors are we might be getting a coffee shop, too. Not a Starbucks, but those are overpriced anyway.

I always thought that Broken Spoke didn't have much to it, but now I realize that it had everything I needed. I wonder if I'll have time to have an egg roll at Chin's (which are way better than any I had in New York) or drop by Sonic to work out my schedule for the fall. Feelings of belonging and familiarity wash over me.

When we pull up to the field, Kiki starts running toward Billie Jean the Third from a quarter of a mile away. Seeing him is the best homecoming I could ask for.

As soon as I open the car door, Kiki flies into my arms. I hold him tight.

"Where are my presents?" he yells. "Is Slimer in your bag? Does he feel oozy?"

I finally release Kiki from our hug and pat him on the head. "I missed you, too," I say. "I'm only giving you one present now. I'll bring more treats when I come next week."

When I pull out the iconic I ♥ NEW YORK T-shirt I

bought from the airport store before I boarded, Kiki squeals in delight.

"I'm wearing this on the first day of third grade. And the second day, and the third day, and the fourth day."

Mr. and Mrs. Houston start walking toward the football field and wave at us to follow.

"C'mon, Kitsy," Mr. Houston says. "Let's see how hard you're going to need to cheer next year."

From our distance, I see Hands catch a tight spiral and run. There's my number 18. When Hands sees me, he keeps running past the goal post and into the parking lot where I'm standing. With one (large) arm, he picks me up and kisses me on the mouth.

"I thought it was you!" he says, laughing. "But *why* are you home?"

"I need to deal with something," I answer as best as I can. He doesn't stop looking at me. How do I explain that I'm doing this now? "Amber," I say simply.

Hands raises his eyebrows in a way that I know means he thinks she's crazy, but hey, she's the only parent I've got.

The guys are calling for Hands from the field to get back to the scrimmage. Reluctantly, Hands lets me down.

"Field tonight?" he asks me with a wink.

"I'm leaving tomorrow. I really want to see you and talk to you, too. Pick me up after dinner?"

Hands grows a little more still and asks quietly, "Sure, but is everything okay, Kit-Kat?"

"It will be," I say. I give Hands a hug and move back toward the Houstons' truck, where Kiki's hopping up and down in his New York shirt, which he already slipped over his head. Mr. and Mrs. Houston ask me if I'm ready to go home. I nod, not sure if I actually am.

After I profusely thank Mr. and Mrs. Houston for the ride, Kiki and I go inside the house. Part of me braces myself for a scene out of that show *Hoarders*. Taking out the trash, washing dishes, and basically doing anything domestic has always been my responsibility. Before I left I taught Kikster how to do dishes because we don't have a dishwasher, but I wasn't exactly depending on a nine-year-old to hold it all together.

Releasing my breath, I'm amazed to see that the house is completely habitable—although it could definitely benefit from a good Swiffering and a dose of Lysol to mask the smell of cigarettes.

"Amber?" I call out.

I didn't expect Amber to be waiting with open arms, warm milk, and a platter of Toll House cookies, but I was hoping that she'd at least be expecting me.

"You made it!" I hear Amber shout back from her bedroom.

"Yup," I say to myself, awkwardly.

Amber comes out from her room. She's wearing her robe, but I can tell that she curled her hair and put some lipstick on, which means it's a good day in Amber terms.

Then she does something that surprises me: She embraces me even tighter than Hands did, and he's the bench-press champion at Broken Spoke High.

"Kitsy," she says. "You look so much older and sophisticated than before. I can't believe that you're my baby girl."

Sometimes I can't either.

"Are you now going to tell me why you came all the way home?" she demands impatiently. "What's going on?"

I know I need to speak directly with Amber. I'm home for this.

I'm realizing for the first time that I can measure home in both physical and mental distances. I feel so tired from traveling them both.

"Wait a minute, Kitsy," she whispers. Then, a little louder, she says, "Hey, Kiki, do you want to watch one of those movies I rented? I'll put some popcorn in the microwave. Me and Kitsy need to talk for a minute."

Amber throws a bag of popcorn into the microwave. Then she slides a DVD of *Miracle on 34th Street* into the player.

"He'll only watch movies about New York," Amber explains to me as Kiki plops in front of the TV. "I think it makes him feel closer to you."

Looking out the front window, Amber smiles and says, "Looks like the sun is almost setting. Days are getting shorter again. Let's go sit outside."

I haven't said anything. Where did the old Amber go?

Sitting down on an old folding chair, Amber lights up a cigarette. Before she takes a drag, she says, "So what's up, Kits? I know you wouldn't just come home from your big adventure for nothing, right? I know this trip meant a lot to you."

I reflect back to all my planning and poring over New York books at the library. My trip didn't end up being anything like I thought it would be, but turns out that that's part of what I love about New York—the unpredictability.

"What's it like?" Amber asks after a moment. "Have you really not seen any celebrities?"

"This isn't about New York. Well, it is and it isn't. While I was there, I realized that I wasn't really *all there*. I kept worrying about you and Kiki. And I know now that if I don't confront this—what's happening here, at home—that it's going to haunt me."

Amber buries her face in her hands. "I know I haven't been the perfect mother. I'm sorry," she says, peeking out.

The only time I've ever heard Amber use the word *sorry* before was when she called my dad "a sorry piece of a human."

Amber breathes in, takes her face out of her hands, and continues.

"When you were first gone, I didn't know what to do. The house started to get to be a mess, and Kiki was getting all worked up about how he missed you. The Houstons and Hands kept showing up at the door, acting like they weren't sure that I could take care of him. After a while, I realized they were right. I haven't been caring for Kiki. *You* have. You've been caring for all of us, but not taking care of yourself. It isn't right." She wipes a tear from her eye.

I reach into my pocket and give her a Kleenex. I'm used to carrying them around on account of Kiki's permanently runny nose.

I try to remember for a second if Amber had always been . . . messy. In more ways than one. I can't remember if my dad left because of the drinking or the drinking happened because my dad left. But it was Amber who stayed and that has to count for something.

"Oh, Amber," I say, wiping her eyes with the Kleenex. "I don't mind doing housework and I love hanging with Kiki. You know that. I understand that sometimes you really struggle. And obviously, nothing's been easy for you since Dad left. It's just I worry about your health and if you'll be able to do all this on your own if I ever leave. After this summer—well, I've decided that I *really* want to go to art school, which means leaving you and Kiki for at least a few years."

Amber puts out her cigarette in a bowl next to us and shakes her head. "I'm not a good mom now, but I'm going to try to become one. I know what it's like to feel stuck, and I don't ever want you to feel that way."

Her words mean a lot to me, but I know this won't be easy. We'll need to face this head-on if it's really going to work.

I scoot my chair closer to hers and soften my voice. "You being able to handle Kiki on your own isn't just going to happen magically. It's not that simple. You're going to need help from professionals. I've had this DVD in my room for a long time. It's about a wellness center at a medical facility. If I give it to you, will you watch it and think about it? We need a plan and a promise."

"Yes," she chokes out. "I'll watch it and give it some serious thought. I want you to be able to follow your dreams. Every mother wants that. I was in your room looking for something, Kitsy, and I saw some of your sketches. They're really good. I remember you being a talented artist as a little girl, but of course all moms think that. But I realize now that you have something special. I guess I've been looking at you without really seeing you. I'm going to change, Kitsy. I promise."

I rub Amber's back. "I'll help in any way I can," I say.

I'm surprised how well Amber is responding. After a while of living a certain way, you figure it'll be that way forever. You hope otherwise, but you never expect anything. "Thank you so much for talking to me about this. I know it can't be easy."

"No, thank *you*, Kitsy, for all your help and support. It's about time that I start acting like the adult, and you start acting like the teenager."Amber stands up and wipes the last of her tears. "We will talk more about it before you leave. But right now, how about a family supper?"

I stand up next to her and put my hand on her shoulder. "That sounds nice, Mom," I say before I realize that I didn't call her Amber.

When we sit around the table for supper, three no longer seems off balance.

Later that night, after Kiki and Amber have gone into their rooms, Hands picks me up in his truck. Driving down the dirt road sounds like more than a familiar soundtrack. It feels like a lullaby.

Hands drives to an empty cul-de-sac, the very first place we drove when Hands got his license. On the trip there, I fill him in on Amber. He tells me how glad he is that she is finally "taking her place on the starting line." Hands describes everything in football terms.

When we arrive, Hands turns off the ignition and

wraps his muscled arms around me in a big hug. "Tell me everything. Are you ready to leave me for Gotham?"

Oh yeah, Gotham is code name for New York in *Batman*.

"Here's the thing about New York. It's nothing like the movies. Glamorous or wonderful things don't happen there every day, but somehow you feel like they *could*. There are so many opportunities."

Hands nods. "I just wish following your dreams didn't mean you have to leave the Spoke but it seems like more often than not, it does."

"That's just it! When I was there, I felt like I could be someone more than Broken Spoke's cheerleading captain. I don't want to stress you out, especially since I'm only home for the night. But I need to ask you something. Why are we together? And please don't say because you asked me to dance back in the sixth grade."

In New York, I started to think that the reason that Hands and I were together was because it made sense. I'm the cheerleading captain and he's the football captain. Maybe that was enough for us earlier on in high school, but what about now?

"Kit-Kat," Hands says, drumming his left hand on the steering wheel. He looks a little nervous. "I didn't just *happen* to ask you to dance. I'd been waiting to since kindergarten. It just took that long for me to get up my courage and for the right situation. I have been sweet on you since you wore pigtails with one pink bow and one purple bow when we were little kids on the playground."

"That's the kindest thing," I start to say. I watch a montage of Hands and me growing up together in my mind. We do go way back.

"*But* you didn't let me finish, Kitsy. I'm with you because you feel like home. I know saying that could get me beat up by the boys, but you're home to me. I feel the best when I'm with you. I swear state on it." He knocks his state championship ring on the dashboard for emphasis. "If someday, you want to move to New York, I'll try to get there as soon as I can. I'm sure New York could always use a few big guys like me to bounce thugs out of bars."

The image of Hands in New York makes me smile. He'd hate it; the football field is his favorite place in the world and I didn't see one my entire month in New York. It's not fair for him to plan his life around me. Just like it's not fair for me to plan mine around him.

I hesitate. "You're my best friend, Hands," I say finally.

"This doesn't sound good." Hands looks like he's been tackled without warning. "I'm sorry," he spits out, "if I wasn't supportive enough about your trip and your art, I'm sorry. I was just scared of losing you."

"Stop," I say and hold up my hand. "I couldn't have left Broken Spoke if it wasn't for you. You helped keep me sane knowing that someone was looking after Kiki. And of all people, you've been the most supportive of me and my art."

"Is it another guy, then? Because I promise you no one ever will love you like I love you. Or actually, I'm sure a million guys would, because it's you and you're so amazing. But if you're breaking up with me, please know that I'll think about you every single day for the rest of my life," he says in a shaky voice.

Hands hangs his head, waiting for an answer. And the answer is no, it really isn't another guy. I would give back all the adventures with Tad for my memories with Hands. This is about me.

"There's nobody else, Hands," I say to him earnestly. "We can't get lost in confusing what we do in Broken Spoke with who we are. You might want to play football in college, but I don't want to cheer there. I want to study art, so I'm probably going to leave Texas . . . for at least a while. It's time for me to focus on myself."

"Haven't I always been telling you to do that?"

"Sometimes you can't be told something, Hands," I say. "You have to learn it for yourself. What happens after this year, I have no idea, but I want to make sure that we both choose our own futures. I couldn't have made it this far without you, but I want to make sure that I can make it on my own, too."

"I get that, Kitsy," Hands says, but he doesn't hide

the tears in his eyes. "It's about time you come first. But remember, no matter where we are, I will be thinking about you every day for the rest of my life. And even if you played clarinet in the band, I'd still love you just as much. I'm not with you because you're on the top of the pyramid . . . literally."

"No matter where we go, you will always be a part of me. So will the Spoke. Nothing can change that."

It's nearly nine o'clock. We sit arm in arm and watch as the sun approaches the bottom of the sky, and begins to fan out over the horizon. In New York, you feel like the possibilities are endless, but in Texas, it's the land that feels that way.

And then I start to realize exactly what Iona, Professor Picasso, Mrs. Corcoran, and even Tad were trying to get me to see: Art comes from the inside. Taking photographs of Hipster Hat Trick was just me trying to see myself through Tad's eyes. I remember that I brought the school's camera with me to take a few landscapes for Mrs. Corcoran. Then it hits me that my best portfolio has probably been in my own backyard the whole time.

"Hands," I say urgently, "I can't go to the field tonight." There will be other nights for kegs, Mockingbirdettes, and hanging out with Hands in his pickup at the field.

"Can you drop me off at home? But, first let's swing by Sonic because I can't wait another week for a Blast."

"As long as this isn't a final good-bye," Hands says, revving the engine.

"We'll never have a last good-bye," I say. And I mean it as much as any other hopeful teenager who has ever uttered those words.

After swinging through Sonic—where I happily find out that my replacement can't Rollerblade half as well as I can—Hands drops me off at home.

I kiss him on the forehead and say, "It's only nine days."

He kisses me back on the cheek. "A lot happened in the last twenty-one days," he reminds me and I nod because he's right.

A lot can shift even in a single day. Take today. Sneaking back into the house, I'm careful not to wake Kiki or Amber. In my room, I pull out my camera, confident I'm at least beginning to be myself with my art. I thought it was who I was with or where I was that defined me in some way. I realize now that I decide who I am, no matter the company I keep or the place I am.

As I wait for the earliest signs of morning light—"The Golden Light" as Professor Picasso explained it—I begin to snap photos of my room. When I finally think the light will never come, it shines through and the sun begins to illuminate the morning sky through the curtains. The sunrise is composed of a dozen shades of red. It's breathtaking.

Maybe it *is* true you can never go home again because even home is an ever-changing landscape, a place that's sometimes troubled and other times happier. But that doesn't mean it's not possible to capture fragments of home with my work, and I aim to try.

Click.

To: kkidd@gmail.com

From: corrinnec@gmail.com

Date: Sunday August 5

Subject: Hellooooo . . .

Where in the world is Kitsy Kidd? I know you're alive because I got an email from my mom about you. Can you please write me? I'm having serious cravings for contact from the Real World. And I need to hear what's going on from you. I can't WAIT to see you, Kitsy.

# Chapter 15

# The Best Place to Start Over

ON THE PLANE BACK TO New York on Sunday afternoon, I fidget the entire time, but not because I'm nervous about flying. After three flights in three weeks, I'm feeling confident about my aviation know-how. But I'm jumpy because I want to get back to Parsons to start editing my new photos. I genuinely can't remember the last time I was so excited to work on something.

I should be exhausted since I didn't sleep a wink last night, and I spent the whole car ride to Dallas clicking away and reviewing my photos, but somehow I'm still bright-eyed. During the flight, I alternate between brainstorming for my portfolio project and gleefully looking at my photos. When the announcement to turn off all electronics is made, I reluctantly put away my camera and prepare for landing.

Once off the plane, I meet Ivan at the baggage claim.

"Starbucks, Kitsy?" he asks.

"No, thank you." I never fell victim to the green-and-white beast. "Besides, I'm on a tight schedule. I have exactly eight days to win a scholarship and see more of Manhattan."

Taking my bag from me, Ivan grins and says: "Let's get going then. It's a good thing that New York can handle a take-charge girl."

I wake up very early on Monday, the first day of my last week of school. Since it's portfolio week, we're not having class. There are just optional lab hours for us to work on our portfolios and get help from Professor Picasso. Since I got a lot of planning done on the plane, I'm taking some *me* time this morning and being a tourist.

Where's the best place to start anew? For a long time, the answer was the United States of America—Ellis Island to be exact—so I make that my first stop.

After quietly slipping out of the apartment, I stroll down the pathways along the West Side Highway to Battery Park, where the ferries depart for Ellis Island. From the harbor, I can see the Statue of Liberty, which even from this distance seems a hundred times larger than it did from the plane. Luckily, I don't have to use my rusty trigonometry to figure out how tall she is; the brochure that came with my ticket informs me that she's 151 feet tall from head to base. Given to the United States by the French, she most certainly has the *je ne sais quoi* that Iona once said my art lacked. Hopefully, my new photography project will have a touch of it.

On the ferry I imagine the difficult journeys that the immigrants endured to get to New York City, and my flight from Texas suddenly seems like riding a cloud. After docking, I walk around the outside perimeter of the island. There's a large memorial wall of honor that surrounds the museum and I read that people have donated money to have their ancestors' names etched on the memorial. According to my brochure, it's the longest list of names in the world.

As I pass panel 222, something catches my eye. Moving closer, I see THOMAS KIDD engraved into the wall. I have only met three other Kidds in my life: Amber, my dad, and Kiki. I always assumed that there were other Kidds, but it's crazy to actually see my last name etched in stone, and to be on the same island where a Kidd entered the United States. I may not be related to Thomas Kidd, but I want a record of him anyway. I place a piece of tracing paper over his name and carefully make an etching. I wonder where Thomas Kidd went after he arrived at Ellis. Did he find what he was looking for in New York, or did he go searching for it somewhere else?

I feel connected to New York City, and also to America and its past. Many people who came here left places with terrible conditions. They weren't so much running away as they were moving toward hope. Once in America, many of them worked hard to maintain their native cultures and share them with others. Ellis Island makes me realize that everyone carries baggage, both good and bad. And you don't have to leave who you are and where you're from in the dust when you come here. New York is called the Melting Pot for a reason. I could live here for the rest of my life, but I hope I'd always keep my accent and still call all carbonated drinks Cokes.

On Tuesday, I set up camp at our school's lab to edit my photographs. If you had told me at the beginning of the class that my project would be on Broken Spoke, I would've laughed. Now, looking at my two hundred shots from home, I'm having a hard time narrowing them down to only ten coherent images.

Just like Van Gogh and Monet, I'm amazed at the view from my own backyard. As I'm cropping a photo of the football field and deciding if it's better in color or black-and-white, I feel a tap on my shoulder.

"Kitsy," Ford says. "It's time for a break. Your work ethic is scaring me."

Looking at my computer screen, he says, "Hey, I

thought you were doing your project on a band."

"I changed my mind," I say, laughing. "I think my judgment might've been clouded when I decided to do that one."

"Let me guess," he says as he cleans his green frames with his shirt. "You were doing it for a guy? I once pretended to love Japanese anime for six months because this kid I crushed on was totally into it. Total waste of time."

"You're right about the guy thing," I admit and save my work. "But it didn't end up being a waste of time for me. Sometimes you have to go to point C to find point A again. So, where are we taking our break?"

"Have you been to a Mister Softee yet?" Ford asks.

"No, but I've been eyeing them since I got here. Let's do it!"

I follow Ford out of the building.

Outside, Ford looks left and then right. "It shouldn't take us long to find one," he says. "Sometimes, you'll see three on the same block."

Ford spots a Mister Softee truck parked on a corner near Union Square. "Jackpot." We both get twisty cones and stand listening to the truck's jingle and eating our ice cream quickly before it melts in the sun.

"So why didn't you answer my texts this weekend? I think my boyfriend's starting to believe I made you up!" Ford asks as he wipes his chin.

"Ohmigosh, I'm so sorry. I went home for like

twenty-four hours to deal with some stuff and I forgot to text you back."

Ford makes his way to an unoccupied bench and waves me over. "What kind of stuff?"

I walk over to him and brainstorm a lie, but once I sit down, I feel the whole truth falling from my lips as I tell Ford about Amber, Kiki, and Hands. Ford's been a good friend, and I shouldn't hide the true Kitsy from him.

Ford finishes his ice cream as he patiently listens. "Wow," he says. "I'm impressed. Sometimes it's harder to be honest than it is to lie."

I toss my cone's wrapper into the trash. "I agree," I say. "But it does feel better."

And as delicious as Mister Softee was, I'm still loyal to my employer. Nothing beats a Sonic Blast.


On Wednesday, with two days to go before the show, I'm feeling confident about my progress. So I decide to take an extended lunch break and I know exactly where I want to go: to see the pigeons at Central Park. After all, Tad told me that they're the city bird. I wonder if any high schools around here have pigeons as their mascots and cheerleaders called Pigeonettes.

I think back to when Tad and I came here together. He hasn't tried to contact me since the incident with Annika, but I think that's for the best.

At Central Park, I spot more than three dozen pigeons near a set of benches. I decide to take some photographs for Kiki and print them at the school's lab. He'll flip.

A group of men in business suits walk by just as the pigeons take flight. "Holy cow," squeals the tallest of the group as he runs from the flock.

I find it comical that in this big city it's the pigeons that scare people. I abandon my plan to feed the pigeons when I read a sign that says FEEDING PIGEONS ALSO FEEDS RATS. I don't want to be responsible for the next bird flu epidemic.

Wandering up and down the trails in the park, I keep forgetting I'm still in the city until my eyes run across the skyscrapers boxing the park in. I heard there was a zoo, so when I stumble upon it, I decide it's worth the ten dollars to visit.

There's Ida and Gus, the polar bears; Nicky, the harbor seal; a newborn goat named Funky. There are pandas, snow leopards, and lizards. I reckon there's a place for every person and animal in Manhattan.

I'm on my way out of the park when I remember that I still haven't seen the *Angel of Waters* statue. Finding a map, I pinpoint it to the Bethesda Terrace, a section near the lake. With a bit of navigating, I spot the large fountain up ahead. Behind it, rowboats and ducks float in a lake.

Approaching the pool of water, I see the angel on top

of the giant fountain. Beside me, an Australian couple is huddled around a guidebook. The woman is reading out loud: "'The idea comes from the Gospel of Saint John when an angel bestowed healing powers on the waters of Bethlehem. This angel is supposed to protect New York's waters.'"

I like that. New York City has most certainly had healing effects on me. I toss a coin into the fountain to thank the angel, but I don't make a wish. I've had enough dreams come true recently; I'll give someone else a turn.

As I turn to leave, I see an older man and lady row by in one of the same green boats that Tad and I rented earlier this summer. Their laughter echoes over the water and reaches me. Thinking back to my time with Tad on this lake, I remember it like a painting, a snapshot in my mind. But really, all memories are like paintings: They can be incredibly vivid and lifelike. But in the end, they both just remind us that we only get to live any particular moment once, even if we remember it forever.

After getting another Mister Softee, I head back to school to spend the afternoon editing and cropping photos. I can't believe the exhibit is in two days and Corrinne will be here. Hopefully, her time at fancy horse camp hasn't reverted her back into Country Club Corrinne.


I'm putting my last photograph—one of my oak tree—on its mat, when Professor Picasso appears in the classroom.

Over the course of this week, he's given us our space, only coming around if we have questions. But I've been nervous to ask him about what he thinks of my project.

His opinion really matters to me. I know he liked my admissions sketch, but how will he feel about this project?

"Kitsy," he says, leaning over my shoulder. "It's your oak tree!"

"Do you recognize it?" I ask. After the golden light arrived in Broken Spoke, I biked out to the field and took this photo while lying on my back. It's a shot of my oak tree trunk with an upside-down view of the leaves.

"Of course, I love that oak tree and I like this interpretation even better than your admissions sketch," he says. "It looks like you—and your art—found its roots."

I beam inwardly. He's exactly right. And I found out that my best art says something about me, not someone else.

"Hopefully, we'll be seeing each other again, Kitsy," he says. "There's a lot of talent in you. I can feel it as much as I can see it."

"Thank you, sir," I say. "You don't know how much that means to me. Where I'm from, there are not a lot of people who share my interest in art. This has been the most incredible experience of my life."

"You're more than welcome, Kitsy, and your journey is just beginning," Professor Picasso says with a nod.

As he walks away, Iona comes over from where she's been working on her own project. She's being super secretive about it and has built a wall around her working space so no one can see it.

"I've never seen Professor P. act so complimentary," she says. "Someone must've prescribed him some Xanax. That stuff works wonders. My parents are huge fans."

I like to think it was my photo that gave him hope, just like it did for me. But I just nod. I don't want to rob her the chance of reading people. Besides, Iona's definitely turned out to be pretty cool. She gives me the slightest smile and starts to head back to her corner.

"Wait, Iona," I call out. "I never said a proper thank-you for giving me that scholarship information. It means everything to me. I'm about to go to the Empire State Building. I know that you're from New York and probably think that's lame, but do you want to go?"

"Thanks, but I'm going to pass," Iona answers. "I've never actually been up there. It's funny what you don't appreciate in your hometown."

After I pack my sketchbook into my purse, I give Iona a small smile and move toward the door.

"Wait, Kitsy," Iona calls out. "Do you have time before you go for me to take you somewhere you'll never find in any Frommer's guidebook? It's close by."

We make our way southwest and walk down West

Tenth Street. As we near the water, the street becomes speckled with tiny coffee shops and a dark Mexican restaurant. I'm sad that I don't have enough time (or money) to visit all of them during this trip.

Leading the way, Iona explains, "This is where I go when I'm trying to get over something. It's my favorite place. Second only to my therapist's couch."

"Corrinne calls those mental happy places," I say.

"That's a lot more creative than I-don't-wanna-know-you Iona," she says with a smile.

"Totally agreed," I say and laugh. "My mental happy place is MoMA but I love this street, too. The brownstones are so beautiful."

Iona looks ahead and lowers her voice: "There's only one rule about my place: You can't tell a soul. It's totally underappreciated, which is what makes it special. I've never actually brought a friend here," she says as we wait to cross the street.

I use two fingers to pantomime zipping my lips.

"It's up ahead." Iona points to a redbrick church with ivory doors in the distance.

"A church?" I ask, trying not to sound too surprised.

"No, the church just owns it. You see that stone archway? It's an entrance to a secret garden. It's only open sometimes, but when you go in, it's like walking into the jungle from *Where the Wild Things Are*. You can hardly believe you're in New York."

"Awesome," I say as I walk through the wide-open iron gate.

Iona hesitates. "This is somewhere you have to go by yourself," she says. "It's your turn to see it, so I'll head home. Good luck finishing your project. And who knows—maybe after the exhibition, we'll meet up again in another world."

"Are you on Facebook?" I ask.

Iona shakes her head: "Nope," she answers. Somehow, I'm not surprised. "I bet our lives will intersect again one day, but let's leave it up to chance. Isn't that more fun? Twenty-first-century technology takes the fate out of life. Besides, I've got a feeling that Kitsy Kidd will someday be coming to a gallery near me soon. It's just a hunch. I want to be a shrink, not a psychic, although sometimes my parents think they're both."

I cross back through the gate and give Iona a hug. She only holds it for a second; then she pushes me off.

"See you at the exhibition tomorrow," she says, already heading down Hudson Street.

Walking into the garden of the Church of St. Luke in the Fields is like opening a treasure chest. In the middle of this concrete jungle, there's a lush green sanctuary where an archway of cherry trees creates a tunnel for you to pass through. It's "ah-mazing" as Ford would say.

I don't see a single person as I sit under an ivy-covered tree and listen to a sparrow as he feeds from a homemade birdhouse. Admiring the flowers that come in as many varieties as there are people in New York, I think about having a Georgia O'Keeffe moment and sketching a solitary flower, but then I begin to draw a subject I've never dared to try: a self-portrait. I do it entirely from memory.

After I finish my portrait, I impulsively decide to text Tad to see if he wants to meet up at the Empire State Building to say good-bye. Even though the scene at the Mercury Lounge hurt, it would be worse not to see him one last time.

Tad texts back right away.

I'll see you there!

I leave the garden and try to pretend that I'm not nervous.

While I'm waiting on Tad near the Empire State Building, I think about what Annika said. Should I feel lucky that Tad liked me as a friend with no strings attached? The more I think about it, the more I realize she's right. Although it would've been nice to have a song written about me.

"You just love getting high, don't you?" Tad's voice whispers in my ear.

I whip around and shake my head at him.

"I'm sorry about the scene at the lounge," Tad says. "I acted like an asshole."

"Forget about it. It's in the past." And it's true. Just like whatever feelings I had for Tad. I was just as sweet on Tad's being a New Yorker and interest in art as I was on him. I think that made my heart wires cross.

I look up at the Empire State Building. While I've seen it, this is the first time I've been this close to it.

"We're going up. It's my treat. I'm in the money. I just sold my song," Tad announces and does a little dance. "That's what I was doing in Midtown. I'm sure it'll end up a Justin Bieber remix or something, but still. Pretty sweet feeling, I must say."

"But I thought you were going to sing it? It's your song!" I try but can't imagine anyone else singing Tad's lyrics.

"The important part for me was writing it," Tad says seriously. "I don't care who sings it. Honest. It's about my dad, so I don't know if I could get through it without crying. Sometimes, you can actually be too close to something."

*His dad?* Of course. I feel like a *total* idiot right now. His dad was his buoy. I want to burst out laughing at my own stupidity, but I hold my breath and tell him honestly, "Congratulations. I'm sure your dad would be proud of you."

"Thanks, Kitsy," Tad says. "You always know what to say. Now let's go see New York from over a hundred and two floors up. By the way, did I ever mention that I have acrophobia? You might have to hold my hand."

I put my hand in his without regret because I know it doesn't mean anything, and there are definitely no Tad tingles when our palms touch.

On the way up, my ears pop. That's how high we are.

At the observation deck, I spot a dozen giant binoculars you can use for a quarter.

I start digging through my purse when Tad gently slips a quarter into my hand. "Growing up in the city, my parents taught me to never leave home without a quarter to make a call. Of course, this was all pre–cell phones, but I still do it out of habit."

Sliding the quarter into the slot, I smile and thank him.

As I turn the binoculars toward Central Park, my view transforms from a glob of green to a clear picture of tiny people moving around the park. The people look like chess pieces in the game of life. Seeing through the binoculars reminds me of looking through a camera and how I finally realized that the hardest job for an artist is to choose the right subject. For me, the best one turned out to be in my backyard. Who knows what my next subject will be?

"Are you coming to my show tomorrow?" After the Annika thing, I wasn't sure if Tad would still come to my show, but I did have a few fantasies of him showing up and realizing that photographs on the wall *weren't* of him.

"Unfortunately, I can't. I'm sorry, Kitsy, but I have a contract meeting about the song." I can't read his eyes. "I'm sure your project came out great though. What did you decide to do it on?"

"What do you mean?" I ask with a half grin. I never told Tad how I switched portfolio subjects.

He loops his arm in mine and pulls me over to get a closer look at the view.

"I knew that you would eventually find something else that would be more Kitsy," Tad says.

"You're right," I admit. "My project is on Broken Spoke. There's nothing like your hometown, right?"

Looking down at the city below us, Tad nods his head in agreement.

"My hometown is pretty awesome," he says, gesturing around to the spectacular view.

"Okay, okay, there's nothing like *New York*," I correct myself.

Tad shakes his head and turns to face me. "There's nothing like Broken Spoke either, Kitsy. Just because you're from a small town doesn't mean that you're small. Don't ever think anyone's more important than you are or has more valid experiences."

"For a while," I admit, "I do think I was worried about

that, but I've realized there's something special about making art that reflects you and where you came from."

"I totally agree," Tad says, nodding. "Trust me, I've done enough cover songs to know that the best kind of music to play is your own. I'm finished singing other people's songs. I told the guys to go on tour without me so I can focus on my writing. I've got to admit that you've helped me refocus my energy. There are people here for both the right and wrong reasons. You helped me reevaluate mine."

Goose bumps grow on my arm, and not from the breeze. "I have a question. When something happens to you, do you think about how to use it in a song?"

Tad points toward the view. "When I look at anything," he says, "all I see are notes and lyrics. I bet you see everything in angles and colors."

"I like that," I say and mime taking pictures. I realize if I learned anything this summer, it was to trust my own artist's eye.

Tad sighs. "Whatever guy that ends up with you, Kitsy, is lucky. I just want you to know that. I love how you see this city, but even more, I love how you see people."

"Thanks, Tad," I say. Maybe I didn't imagine *everything* between us, but I'm still happy that nothing actually happened. I want to remember this summer as being about art, this city, and me.

"Hey, Tad. Can you do me a favor?" I ask, pulling out my phone. "I want a picture of me here for my little brother. *King Kong* is his all-time favorite movie." I know my camera's phone won't do the view justice, but I'll make sure to describe to Kiki just how amazing it was.

"Sure," Tad says and snaps a photo of me. He looks at the image on my camera a long time before he finally hands it back to me. Maybe he's trying to figure out where I fit into his life.

When we get on the elevators, I turn to Tad and say, "If you're ever coming through Texas, look me up."

"Are you on Facebook?" Tad asks. "I feel lame-o even asking that."

"Let's leave it up to chance," I say as we step back out onto the ground level. I'm only a little bit dizzy.

"Good-bye, Kitsy Kidd," he says as we near a crosswalk. "I hope you make it back to New York soon. You definitely added something to my city."

"That's my plan," I say, realizing that I *can* do something if I work at it. I made it here once, so I definitely think I can do it again.

Tad gives me a quick hug and one last smile; then he gets swept up in a crowd crossing the street. I can't spot him any longer so I don't even know if he's looking back at me. I'm still not sure why Tad came into my life or what he means to me. Some things I've learned are only clear in reverse. Of course, Hollywood never tells you this. If this were a movie, I'd end up with a guy, but this isn't the story of a girl and two guys. There'll be no credits because the truth is that this is the middle—not the end—of my story.

(On the back of one of my photographs of the Statue of Liberty)

Dear Dad,

This is a picture I took. Yup, I made it to NYC—just like we talked about. Cool, huh? I've also resolved to stop running from anything anymore—the past or the truth. I hope that you're okay and that you stop running one day, too. You know where to find us.

Love,

Kitsy

# Chapter 16

## *Que Será Será*

WHEN I WAKE UP ON Friday, it feels like everything is both happening and ending at the same time. Maybe that's what growing up feels like. By this time tomorrow, Corrinne will be home from camp, school will be over, the scholarship will be awarded, and I'll need to start packing to head home to the Spoke.

After I hang my photographs in the school's art gallery, I run home—literally. It's strange how I find myself calling the Corcorans' apartment "home" now. But who says you can't have more than one place where you feel like you belong? Luckily, I'm wearing my tennis shoes, so I make it to the apartment's courtyard just as Ivan's town car is pulling up. As it turns out, Waverly is waiting for Corrinne, too. I guess if you can have two places that feel like home, you can have two best friends—two very *different* best friends.

When Corrinne rolls out of the car, both Waverly and I gasp a little bit. She's wearing a pair of grass-stained jeans, a T-shirt that reads CAMP HOPE: WHERE NOTHING IS IMPOSSI- BLE, and her hair is either very messily braided or matted to her head.

"Um, what happened?" Waverly asks as she gives Corrinne a side-hug.

I go for the full bear hug since I'm already sweaty and I'm just happy to see her. I don't care what she looks like. I just know I've missed Corrinne so much.

"I had the best time of my life. That's what happened," Corrinne says, then gestures to Waverly and me. "Well, minus my times with you girls, of course. Those memories are priceless, too."

"Earth to Corrinne! I repeat: *What happened* to you?" Waverly asks again. "You look like you lost a battle with a circus."

Corrinne laughs. "I think you're referring to a rodeo, Waverly. And basically, I did. I had to rush from the camp- ers' award ceremony at the horse ring straight to the car to make sure I made Kitsy's event. Do I look like I've been crying?" Corrinne asks.

"About what? Your reflection?" Waverly asks seriously. "It's okay. I can work some of my style magic on you. You should've *seen* the number I did on Kitsy!"

Maybe I will just have to go into fashion with Ford. Seeing the look on Waverly's face at our debut fashion show at Lincoln Center would make it all worth it.

Corrinne rolls her eyes at Waverly. "No, Waverly. I'm a wreck because I bawled all the way home after saying good-bye to my campers. Seeing kids who have disabilities get up on a horse for the first time is amazing." She looks down at her outfit and adds, "As for my clothes, you're right, I need a serious wardrobe change, stat. If I don't wear jeans and a T-shirt ever again, it'll be too soon. Oh, and at camp everyone wore these *hideous* beaded bracelets. I 'accidentally' left mine behind."

Waverly and I both laugh.

"We'll have a Bloomie's date soon. I need to hear about the hot cocounselor! Did you guys make out in a teepee?" Waverly teases before moving to the front door. "It's too hot for me outside, so I'll get the details later."

"Wait, Corrinne," I say, confused. "I thought you were at horse camp doing that horse dancing thing."

"Dressage?" Corrinne asks. "No, it wasn't a dressage camp at all. I helped kids with physical and mental disabilities learn how to ride."

"How come I didn't know that?" I ask her, genuinely curious why she didn't tell me.

"Because you were busy following your dream,"

Corrinne tells me with a hand squeeze. She takes one enormous bag from Ivan and hands another monster one to me. "I'll tell you *all* about it later. I must say it's awesome to have a bunch of little kids listen to your every word and tell you how they want to be you. I know this is going to sound crazy, but I found myself thinking about being a teacher!"

"*Really?*" I ask with an incredulous smile, trying to imagine Corrinne with a room full of screaming kindergartners and finger paint. But then I remember how Corrinne's always supported my art dream, so I add, "That's so great."

I start moving at a snail's pace to the door, slouching under the weight of Corrinne's two-ton bag. "Thanks for everything you did for me this summer, Corrinne," I tell her.

"I was in Virginia at horse camp. I didn't do *anything* for you," Corrinne says seriously. "By the way, I've been meaning to ask you something. Waverly told me you were at a totally exclusive fashion magazine event. That's T.M.F.G."

In Corrinne-speak, T.M.F.G. means Total Material For Gossip.

All I can say back is "It was a weird summer."

"Speaking of weird," Corrinne continues, "I saw a picture in *Us Weekly* of this new 'it girl,' and there's a girl in the background who looks just like you, but a New York version. You either have a lot to fill me in on or you must have a doppelganger."

"That is strange. We definitely *do* have a lot of catching up to do," I say, relieved that Corrinne's here. "I can't believe *everything* that happened in just four weeks."

Corrinne moans a long "ahhh" every time I bring the makeup brush to her face.

"I really loved camp," she says, eyes closed. "I really did. But this feels *so* good. There's only so much natural beauty in the world. I'm happy to get a little help from Chanel."

I add the last touch of blush and say, "Ta-da. You look *gorgeous*."

Corrinne inspects herself carefully and then winks at her own reflection.

"Are you sure you don't want to do *this* for a living? Just teasing," Corrinne says, pointing to her face. "I know you're on your way to being a famous artist. By the way, my mom sort of mentioned that a lot has been going on with you. You *know* that I'm always here for you even if we aren't in the same place."

"Hopefully, one day we'll *both* be here," I say. "I'm definitely not done with New York. I do have a ton to tell you about Amber and Hands and everything, but I've got to run to my class meeting before the show tonight."

"All right, well, we'll have to talk later," Corrinne says as we make our way into her bedroom. "Are you sure you don't want to borrow a dress for your big night?"

Slipping my red Charlotte Russe dress over my head, the one I got in Texas bargain-shopping with Corrinne, I shake my head.

"Thanks, Corrinne, but I think I'll feel my best tonight if I'm wearing my own clothes." My dress might not be couture, but I feel like me when I wear it.

Taking my front-row seat next to Ford, I turn and look around the classroom. Whereas the first day, it was a sea of intimidating faces, now it's a small group of faces I know well, who were there with me from day one of the shocking nudes to my disastrous clay explosion. Maybe we'll meet again in art school, or in a gallery one day. The door opens and Professor Picasso enters grandly one last time.

"I think students sometimes forget how attached we teachers become to them. Thanks for being such a great class," he says, looking out at us.

Ford coughs and mutters under his breath, "Picasso has emotions? That surprises me."

He does have a point. You have to pass through a lot of curmudgeonly layers before you get to the supportive Professor Picasso, but I'm so glad I did.

Professor Picasso gives Ford an icy stare. "You should

know that your successes are our successes, too, so don't be strangers. I want to vicariously live through you all as you change the art world. On day one, I said this wasn't summer camp. But I still hope you did make a few friends and had at least a little bit of fun. As for the exhibition in a few minutes, don't be nervous. Even if the art world doesn't love you, I'm sure your family still will. *Que será será*," Professor Picasso says.

I look back to Iona, who's wearing her signature boots with a white lace dress. I raise my shoulders. She mouths back, "What will be will be," and winks.

I like that. Maybe I'll start learning French on the internet. If I can do New York, I can *definitely* do Paris, and I read Parsons has a program there.

Professor Picasso continues: "The judges will circulate like everyone else at the showing. At eight o'clock, the scholarship winner will be announced. After that, you're free to take your pieces with you, although I do ask that you might consider donating one to the school for display. That's it, class. Have a great rest of the summer. Thank you."

For a few minutes, we all sit there in silence. It's nothing like the last day of regular school, when students fly out of their seats like they are on fire. I'm thinking about how special this summer was and how lucky I was to have it. I don't know what anyone else is thinking about, but I can tell everyone has something on their mind, too. Finally, everyone quietly gets up and walks together to the school's gallery, where friends and family have already begun to gather.

I walk slowly through the gallery and check out my classmates' work. First, I stop by Ford's project. He's photographed mannequins wearing designer clothes and contrasted those images with photos of real people wearing the same clothes. I think he definitely made the statement he was trying for. "I want to show that real people, not anatomically impossible mannequins, wear clothes best," his artist statement reads.

A small crowd has congregated around Iona's series of figurative self-portraits. Only Iona would have the confidence for this project. In each drawing, she's making a different unattractive face, which is my favorite part. In one, she's sticking out her tongue defiantly. It's as if she's looking at the viewer and saying, "It's okay. You're not objectifying me. I'm in control because I'm the artist."

"Provocative," remarks a well-dressed woman, probably someone from the *real art world*.

I'm thinking how Iona would love to hear that, when I realize she's come to stand next to me.

"I thought if art is about revealing yourself, I might as well do just that. I also think it's a nice reversal on society objectifying the female," Iona says. "By the way, I looked at your photos earlier. They have a lot of heart."

"Thanks, Iona," I say.

"Stop hanging around here," she says. "Go show off your art."

I round the corner where I installed my project and see the Corcorans. I stand back for a minute and I watch them take in my photographs. Seeing my art on the wall makes me feel both proud and exposed at the same time.

Pointing to a shot of a farm silo at sunrise, Mr. Corcoran says loudly enough for me to overhear, "J.J., is *this* Broken Spoke? It's breathtaking. How come you never mentioned it was so beautiful?"

"It's not," Corrinne starts to say, then gets distracted by a new photograph. "Well, it's usually not."

Mrs. Corcoran doesn't say anything, but she gazes at a panoramic picture of Broken Spoke's strip. I edited the photo so that only the storefront's American and Texan flags are in color, and the rest is black-and-white.

"American by birth—" Mrs. Corcoran starts to say.

"And Texan by the grace of God," I finish for her as I finally approach them.

"Holy Holly Golightly!" Corrinne says, hugging me. "These are amazing, Kitsy. I didn't realize that you knew how to take photographs. I mean, how did you get Broken Spoke to look so good? No offense or anything."

"I just tried to see it from a different angle," I answer, looking back at the wall covered in scenes of Broken Spoke.

The photo of the football field at dawn with mist rising off the grass. The first car at Sonic in the morning. Mr. Chin sweeping outside his restaurant. A photograph of the view out my bedroom window. I don't think I figured out how to make a political statement or anything, but I do think I finally figured out how to make my art about me and about more than me.

I notice a few older, well-dressed people approach. Instead of sticking around, I leave and let my work speak for itself.

"Let's go get free cheese," I say to Corrinne. I know that we don't have much time together and I want to make the most of it.

"Okay," Corrinne says, looking at the photographs one more time. "These are making me miss Broken Spoke. I need to plan a visit. You'll have to give me the football schedule because I definitely want to go to a home game. I'm in need of a good field party, too."

"You know what? I kind of miss it, too."

"*Really?*" Corrinne asks me.

"Really. It's still home at least for another year," I say. "And it'll always be part of me even if I'm not living there."

As we round the corner, we run smack into Iona.

"Hi, Iona!" I say. "Of course, you know Corrinne."

I give Corrinne a look and she forces her frown into a small smile.

306

"Kitsy," Iona says, motioning to a man and woman standing next to her. "These are my parents. Mom and Dad, this is Kitsy, the girl—I mean my friend—from class I keep telling you both about."

Iona's mother and father, who look nothing like her, nod knowingly. Her mother, dressed in a pencil skirt and cardigan, gives me the same look Iona gave when I first met her. She's definitely analyzing me, but I'm okay with it. I'm proud of who I am.

"So nice to meet you," I say. "Iona's been very kind."

After a few polite moments with Iona's parents, Corrinne and I excuse ourselves. She whispers to me, "Tell me you didn't become BFFs with Iona."

"Not BFFs," I say. "*You* are my only best friend . . . but Iona's cool. You might try to get to know her."

"Remind me *not* to leave you alone in Manhattan next time," Corrinne says, rolling her eyes and tossing a cheese cube in her mouth.

I'm glad I spent some time here alone. I don't think I would've figured out so much about myself if Corrinne had been in New York all summer.

Professor Picasso walks up to the podium and taps the microphone. As much as I keep trying to ignore that this exhibition is also a competition for a scholarship, it does keep popping back up in my mind.

"Hello, students, family, friends, and patrons of our

program at Parsons. I hope you've enjoyed the exhibition. I know that I'm most certainly impressed by this crop of young talent and I hear that they have a wonderful teacher," Professor Picasso says. He pauses and waits for the polite laughter. "With many thanks to an anonymous donation, we're proud to grant a ten-thousand-dollar scholarship toward an art education to one promising student."

"I didn't know there was *money* on the line," Corrinne whispers. "I would've totally helped you suck up to the judges. Flattering authority is an extremely important skill of winners. If you want to *win*, you have to play the game, Kitsy."

I laugh and shake my head. "Art's not a game to me," I whisper.

"I'll have one of our judges, the esteemed potter Maureen Arden, announce the recipient. Thank you all for coming tonight," Professor Picasso says and smiles, which is definitely the first time I've seen that happen.

"My mom has one of her vases," Corrinne hisses. "It's *awesome*."

My shoulders slouch because I can't help but assume this means the scholarship will go to someone who works with clay. But I don't regret doing photographs, because it changed how I saw art. It made me into an active creator rather than someone who just copies what she sees.

"Thank you, Professor Picasso," Ms. Arden says,

looking out at the crowd. "All of the art was impressive both on technical and artistic levels. If this is what these teens can do now, I can't imagine where they'll go next—especially if they are afforded a great art education. The recipient of this year's scholarship was chosen for her ability to capture simple landscapes that we can't rip our eyes away from. It might be the photographer's technical facility, but there's something else, something intangible, going on there within the film that's so beautiful."

Corrinne is nudging my ribs so hard that she's going to leave bruises. "It's you," she keeps whispering in my ear. "It's you."

I refuse to let myself believe it until Ms. Arden pronounces, "This year's recipient is Kitsy Kidd for her landscapes of small-town Texas."

Then I hear applause. People are cheering for me. Corrinne is loudly whistling and hollering on as if we were at a Mockingbird football game rather than in an art gallery. For the first time in my life, it's not me who's the cheerleader. Instead I'm the one being cheered for. It feels *really* good to be on the other side.

Awkwardly, I walk to the podium to accept the award from Ms. Arden and shake her hand firmly. "Thanks, y'all," I say to the crowd, where the anonymous judges must be.

In a blur, a bunch of my classmates come up and congratulate me.

"Where are you going to apply for school?" a girl who wore paint-speckled coveralls nearly every day of class asks me.

"I'm not sure yet," I say honestly. "I'm keeping my options open." I have a year to figure out how far or how close I'll stay to the Spoke. This year, I'm going to focus on working overtime at Sonic so I can buy a camera of my own. All I know is that wherever I am, I want to be doing art.

"Congratulations, Kitsy," Ford exclaims as he pushes through the crowd and gives me a kiss on the cheek. "I guess this means that you're going to become a famous photographer, and you'll be too busy to start Ford and Kitsy."

"Hey," I say, giving Ford a pinch on the cheek. "You said it would be Kitsy and Ford. I'll probably be busy with my photography, but I'm always happy to be a highly paid consultant for whatever fabulous fashion line you start."

"How about I pay you in clothes?" Ford says.

I reach out my hand so we can shake on it.

"I'm going to look for my family," Ford says. "So I guess this is good-bye?"

"Never," I say. "You need my color savvy, and I need your sunnier outlook. Whenever I'm down, I'm going to remember to hear the good stuff, just like you told me."

"I bid you adieu. Until next time, Kitsy," Ford says, giving me an air-kiss.

I watch Ford blend into the crowd until I lose sight of him, but I know that, like New York, he'll be in my future.

When I meet back up with the Corcorans, they all give me huge hugs.

"See, you're a great investment," Mrs. Corcoran whispers in my ear when Mr. Corcoran asks if he can buy the photograph of the silo.

"It's free," I say, removing the photograph off the wall and handing it to him. "It's the least I can do."

Remembering Professor Picasso's request to leave a piece of art behind, I decide to leave the landscape shot of Broken Spoke's strip on the wall. It's no Manhattan skyline, but it has everything someone needs. I like the idea of both leaving a bit of Broken Spoke at Parsons and taking a bit of New York with me to Broken Spoke.

"Are you dripping happy?" Corrinne asks. "That was the big word at camp. *Dripping.* It means awesome."

"I only know how to describe how happy I am if I speak Texan. Corrinne, may I?"

"Sure," Corrinne says. "It's your day. If you want to speak Texan, go right ahead."

"Corrinne, I feel like I'm riding a gravy train with biscuit wheels."

"All y'all Texans are nuts."

"Well, you New York *guys* are crazy, too," I say, looping my arm in hers and heading for the door. "The stories I could tell . . ."

When the exhibition's slowing down, I step outside to call home.

Kiki picks up on the first ring.

"Kitsy!" Kiki squeals. "You come home in exactly thirty-two hours. I counted. And guess what? Mom and I are going to the park. Isn't that cool?"

"That's super cool," I say, smiling. "Do the monkey bars for me. And guess what, Kiki? I won a scholarship for my photographs of the Spoke."

"Of course you did! You're the best artist in the world."

I get choked up thinking how Kiki's not only the best brother but how he's also a great cheerleader. It must be in the genes.

"You're the best brother in the universe," I say.

"Kitsy, I forgot to tell you. Last night, the stars told me that they've missed you. I'm sure New York is really cool, but I think it stinks that you can't see the stars."

"I agree—"

"You won!" I hear Amber's voice cry.

She must've grabbed the phone from Kiki.

"*Ten thousand dollars!*" I exclaim.

"I'm so proud of you," Amber says.

That's the first time Amber has told me she's proud of me, and it feels just as good as I always imagined it would.

"I've got to go," I say. "But I think we're going to have a great year."

"I think you're right. By the way, I watched the DVD. They have a lot of success stories. It's definitely worth looking into it. I love you, Kitsy."

"Love you, too." When it's out of my mouth, I realize it's been a long time since I've told her that.

I start typing a message to Hands, but I stop, delete it, and decide to call him after dinner. I need to focus on savoring my last moments in New York.

"Kitsy," Corrinne calls from down the block. "We've got to find a cab *stat*. Our reservation is in T minus five seconds."

The Corcorans and I have plans for a celebration supper at The Little Owl, a tiny restaurant tucked away in the West Village.

As we stand on the corner to catch a cab (because I totally mastered the taxi-light system), I notice a girl sitting on the sidewalk begging for change. She doesn't look a day older than me. While I have been in New York long enough that the sight of a homeless person doesn't shock me anymore, there's something about her that draws me closer. I notice her cardboard sign has only four words: TRYING TO GET HOME. Reaching into my purse, I pull out the twenty dollars that I've been saving to buy myself a souvenir from MoMA.

Corrinne watches me and warns, "She's going to buy drugs."

I shake my head. "She's just trying to get home." I put the bill in her empty Dunkin' Donuts Styrofoam cup.

I don't need any souvenirs. I have my experience.

"Bless you," she says.

"I know what it's like to want to get home," I tell her. She doesn't acknowledge me, but maybe I'm not talking to her anyway.

# Acknowledgments

To my readers, thank you for allowing my characters to visit your imagination. Please email me your thoughts at gwendolyn.heasley@gmail.com. I write for you all, and would love to hear what you think!

To my friends, thank you. I believe E. B. White said it best in his beloved children's classic *Charlotte's Web*: "'You have been my friend,' replied Charlotte. 'That in itself is a tremendous thing.'" Thank you also for encouraging my writing career and, most importantly, for peddling my books.

To Sarah Burningham, thank you for being my little bird and helping to launch my career.

To Leigh Feldman, your presence in my life continues to be a gift, and I'm always grateful for your wisdom.

Thank you for helping me get the world's greatest job. I'm indebted.

To HarperTeen, I know it takes a village to publish a book, so thank you all from the bottom of my heart.

To Alison Klapthor, I'm happy to let anyone judge my books by their covers as long as you're the one designing them. Thank you for your—and your team's—beautiful art!

To Sarah Dotts Barley: It seems like just yesterday we were classmates in German class, and now you're my editor! What a beautifully small and crazy world it is. Thank you for adopting *A Long Way from You* and raising it like your own. Your vision, intelligence, and attention to detail wow me on a daily basis. It's actually very hard to believe we went to the same school. I'm beyond grateful to have you as my editor on this novel.

To the O'Sullivan sisters, thank you for the countless reads.

To Cory, you make (my) life better. I love you.

To my mom, my dad, and Aliceyn, I really like being enmeshed, and I'd have it no other way. Thank you for your enduring support, confidence, and, most of all, love.

READ AN EXCERPT FROM THE BEGINNING
OF KITSY AND CORRINNE'S STORY IN

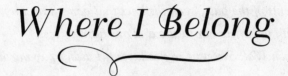

# Where I Belong

*Dear Reader,*

*Have you ever heard of the Butterfly Effect? I learned about it in science class last year. Probably the only lesson I remember because it's way more relevant to real life than the three types of sediment rock or the properties of noble gases. And it's also not revolting, like dissecting a frog. Basically, the butterfly effect is a chaos theory, attributed to a guy named Edward Lorenz. Here's the CliffsNotes version: A butterfly flaps its wings in Brazil, and it sets off a tornado in Texas. It means the smallest moments of the past, even the ones that don't have anything to do with us, affect our future and our future selves.*

*When Wall Street nearly collapsed, I didn't pay much attention. I used to care a lot more about the hottest starlet's weight fluctuation than the current prices of stocks. But when the economic problems caused my dad to lose his seven-figure job and me to move to a Texan town that's so teeny tiny it's not even on Google Maps, I realized how seemingly distant events can change your life forever.*

*This is the story of how I was transformed. How the pieces of the global economy toppled like dominoes and made a teenage ice princess from Manhattan (me) melt and find her long-dislocated heart. So if you hate me at first, keep reading. You might just surprise yourself. I know I did.*

*And just think, somewhere right now a butterfly might be flapping its wings and altering your future in some peculiar, yet beautiful, way.*

*Sincerely,*
*Corrinne Corcoran*

# Chapter 1

## Family Meeting

My iPhone loudly sings a little ditty.

*She got diamonds on the soles of her shoes.*

The Barneys saleswoman, dressed in a hideous avocado green dress, gives me a look of disgust. Maybe she doesn't like Paul Simon's music. Stupid, it's a classic, and I don't have to change my ring tone each time Lady Gaga makes a costume change. Have you ever been to a party where twelve people have the same ring tone? So pathetic, it's almost as bad as two girls having the same signature scent.

From a distance, I am pretty sure the avocado lady is rolling her eyes: Maybe she's one of those people who don't believe in using cell phones in public? Please, isn't that why they were invented? To make us mobile? And look around, Miss Barneys employee; I am the only customer on floor three, the designer collection department. It appears that whole recession thingamajig scared everyone else away.

She keeps staring at me, and I know it isn't my clothes: I am wearing an Alice and Olivia summer white dress and Jimmy Choo pink heels with my mousy brown hair slicked back. And she's the same shopgirl who still hasn't brought me the pair of Hudson jeans that I asked for more than twenty minutes ago. She's probably ignoring me because I am a teenager. I just *hate* age discrimination, but I still refuse to shop in Juniors. First of all, I am a size five in Juniors and only a size four in Womens. Second of all, most of the clothing in Juniors is cheap. I might be only sixteen years old, but I own plastic. That should count for something. The saleslady keeps on glaring at me like it's a new pastime, so I finally silence my phone. It's my mother anyway, and I don't want to talk to her.

I don't want to talk to anyone. I shop alone. Sure, I'll occasionally have lunch with friends at Fred's, the restaurant at Barneys. And I'll be sociable and make a courtesy loop or two of the store afterward, but I won't wardrobe (aka power shop) with them. They'll either move too slowly or claim they spotted that yellow eyelet Milly dress first. And right now, I am shopping for my first year at boarding school. This is serious. There are no Barneys in the middle of Connecticut, and online shopping should always be a last resort. And of course I don't do malls on principle.

When "Diamonds on the Soles of Her Shoes" booms in once more, I silence it again. . . . I mean, really, Mom? We just spent the first two weeks of August in Nantucket, and I have less than three weeks before I need to leave for Kent, my new boarding school. I haven't even finalized my bedding and drapery because Kent has yet to tell Waverly, my best friend, and me if we are permitted to be roommates. Having never shared a room before, I totally tried to finagle a private room by lying and saying that I have a serious snoring issue. But the dean of students said all roommates have to work out differences and mine will just need to wear earplugs or I'll have to wear one of those nose strips. Since a private room isn't going to happen, bunking with Waverly is a better option than some foreign exchange student who doesn't shower daily.

Moving over to accessories, I model shades in the tiny mirror. After trying to remember if I have the tortoiseshell Ray-Bans at home or if I just have the white, the black, and the neon pink, I decide to buy the tortoiseshell ones just in case. I should look at round Jackie-O glasses, too, because I totally hear they're having a revival.

*Bing!* bounces from inside my neon blue Marc Jacobs purse.

A text message from "her." That's how I put my mom into my phone. Funny, right?

Her: Family meeting, 7 pm, get home

It's six, and I am supposed to do seven thirty sushi with the girls at a BYOB (bring your own bottle) restaurant in the East Village. My friend Sarita's older brother taught us to frequent BYOBs, so we don't get our fakes swiped because when you bring your own booze, the restaurants don't even card. I guess I'll have to be a little late to my friends' dinner since I'll need to swing by home.

I text her back.

Corrinne: Fine. The meeting better last only nanoseconds. I got plans.

I bring my purchases—two pairs of Notify jeans, the tortoiseshell Ray-Bans (why not?), and the orange Tory Burch flats—to the counter where Little Miss Bitter Saleswoman sits perched.

"I'd like those Hudsons I asked for," I try to gently remind her how to do her job.

The saleswoman huffs off to find my jeans. After she packages up everything into two Barneys white and black logoed bags, I decide that I am definitely cabbing it. Those bags look heavy! And August in New York is too hot for the subway. Even though I could use the subway-stair exercise since I didn't ride or go to the gym today, I simply can't bear the thought of descending into hot, crowded mugginess. And especially not on a weekday: there are too many sweaty worker bees in tacky, cheap suits.

After I catch a cab outside, I text Waverly and tell her that I might be late.

Waverly: Don't B 2 late, we might drink all the vino. And it's never fun 2 B the sober kid.

I want to call Waverly and say there had better be wine left when I arrive, but the cabbie's blasting the radio news. All I hear is "layoffs" this, "layoffs" that, "another Ponzi scheme." Gross. I am sick of all this bad economic news, and it doesn't even make any sense. Our math teacher, Mrs. DeBord, tried to explain last year when things got really bad: something about defaults, mortgages, shorts. I definitely didn't get it. But hey, I don't even understand algebra. Letters for numbers, really? We might as well learn hieroglyphics. At Kent, I am going to need a math tutor if I want to get into the Ivies. And I for sure want to get into the Ivies because that's where the boys are not only cute but smart and rich.

When the recession first began last year, some kids' parents had to pull them out of school. But it's hard to tell who left because of money fiascos and who left for other reasons, like rehab and divorce. Thank God my dad made it through all the layoffs, and he even still got his bonus. I was scared that it was going to be a pauper's Christmas like Tiny Tim had in *A Christmas Carol*, but everything I asked for, all four pages (single spaced), sat right under the tree.

The cabbie pulls up to my building at Morton Street and the West Side Highway. I bound out of the cab, buzz to open the gate, and jog up to the marble front desk.

"Rudy, favor, please: Hold on to one of these for me," I say, extending a Barneys bag.

Rudy, our hot 6'6" doorman who models on the side, takes the package out of my hands and puts it behind the desk. I always leave one bag downstairs with Rudy so my parents don't know how much I am shopping. Then I retrieve it when I know my parents aren't around. This way, they're only mad at me once a month when the credit card bill arrives versus every time I make a big spree. My mom says my shopping is "O.O.C.," which is an abrevs for out of control; my dad says that "maybe she'll go into fashion, and it's an investment." They argue about it. Actually, they argue about me a lot. Yeah, I've gotten a few detentions and had sit-downs with the parents over learning to filter my comments, but compared to other teenagers I know, I am practically a wunderkind. No mug shot in the *Post* like the girl at school who got busted for smoking pot in a club. Good thing because mug shots, as a rule, find your most unflattering angle and make even celebrities look homeless.

I nudge Rudy with my elbow: "Thanks, Rudy. You

totally help my publicity with the parents," I say, and head to the elevators.

Rudy is awesome; he keeps all my secrets, like the fact that I come in right before curfew, make sure my parents know I am home, wait for them to fall back asleep, and then leave again. And then there was the time I drunkenly threw my keys down the trash chute with the late-night pizza box. Rudy even dug them out for me. If he weren't a doorman, I'd totally marry him. Waverly's doorman will rat her out to her parents for a good Christmas tip, so I know how fortunate I am.

Stepping out of the elevator onto the thirteenth floor, I smell chicken. I haven't eaten all day because I am trying to go vegan to shed some poundage for back-to-school. But still, it smells divine, and I'd kill for a little piece. I am shocked to find the aroma's coming from my own kitchen where my mother, J.J. Corcoran, stands over a stove. She's wearing a seriously unglamorous apron that reads "Kiss the Cook" with a gigantic lipstick mark over her perfectly coiffed clothes, a black Diane Von Furstenberg dress with a full skirt, and a long string of pearls. The black-and-white color combo highlights her naturally honey blond locks. It makes me mad to see that dress because I had picked it out on a rare shopping excursion with my mom, but the store only had it in her size: a size *two*. She told me that she would order me one in my size, but I couldn't bear the depressing notion that I would be Jumbo-J.J. Being fatter than your mom is a common issue for the kids at my school. And even worse yet, my mom told my hairdresser that I couldn't get blond highlights until I am in college. "You have such beautiful brown hair, Corrinne; you'll thank me someday," she said. So I am fatter than my mom and a brunette. I imagine that I will spend a great portion of my adult years on a couch discussing these two injustices with my shrink.

"Corrinne, is something wrong with your phone again? Why didn't you answer when I called twice? You know I don't like texting," my mom says as she stirs the chicken steeped in red wine. She stops churning to take a sip out of a very full glass of white wine.

"Why are you cooking, Mom? And where'd you get that apron? Is Maria okay?" I say, looking around for our fifty-something Mexican housekeeper, who's always at the apartment until at least eight at night. She's worked for our family for years and helps to keep our lives out of madness.

"Maria's fine. She took the train back to Coney Island this afternoon. And I've cooked before, Corrinne. Just not in a while. Besides, I thought it would be nice to have some real food for our meeting."

"Whatever; I have a dinner date at seven thirty, so let's make it quick."

"Corrinne, this is important. Your father's home, um,

he's home early for it," my mom says, and turns back to the stove.

This must be a big deal because my dad and I usually only exchange glances on Saturday mornings.

"Corrinne, one more thing: Set the table."